WITH THIS
RING

Dear Reader:

What can I say about Allison Hobbs other than she is phenomenal? There are very few writers that I can say that I actually admire. She is a powerhouse of a writer and she keeps churning out one masterpiece after another; year after year.

With This Ring continues to entice my literary palate with the theme of women seeking that diamond ring to be validated by marriage. Now the three characters Allison introduced us to in *Put a Ring on It*—Vangie, Harlow and Nivea—return in the follow-up with one who has finally made it to the altar. The other two continue to strive to make it down the actual aisle, but it is the least of their problems as they have to contend with baby daddy drama. *With This Ring* contains all of the signature elements of an Allison Hobbs novel: scandal, lust, surprises and shockers.

Allison's a prolific author whose latest title, *No Boundaries*, features a young law school student who stumbles into an alternative lifestyle. With her Eternal Dead Series, she explored the supernatural genre writing under the name Joelle Sterling. With twenty-one titles under her roster, she has surely created a thriving writing career.

As always, thank you for supporting myself and the Strebor Books family. We strive to bring you cutting edge-literature that cannot be found anyplace else. You can find out about our other authors on www.zanestore.com and you can find me on Facebook @AuthorZane and on Twitter @planetzane. Or you can email me at zane@erotica noir.com.

Blessings,

Zane

Publisher
Strebor Books
www.simonandschuster.com

ZANE PRESENTS

ALLISON HOBBS

WITH THIS RING

SBI

STREBOR BOOKS

NEW YORK LONDON TORONTO SYDNEY

Strebor Books
P.O. Box 6505
Largo, MD 20792
http://www.streborbooks.com

ISBN 978-1-59309-467-6
ISBN 978-1-4516-9702-5 (ebook)
LCCN 2013933666

First Strebor Books trade paperback edition October 2013

Cover design: www.mariondesigns.com
Cover photograph: © Keith Saunders/Marion Designs
Wedding bouquet: © LanKS/Shutterstock Images

10 9 8 7 6 5 4 3 2 1

Manufactured in the United States of America

For information regarding special discounts for bulk purchases, please contact Simon & Schuster Special Sales at 1-866-506-1949 or business@simonandschuster.com

The Simon & Schuster Speakers Bureau can bring authors to your live event. For more information or to book an event, contact the Simon & Schuster Speakers Bureau at 1-866-248-3049 or visit our website at www.simonspeakers.com.

For my fellow author and friend, Daaimah S. Poole

NIVEA

NO! Nivea groaned as she scanned the paper. She felt the blood leaving her face and the room began to spin. She anchored herself against her baby's crib as she read the DNA paternity test results for the second time: *Based on DNA analysis, the alleged father, Knox Bowers, can be excluded as the biological father of Mackenzie Westcott. They do not share the same genetic markers.*

Despite the scandal and the dissention that she'd caused within her family when it was discovered that she'd had an affair with her sister's husband, Nivea had desperately wanted Knox to be the father of her baby. It wasn't that she had genuine feelings for him; she didn't. The thought of him having to pay her child support for the next eighteen years had given her malicious pleasure.

But now those dreams were destroyed. She glanced at her sleeping daughter and shook her head. She should have known that Mackenzie was too pale to have been fathered by a black man. Knox was light-skinned and all, but still…the baby should have had a little more color if it were his.

Livid about the test results, she balled up the paper and flung it in a waste bin that was decorated with images of Tinker Bell.

No doubt, Knox had received the news, too. He and her sister, Courtney, were probably gloating. Luckily, Nivea wasn't speaking to anyone in her family, except her father, and it was a relief that she wouldn't have to bear witness to their smug faces.

What should she do, now? She didn't know how to get in touch with those two bartenders she'd had a threesome with on New Year's Eve. She barely recalled what they looked like and didn't even know their names. And what could their broke asses do for her, anyway? Absolutely nothing! Nivea pondered her dilemma. Someone needed to be held accountable. Why should she alone bear the financial burden of raising a child?

She thought about the list of men who could potentially be her daughter's father and decided to go after Dr. Bertram Sandburg. He had a thriving practice, was on the staff of several hospitals, and probably had other streams of income. The man made a shit-load of money, and his support payments would far exceed the measly pittance she would have gotten out of Knox, who was still in school and only working part time. She had wanted to hurt Knox and Courtney so badly, she hadn't thought about the bigger picture.

Four-month-old Mackenzie began to fret and Nivea lifted her from the crib. The nursery was decorated in shades of pink, cream, and lilac. Nivea had put a lot of effort into making the room beautiful and cheerful, yet it was rare for Mackenzie to sleep in her own room. She preferred sleeping with her mother.

A wave of overwhelming love and protectiveness surged through her as she kissed her child. "Are you hungry, Kenzie-Ken?" she cooed, patting her daughter's back.

She sat in a cream-colored rocking chair with plump, lilac cushions. She lifted her top and began to nurse her daughter. She hadn't planned on breastfeeding, but moments after giving birth, she'd bonded with her daughter in a way she would have never thought possible. At that moment, she decided that synthetic baby formula wasn't good enough for her precious bundle of joy.

With the baby nestled in her arms and feeding, Nivea rocked

back and forth, her thoughts running a mile a minute. She made a good salary—more than enough to provide a decent life for her and Mackenzie. But her daughter deserved better than a decent life. She deserved a fabulous life—a life that included a big house with lush grounds, the best private schools, music lessons, dance lessons, horse riding lessons and her very own pony. Mackenzie would be a refined world traveler, envied for her discerning taste and sophistication. And of course, she'd be the best-dressed little girl among her playmates.

And someone with Dr. Sandburg's means could provide the extravagant lifestyle that Nivea believed her daughter was entitled to.

She'd taken an extended maternity leave, but was scheduled to return to work in less than thirty days. There wasn't a chance in hell she was going to put her beloved baby in a germ-infested child care center that was run by incompetent high school dropouts. She needed a full-time nanny to come to her home and take care of Mackenzie, and she would watch the woman like a hawk on the nanny cams that would be installed in every room. Nivea frowned as she imagined the huge expense of having to pay a nanny.

She needed a big payday…and soon!

Dr. Sandburg would want to avoid the scandal of a paternity suit, wouldn't he? Maybe she could convince him to forego the paternity test and persuade him to give her a hefty, lump sum in lieu of a lifetime of monthly payments. It was a pretty good deal, Nivea thought.

Surely, he wouldn't want his wife and colleagues to know that he'd fathered a biracial child outside his marriage. From what she recalled, the doctor was a softie and would buckle under the pressure. How much should she demand from him? A million? No, that wasn't nearly enough. She'd blow through that before Mackenzie was old enough to even enjoy her privileged life.

Perhaps she could figure out a way to get him to agree to an outrageous monthly support payment for the next eighteen years. It was worth a try. And if the doctor wanted to play hardball, she'd take him to court. After all, there was a slim chance that he was actually the father. And if he was, she'd get a high-powered attorney who would show him no mercy and bleed him dry.

Feeling better, a smile formed on Nivea's lips. She hadn't succeeded in marrying a doctor, but she'd done even better by having unprotected sex with one. She planned on getting all the benefits of being married without being tied down to a boring, old physician.

❤ ❤ ❤

The next day, swathed in Dolce & Gabbana with Mackenzie making a fashion statement in a Little Marc Jacobs heart-print dress, Nivea paid Dr. Sandburg a visit.

"Good to see you, Nivea," the doctor said although his sour expression contradicted his statement.

"Good to see you, too, Bertram," Nivea said, pointedly using the doctor's first name as she took a seat in his private office. Her skirt rose up and she adjusted it. The ten extra pounds of stubborn baby weight had accumulated around her hips, tightening her wardrobe, but Nivea refused to move up to the next size. She'd get back to the gym eventually, but in the meantime, she'd have to start wearing Spanx or some kind of shapewear.

"Have you returned to work? Your replacement…a fine young man, told me you were on maternity leave." He sat behind his desk, hands folded calmly, while his eyes shifted warily to the baby in Nivea's arms.

"Not yet. Listen, Doc, I didn't come here to discuss work. I came to introduce you to your daughter."

"Are you insane?" Dr. Sandburg bolted from his chair and stood up, pointing to the door. "I advise you to leave my office right now, young lady."

"I'll leave, but don't you want to meet your daughter first? I think you should. Otherwise, it may get ugly, and I don't think you want a mandatory paternity test, do you?"

"Think long and hard before you try to ensnarl me in a paternity suit."

Startled by the boom of his angry voice, the baby wriggled and began to fuss. "Aw, what's the matter with my little Boo-Boo? Don't cry, sweetie. Daddy's a little upset right now, but he'll calm down."

"Do not refer to me as Daddy," Dr. Sandburg bellowed. His voice seemed to shake the walls and his face was bright red with indignation. "We were intimate only once, and I'm not going to allow you to pin your illegitimate daughter on me."

Nivea rose abruptly. "I thought we could talk like civilized people, but since we can't, I'll have my attorney contact you regarding the DNA test. She's a real barracuda, and of course, she'll hold a press conference to alert the public that she's representing a young woman—a hardworking pharmaceutical sales rep who was lured into a sexual relationship by a prominent physician who coerced her into an illicit affair. A doctor who forced her to whore herself before he agreed to conduct business."

"That's an outrageous lie. I never forced you to do anything."

Nivea narrowed her eyes. "The public loves a juicy scandal. My lawyer will also mention that you're addicted to painkillers. The medical review board should find that interesting. Who knows, before this is over, you might lose your license to practice medicine."

"This is blackmail."

"It's not. I'm a mother fighting for her child's rights. But since you want to play hardball, I'll contact my attorney. She can probably get a statement together in time for the five o'clock news."

Dr. Sandburg dragged his fingers across a ruddy cheek. "Tonight's news?"

Nivea nodded. "My attorney is a real alpha-female type. She's particularly aggressive when it comes to men who try to shirk their parental responsibilities."

"There's no need to involve lawyers," he said, beginning to back-pedal. "Sit down, Nivea. Let's keep this between the two of us."

"No, I'm not sitting down. I want you to look at your daughter. She's your spitting image," Nivea said, approaching Dr. Sandburg and holding up Mackenzie for him to get a better view of her face. It was such a lie. Her gorgeous child looked nothing like the wrinkly, pot-bellied, gray-haired doctor, and he should have been honored to be associated with her little diva!

"I don't see any resemblance," he said, recoiling and barely looking at the child. "How much will it take to make you go away? I can't let my wife find out about this; she'll die from humiliation."

Nivea inhaled excitedly. This was going exactly as she'd planned. "Your wife doesn't have to know about this if you agree to my terms and conditions. Now, I was going to ask for a one-time, large sum, but I have to think long-term when it comes to *our* daughter's future."

Dr. Sandburg made an inpatient sound. "How much?"

"A million up front and twenty thousand a month until she's eighteen."

He choked. "You're out of your mind! I don't have that kind of cash on hand. My money's tied up. Give me a more reasonable figure." He waved his hand. "Never mind, I'll tell you what I'm willing to pay. After I pay you, I want you and your baby to go far, far away."

"Let me hear the figure you have in mind?"

"I'll give you two hundred and fifty thousand in cash. Take it or leave it; it's my final offer."

"Two hundred and fifty?" she echoed derisively. "That's appalling. You can do better than that." Nivea paced with the baby and patted her back as if to comfort Mackenzie from having heard how little the doctor thought she was worth. "I bet you spent a hell of a lot more money raising your other children."

"As a matter of fact, I didn't." He looked at Nivea through hard, challenging eyes.

Something about the way he was looking at her gave Nivea a twinge of alarm, and she began to squirm under his sickeningly, confident gaze. She wondered if he had figured a way to outmaneuver her.

"I don't have any children. Long ago, I had a bout with measles. You understand what I'm implying, don't you?" His mouth curved into a triumphant smile.

Oh, shit. The bastard was implying that he's been shooting blanks. Now what? Think, Nivea…think!

"You may have had measles, but that doesn't change the fact that you fathered my child," she said in a voice that lacked conviction. She cleared her throat. "My, uh, attorney is going to insist on a DNA test to…um…you know, prove it." Jesus, why was she stammering? This was not the time to sound uncertain. Guiltily, she glanced away from Dr. Sandburg. She'd doubted that he was the father and now she knew for certain. They both knew it. But Nivea was banking on the fact that he wouldn't want to be publicly accused of being an adulterer, a drug addict, and a whoremonger. The threat of exposing him was the only weapon in her arsenal.

"I'll give you a hundred thousand," Dr. Sandburg said suddenly, his lips pressed together in a tight line of defiance.

Nivea gazed at him, uncomprehending. "Huh? What happened to the two-fifty you offered?"

"That offer is off the table. Take the money or we can battle it out in court," he said with his double-chin jutted out in determination. "I'll risk the damage to my reputation before I give in to extortion tactics."

Nivea opened her mouth to object to the word, "extortion," but then sighed in resignation.

"You're going to have to sign some papers. I want you to sign a gag order, for starters. If my wife ever caught wind of your accusations, my marriage would be over!"

Cradling Mackenzie, she lifted the fingers of her right hand and examined her French manicure as she digested Dr. Sandburg's words. He was terrified of his wife finding out, which gave Nivea even more leverage. She would need more money than he'd offered to keep quiet. Her beauty requirements alone cost a fortune, and now that she'd be caring for two high-maintenance females—her and her daughter—how could she possible stretch a hundred thousand measly dollars?

Nivea had a background in real estate, so perhaps she could flip the money by buying and selling some slum property. Ugh. The thought of being bothered with that made her nauseous. Her father was good with investments; he could help her double or maybe triple her money. But investing took time and she had urgent needs and immediate expenses. *Goddamn this old, gray-haired, sterile asshole!*

Begrudgingly, she extended her hand. "I'll take your offer."

"Good," he said, giving her a flimsy handshake and then collapsing into his chair in exhaustion.

"When will you cut me a check?" she asked anxiously.

"I don't want to leave a paper trail; I'll pay in cash." He slid a prescription pad toward her. "Jot down your address and phone number. My lawyer will be in touch with you after he's prepared the paperwork. I'll pay after you've signed."

Cradling Mackenzie, she scrawled her personal information on the prescription pad, flung the strap of her designer diaper bag over her shoulder, and left the office.

VANGIE

In the shoe department of Saks Fifth Avenue, Vangie tried on a pair of Giuseppe Zanotti platform sandals and modeled them for Alphonso. "They look good on you, ma, you like 'em?" he asked.

She admired the shoes in the mirror on the floor, and then smiled at Alphonso. "Love them, but I can't decide on these or those gem-studded black sneakers."

"Get both of 'em."

"Are you serious?" She glanced from the metallic and suede sandals to the soft leather sneakers.

"I'm dead serious." Alphonso had been upgraded from bodyguard to partner in an international car dealership with Vangie's best friend, Harlow's husband, Drake, and Alphonso spent money like water.

"Thank you, Alphonso," Vangie gushed while inwardly groaning at the impracticality of spending a total of $1,700 on two pairs of shoes. That kind of money could pay for monthly tuition at a private school for her six-year-old son, Yuri. And if she saved up all the cash Alphonso spent on designer clothes and fine dining, she'd have a hefty down payment on a home in the suburbs.

But it wasn't her place to tell Alphonso how to spend his money. At least not now. But if she ever convinced him to take a walk down the aisle, she wouldn't hesitate to voice her opinions on how he spent money. In the meantime, she kept her sentiments to herself.

Leaving the shoe department, they approached the Louis Vuitton boutique. Vangie dramatically closed her eyes and turned her head in the opposite direction.

"Stop playing; you know you want to check out the bags," Alphonso said, indulging her handbag obsession.

"I only want to look." But a quick glance at the glass-encased Speedy Cube bag from the Louis Vuitton Spring Collection had Vangie hyperventilating.

"Can I see it?" she asked the associate.

"Certainly. It's a lovely bag with intricate details. The tiny sequins replicate the historic Damier pattern. They're painstakingly embroidered on a mesh base," the associate explained as she unlocked the case. She handed the bag to Vangie, who nearly swooned as she caressed the handle. Thanks to Alphonso's generosity, Vangie had an enviable collection of designer handbags, but her Louis Vuitton bags were her favorites.

"I have to have this," she told Alphonso in a desperate voice. "We can return the sneakers, okay?" Perspiration was beading on her forehead. She realized her eyes were probably glassy and looking crazed. Like an addict needing a fix, she was ready to bargain, beg, or swindle. Times like this, all her thoughts about wasteful spending went out the window. Every fiber of her being screamed to own the luxurious bag. She didn't care how much it cost; Alphonso had to buy it for her.

"You can get it, ma. And you don't have to return the shoes."

"Thank you. Thank you. You're so sweet, Alphonso." She had to restrain herself from covering Alphonso's face with kisses and dancing joyfully around the store.

Laden with shopping bags, Alphonso and Vangie breezed out of the store and headed for the underground parking garage. Alphonso hit the remote and the headlights of a red Jaguar came on. Cars were his business and he always drove a different luxury car when-ever he came to town. She was so excited about her new handbag, she had momentarily forgotten what car they'd arrived in.

"That F-Type Jag is smoking hot," Alphonso said, eyeing the car like he was looking at a beautiful woman.

"Yeah, it's really sexy," she agreed, but was actually picturing the unboxing of her sexy, new handbag.

Inside the hotel bathroom, Vangie called her mother. "Can you keep Yuri overnight?" she whispered into the phone.

Barbara Boyd made a disgruntled sound. "I'm not your built-in babysitter. I have a life, too, you know. I've had your son all day and I could use a break."

"I know, I'm sorry, but something came up."

"I don't care. Mr. Harold and I like to walk around our home naked when we want to…"

Vangie wrinkled her nose at the thought of her mother and old Mr. Harold walking around naked.

"I have a hot love life of my own, and you can't call me at the spur of the moment and ask me to keep your child overnight. Every time that boyfriend of yours comes to town, you start your mess," Barbara continued.

"What mess?"

"Being unpredictable and unreliable. You should have warned me that I might get stuck with your little crumb snatcher past his bedtime."

"Please, Mom. I'll make it up to you."

"You'd better! And in the future, you're going to have to check and see if I have any plans before you dump Yuri on me for an overnight visit." Barbara made more utterances of discontent, and then asked, "Do you plan on taking your son to school in the morning or do you expect me to do that, too?"

"I'll drive him to school. I'll be there at seven-thirty sharp."

"Yeah, all right." From her skeptical tone, Barbara didn't sound convinced. "Oh, yeah. You're gonna have to stop by the store in the morning and pick up something for his lunch. That boy has eaten me out of house and home with his greedy-behind self." Barbara gave a little chuckle, and Vangie realized she had finished with her tirade. She wondered why her mother bothered to fuss so much when she knew good and well she enjoyed spending time with her grandson. She simply loved to complain and give Vangie a hard time about babysitting.

"Guess what that son of yours did?" Barbara said with a chuckle. "I'm telling you, Yuri's too smart for his own good—smart as a whip. He showed me and Mr. Harold how to hack into your Netflix account—"

"He didn't *hack* into my account, Mom. He just put in the password," Vangie corrected.

"Whatever. Mr. Harold is in seventh heaven, watching one movie after another. And Yuri showed us how to stream it from the computer and into the TV."

"That's not rocket science, you know."

"Oh, hush up. It's rocket science to Mr. Harold and me! We don't need to pay for all those high-behind premium channels now that we have access to your Netflix."

"Glad you're enjoying it. Look, I have to go, Mom. Give Yuri a kiss for me." After ending the call with her mother, Vangie rubbed lotion over her body and then doused herself with perfume. She reached for the flimsy lingerie that was hanging on the back of the bathroom door, and sighed as she slipped on a full-length black negligee. *Why do I bother?* Alphonso only wanted to feel her naked skin next to his; he didn't care about soft music, lingerie, or anything remotely romantic.

Biting down on her bottom lip, she opened the bathroom door and stepped inside the bedroom of his hotel suite. Naked on top of the covers, Alphonso was watching TV. He glanced at Vangie. "You might as well take that shit off," he said in a guttural voice as he leered at her.

She undid the tie in the front of the gown, allowing it to slide off her shoulders. It was time to pay for the $4,000 shopping trip she'd enjoyed earlier that day.

Alphonso sat up and threw his legs over the side of the bed. He gripped his dick and stroked it. "Get it harder, ma," he instructed, demonstrating none of the finesse he displayed outside the bedroom. He was an unimaginative and selfish lover, and Vangie couldn't stand having sex with him. She put up with his crude ways, hoping in time their sex life would improve.

Knowing what Alphonso expected of her, she lowered herself down to her knees and took him inside her mouth. Thrusting and grunting, he cupped her face as he rammed his dick in and out, unconcerned that he was causing her to gag.

Thank goodness, the assault on her windpipe didn't last very long. After half a dozen strokes, he pulled out and roughly yanked her from her knees. On the bed, he positioned her on all fours and then urgently pushed his dick inside her pussy. Clenching her hips, he slammed into her, hard and fast. Like he was trying to do internal damage. There was no warmth between them during sex. Alphonso fucked like he was at war—and Vangie's pussy was the enemy that he was trying to destroy. Fucking Alphonso was a nightmare, but she steeled herself and bore the assault.

When the time was right, she'd coax him into taking his time and making love to her. Right now, she didn't want to hurt his feelings by complaining about his lack of gentleness and his speedy ejaculation.

As usual, after approximately five or six hard thrusts, in quick succession, it was over. Sweating and groaning like an animal, Alphonso collapsed onto the bed and closed his eyes. Five minutes later, he was snoring.

Vangie went in the bathroom to take another shower. Sex with Alphonso made her feel dirty. Hopefully, he'd sleep through the night and not wake up wanting to attack her again. Washed clean, she returned to bed. There was no point in snuggling next to Alphonso, who lay on his designated side of the king-size bed. Vangie and Alphonso never spooned or cuddled. He never slept with an arm draped around her. He was indifferent toward her, like she was a hooker he'd hired for the night.

A few months ago, she had finally mustered the nerve to ask him about his views on marriage, and he didn't bite his tongue. "Marriage is for suckers," Alphonso had said with derisive laughter. "I'm a bachelor for life."

"Oh," she said, crestfallen.

"Do you think you'll ever get married?" he asked, as if she was nothing more to him than a casual acquaintance.

"Yes, I'd like to, someday."

He gave her a pitying smile.

"I want to ask you something?"

He raised his brows.

"How would you describe our relationship?"

He thought about it for a few moments. "We're special friends."

"Oh."

She should have walked away from the relationship right then and there, but she hadn't. She stubbornly believed that with patience and understanding, she could alter his views on marriage.

It was frustrating being his "special friend," but after dealing with his bad sex for six long months, she believed she'd put in too much time to walk away now. He owed her, and one way or another, she was going to get Alphonso to put a ring on it, goddammit!

Remembering that happiness awaited her in another room, Vangie climbed out of bed and went into the living room area of the suite. She rushed toward the Louis Vuitton box and experienced something similar to an orgasm when she lifted the lid.

HARLOW

Harlow's mouth tightened in frustration as she watched Drake organizing suits and shirts in his garment bag. "I wish you could postpone your trip."

Drake gave her a look of surprise. "You've known for months that we were launching an office in London. It's a big deal; I can't cancel."

"I know, but I think I may be ovulating in a few days. Can't Alphonso handle it without you?" Harlow felt stupid not knowing exactly when she was ovulating, but with irregular menstrual cycles it was hard to determine.

Drake stopped packing and gave Harlow his full attention. "It's important that I be there, too. Sweetheart, you're stressing over nothing," he said, sitting down. "Stop putting pressure on yourself. If you simply relax and let it happen, before you know it, you're going to be pregnant with a big, healthy baby boy."

"But we've been trying a long time, and I'm getting desperate." She felt the hot sting of tears but swiped at her eyes before they could spill. Lately, she'd been so emotional.

Drake touched her chin, and gently stroked her cheek. "Everything is going to be fine. We're both healthy and you'll get pregnant when you stop worrying so much." He brushed her forehead with his lips, and then kissed her on the mouth. "We're going to be fine," he said with certainty as he resumed packing. He paused and then nodded, as if struck suddenly by a bright idea.

"Why don't you call Vangie and invite her to spend the weekend with you?"

"Good idea. Vangie loves shopping in New York," Harlow said, injecting false enthusiasm in her voice, and giving her husband the impression that the problem had been resolved. But it hadn't. Being unable to give Drake a child made her feel unfeminine, unattractive, and unworthy. She didn't want to miss this opportunity to try and make a baby. How she longed to accompany him to London. Before they'd become husband and wife, she used to travel with him everywhere. But marriage had changed that.

Harlow's knees shook with anxiety as Drake zipped his garment bag, closed the lid of his Pullman, and then shuffled through papers in his briefcase. Sensing her gaze, he looked up and gave her a considering look. "We're good, right?"

No, we're not. There was another issue she wanted to discuss, but she didn't know how to bring up the subject without sounding like a nagging wife. Harlow gripped his arm reassuringly and produced a convincing smile. "We're good."

After a cursory glance at his watch, he gathered his briefcase and luggage. "My car is here."

Harlow walked with Drake from the bedroom to the front door. "Have a safe flight, and call me as soon as you touch down."

"I always do." He gave her a quick kiss and was out the door.

Alone in their enormous apartment, Harlow slumped into an elegant chair and gazed out the window, which presented a stunning panoramic view of Central Park and New York's glimmering skyline. She stared at the blue sky and fluffy clouds and waited for the sense of serenity that she usually derived from the magnificent view. But all she felt was a deep sense of sorrow and impending doom.

There was another side of Drake that he was keeping secret.

Though it pained Harlow to think about Drake's propensity toward violence, she couldn't deny that he had a dark side. She'd witnessed it firsthand. The night of their wedding, while walking together to their limo, a lunatic woman from Harlow's past, named Ronica, had been waiting in the shadows and suddenly lunged at Harlow, wielding a knife. From inside his suit jacket, Drake drew a gun, shooting and killing Ronica without hesitation.

Ever since he'd defended her from the blade of Ronica's knife, Harlow had been waiting for Drake to fully explain why he'd been carrying a concealed weapon at their wedding! What kind of man would attend his own wedding, armed?

During the first few months, she'd broached the subject numerous times, but Drake always gave her vague and cryptic responses: *I'm a wealthy man, and I have to either walk around surrounded by bodyguards or stay strapped.*

She'd eventually given up on getting the truth out of Drake. Her suspicions that her husband was involved in something illegal and dangerous hadn't stopped her from loving him and hadn't quelled her yearning to bear his child.

She wanted a baby so desperately that her sex life with Drake had downgraded from passionate and steamy to mechanical. And Drake couldn't be blamed for that. For Harlow, sex was no longer an act of love and intimacy; it was the necessary method to procreate. Hopefully, she'd regain a healthy sex drive after she conceived.

God, she wanted a child so badly, it hurt. And the pain was practically physical. An emptiness in the pit of her stomach, as if she'd gone days without food. There was this feeling—this inner knowing. And she didn't need an obstetrician to tell her that she couldn't conceive. The illegal abortion she'd undergone at eleven years old had ruined her insides and left her barren. She knew it in her heart.

Would Drake still love her if he knew that she couldn't give him a child? Drake would never admit it; he'd be noble enough to suggest adoption. But she wouldn't be able to bear the idea of depriving him of his own natural daughter or son.

Then again, suppose Drake didn't take the high road? Suppose he cringed at the idea of adoption and asked her for a divorce? *Oh, God!* Fear as strong as a tsunami swept over her and she fell back against the chair. Worked up into a state of panic, she sprang from the chair and grabbed the phone. *I have to talk to someone*, she thought as she speed-dialed her therapist and requested an emergency appointment.

Two hours later, Harlow sat in her therapist's office and verbalized her fears. Though Dr. Wagner knew the details of Harlow's tragic childhood, until today, Harlow hadn't verbalized her suspicion that the abortion had damaged her and left her unable to conceive.

"It is possible that the abortion caused some uterine damage, but you won't know unless you take the appropriate tests," Dr. Wagner said with a patient smile.

"I'm too afraid to find out."

"Will worrying resolve the issue?"

"No."

"Then make an appointment with your OB/GYN."

"I can't talk about what happened to me with my gynecologist. It's too sordid. Too personal," Harlow said with a frown.

"You don't have to give details. Simply express your concerns. Your doctor will recommend the appropriate tests."

"I don't know."

"You've made so much progress, Harlow. I believe you'll be doing yourself a disservice if you allow shame and fear to prevent you from finding out the truth. Let's say that scar tissue has formed on the uterus and it's impeding your ability to establish pregnancy, your doctor can order tests that check the uterus and fallopian tubes for things like tubal blockage and uterine scarring."

Harlow grimaced and rubbed her forehead.

"The good news is that if there is scar tissue, it can be removed by a simple outpatient procedure. Again, you can't resolve this issue if you don't take any action."

Dr. Wagner was absolutely right. Because of her doubts and fears, she was mired in anguish, and though Drake didn't complain, they both were painfully aware that their marriage was suffering. The weight that was lifted from her shoulders was palpable, and Harlow gave an audible sigh of relief. "Thanks for seeing me, Dr. Wagner," she said, rising to her feet. "I feel a lot better, and I'm going to make an appointment with my gynecologist, ASAP."

At home, instead of making an appointment with her gynecologist, she called Vangie. Despite what she'd told Dr. Wagner, she wasn't ready to be told that she couldn't have children.

"Hey, girl. What's going on?" she asked Vangie.

"Not much. Yuri will be with his dad this weekend, and as you know, Alphonso is handling business with Drake," Vangie replied with a groan.

"Well, jump on the train and come to New York. We could spend a half day luxuriating at the spa, and then check out a Broadway play or go out and have dinner. Drake and I recently discovered a new Caribbean restaurant in Harlem…you'll love it."

"I don't know."

"It's my treat, Vangie, if you're worried about money."

"It's not always about money, Harlow. And I don't need you to pick up the tab for me. I got a promotion, remember? I may not be rich like you, but I'm doing a little better."

"Are you okay, Vangie? You seem overly sensitive."

"I get tired of you treating me like a charity case."

"I didn't mean to offend you, so let's not argue, okay? I miss you and I figured since our men are out of the country, we should get together for some girlfriend time."

"Let me think about it."

"Okay. Try to make it. I really, really miss you."

"I'll let you know," Vangie replied brusquely.

"Vangie, what is it? You seem really perturbed. Are you upset with me for any reason?"

"No," Vangie said, her tone a little surly.

"Is something going on with you and Alphonso?"

"We're fine. Listen, I have to go. My new job is stressful as hell. I'll call you tomorrow. Smooches," Vangie said and hung up.

VANGIE

Vangie stood at the kitchen counter, tearing open a package of frozen broccoli that would go along with the frozen lasagna that was already in the oven.

"Mommy, can I get on the computer?" Yuri yelled from his bedroom.

"Okay, but do your homework before you play any computer games," she replied absently as she dumped the chunk of frozen broccoli into a pan of boiling water. She didn't have the time or desire to cook dinner from scratch, but her method of heating up frozen meals was a great improvement over the greasy fast-food that had sustained her and Yuri for so long.

"Come here for a minute, Mom." Yuri's voice was high-pitched and excited.

Geez, a mother's job is nonstop. Vangie sighed and wiped her hands on a dish towel. Believing that Yuri had logged on to First in Math, an online math resource that students were encouraged to use five to ten minutes a day to keep their math skills sharp, Vangie ambled to her son's bedroom, mentally gearing herself up to provide praise for whatever it was he had accomplished.

Vangie entered her son's bedroom with a smile on her face. "How many more points did my little genius get?"

Yuri looked baffled. "Points? They're not points…they're hits!" His expression quickly switched from puzzlement to pure delight.

"Look, Mom. We might get discovered by Meek Mill or Kendrick Lamar," he said, excitedly pointing to the screen.

Vangie peered at the image on the screen, which Yuri had paused. Instead of the colorful First in Math website, she saw a YouTube video with a mob of teenage boys, their faces frozen in belligerent expressions, their hands, poised in confrontational gestures. And in the center of the young thugs was none other than her innocent, young son.

"Yuri! What are you doing with those teenagers?"

"I was with Uncle Man-Man." Yuri pointed to a chunky teen, around fifteen or sixteen.

"You don't have an Uncle Man-Man." Vangie didn't recognize the kid in the stilled video, and he was certainly no kin to her and Yuri.

"Uncle Man-Man is Jojina's brother."

Jojina was Yuri's father's latest hood-rat girlfriend and the negative influence that she and her three monster-kids had on Yuri was bad enough. Now that a wayward teenage brother was in the picture, there was no telling how much inappropriate behavior Yuri had been exposed to during the court-appointed time he spent with his father.

Vangie unpaused the video and grimaced as she listened to Yuri, standing amidst a throng of thugs outside a housing development that she didn't recognize, reciting rap lines that embraced violence and misogyny.

"We have six thousand hits. When we reach a million, we'll probably get a record deal," Yuri said with innocence shining in his eyes. And that youthful naiveté and innocence was something she wanted to preserve for the duration of his childhood, but if she left it up to his father's lack of wisdom and apparent lack of supervision, Yuri would be headed down a bad path before he reached his teens.

It wasn't that Shawn was a bad father; he wasn't. But he seemed blind to the potential harm that his relationship with his welfare-receiving, project-dwelling girlfriend, Jojina, could cause Yuri down the line. Jojina's children, ages ten, eight, and seven, had already filled Yuri's head with a bunch of ghetto nonsense that he had no business knowing. Every time Yuri came back from a weekend with Shawn, he used new, uncouth expressions that Vangie didn't approve of. It was sickening, the way she had to deprogram Yuri after every visit with his father.

"Does Man-Man live in the same housing projects as Jojina?" Vangie spoke the names *Man-Man* and *Jojina* with repugnance. She already hated hearing Yuri talk about Jojina and her kids who were named Devontay, Javarious, and Starlet. Seriously, who would give their children such ridiculous names except a moronic hood rat?

Lately, Yuri had been referring to Jojina's little monsters as his brothers and sister, which drove Vangie out of her mind. Now, hearing about this teenaged, *Uncle Man-Man* presented a new thorn in her side.

"Log off the computer and read a book, Yuri!"

"But—"

"But, nothing—read a book! I'll call you when dinner's ready."

She stormed back to the kitchen and grabbed her phone. She entered Shawn's number and tapped her nails on the kitchen counter as she impatiently waited for him to pick up.

"Yo," Shawn said in the brusque tone that he used whenever he spoke with Vangie. They'd been mortal enemies ever since Shawn had taken Vangie to court, claiming that Vangie made more money than he did and should be paying him child support. But his tactic hadn't worked.

A few months ago, Vangie had taken Shawn back to court, trying to revoke his visitation rights due to the bad influence the project heifer and her heathen kids were having on Yuri. But the judge told Vangie that she had to prove that Yuri had been harmed while in the care of his father. Unable to prove that Yuri had actually been harmed, Vangie had no choice but to continue allowing Yuri to be around Shawn's ratchet girlfriend.

Since then, Vangie had tried to move on. She tried to act civil around Shawn; she tried to not hold a grudge against him. For Yuri's sake, she would have preferred that she and Shawn treated each other with mutual respect, but Shawn was too stubborn to let go of their past differences. He spoke to her in gruff tones in front of Yuri, giving their son the impression that she was the bad guy.

The chorus of male voices in the background indicated that Shawn was at work at the barbershop, and probably couldn't have a serious discussion at the moment. "When you get a chance, can you call me back; we need to talk about something serious," Vangie said.

"I have a few minutes; what's on your mind?" Shawn softened his tone a little.

Vangie took a deep breath. "Well, you know I've been complaining that your girlfriend's kids are a bad influence on Yuri—"

"Yeah, and you took me back to court, trying to cut off my visitation rights, but the judge told you to chill out. So, what's the problem, now?"

"The problem is—"

"The problem is," Shawn interrupted, "you want to control my life and give approval over who I'm seeing. But you can't, so you need to stop trying."

"I don't care who you're seeing. I'm only trying to look out for Yuri's best interest and would hope you felt the same way."

"I'm not going to let anything happen to my son, Vangie. You know that." Shawn exhaled in frustration. "I said I have a few minutes…not all day. So, what's this call about?" Irritation had crept into Shawn's voice and Vangie realized she wouldn't be able to get through to him without involving lawyers. He could be so narrow-minded and stubborn, it was infuriating.

"Do you realize that Yuri is on a YouTube video?"

"What?"

"You heard me. While he was in your care, his so-called *Uncle Man-Man* included him in a video with a bunch of thugs, and they're all in front of the camera rapping about killing and chopping down women."

"Oh, yeah?" Shawn said with a trace of pride in his voice. "I heard Yuri spitting some rhymes the other day; he might have talent. Time will tell."

"Time won't tell shit. If you can't protect Yuri and keep away from those ignorant-ass future convicts, then you don't need to have visitation with him."

"Here we go with the same old shit. You're no better than the cops, prejudging and profiling the young man only because he's a normal, urban teen who enjoys rap music."

"Don't even go there, Shawn. I like rap music, too, but I wouldn't film a six-year-old kid rapping about illegal activities and sexual stuff he doesn't understand. And I definitely wouldn't post it on the Internet."

"Welcome to modern times," Shawn said in a condescending way.

"Aren't you worried?"

"Worried about what?"

"Yuri's life could be in danger. Suppose some rival gang targets Man-Man when he's around Yuri?"

"What gang? You watch too much TV."

"I don't want that heathen named Man-Man to have any influence whatsoever on my child. Do you hear me, Shawn? If you can't assure me that Yuri will be with you at all times during his visitation, then don't even bother to pick him up."

"If I'm not mistaken, we have joint custody. I don't ask you who you leave Yuri with—"

"Because I only leave him with my mother."

"And what about your man?"

"Alphonso doesn't babysit for Yuri."

"Are you trying to tell me that ol' boy is never alone with Yuri?"

"What are you trying to say?"

"Look, I know for a fact that Yuri has been in the care of ya boy and you weren't with them."

Vangie thought about it. "Well, yeah, Yuri has made a couple of quick runs with Alphonso. You know…like to pick up food or to take my car in to be detailed, but I don't leave Yuri in anyone's care for a lengthy period of time. Your irresponsibility is frightening. I mean…seriously, what were you thinking when you brought those dangerous, uncouth people into our son's life? Couldn't you have kept your disgusting relationship away from Yuri?"

"Disgusting?"

"That's right. I work hard to give Yuri the best life I can offer him. But you're undoing my hard work by taking him to the damn projects, and deliberately exposing him to all sorts of violence and crime."

"I think Yuri is safer with Jojina's family than he is with your man."

"What! Do you know how stupid you sound? Alphonso is an upstanding businessman, not a wannabe thug like you! I have to look out for my child's well-being, so don't even bother to pick up Yuri tomorrow. You're not fit to be a parent!"

"You don't run shit, Vangie. I'll be there to pick up Yuri for our scheduled visit and you can't do shit about it. Oh, and by the way, ask Yuri about the gun he saw strapped to ya boy's ankle. The gun your boy put in his hand."

"What the hell are you talking about?"

"Ask Yuri about it. That gun situation sounds like something the judge would find much more dangerous than Yuri rapping along with a harmless song. Think about it."

The phone went dead and Vangie realized that Shawn had hung up on her.

"YURI!" Vangie screamed her son's name.

Yuri dashed into the kitchen. "Is dinner ready?"

"No." She gripped her son by the shoulders. "Did you tell your father that Alphonso let you hold a gun?"

Yuri took on a guilty expression, and then nodded his head.

"Why didn't you tell me?"

"Mr. Alphonso told me not to mention it to you. He said you'd be upset."

"He was right. I'm very upset. But I'm more upset with Alphonso than you. You're only a child; he should have known better."

"I saw the gun in his ankle strap and asked him if I could hold it."

Vangie grimaced in horror.

"He took out the clip before he let me hold it," Yuri said.

"What do you know about clips?"

Yuri shrugged. "I know a lot."

"A lot?"

"Uh-huh. Devontay, Javarious, and me…we look at guns online. My brothers want to buy Glocks when they get older, but I want a compact Ruger, like the one Mr. Alphonso carries."

Vangie was beyond horrified. She grabbed her phone, ready to call Alphonso, but remembering that he was probably still en route to England, she put the phone down. Incensed, she didn't know who she was more furious with…Shawn or Alphonso.

NIVEA

Mackenzie jolted awake and yelled each time Nivea tried to lower her into her crib. "You have to sleep in your crib, Kenzie. You can't sleep in Mommy's bed forever," Nivea said firmly as she checked to make sure her daughter was dry. "Tonight, you're going to have to cry yourself to sleep."

Since her own mother wasn't speaking to her, Nivea got most of her parenting tips from Vangie. According to Vangie, it was okay to allow Mackenzie to cry herself to sleep as long as she was fed and dry. Mackenzie screamed in outrage when Nivea turned off the light and closed the door. A second later, Nivea rushed inside her daughter's room and plugged in the night light. It took all her willpower not to pick up her baby and put her in bed with her.

Heading to her bedroom, Nivea began stripping out of her clothes. A long, hot bath was in order. Taking care of a baby was exhausting, and she was anxious to hire a nanny. Dr. Sandburg's money couldn't come soon enough. She wondered how long it would take before she had his money secured in her bank account.

The baby's cries began to die down as she ran her bath water, and no sooner had she stuck her toe into the hot, scented water, she heard the dull buzz of her cell phone. Naked, she trekked into her bedroom and picked up the phone. She didn't recognize the number of the incoming call. Maybe it was Sandburg's lawyer, anxious to get the paperwork signed.

"Hello?"

"May I speak to Nivea Westcott?" asked an unfamiliar female voice.

"This is she."

"This is Rachel Sandburg, Bertram's wife…"

Oh, shit! "What can I do for you, Mrs. Sandburg?" Nivea's voice was even and controlled, but her heart was hammering away. *How did this bitch get my number and why is she calling me?*

"Call me, Rachel. Please," the doctor's wife said pleasantly. "Bertram told me about the baby…" The woman paused. "The child he possibly fathered."

Bringing a lawyer into the equation was bad enough, but why would Dr. Sandburg also tell his wife about the situation? She was the main reason he wanted to pay for Nivea's silence.

"I want you to know that I don't harbor any resentment toward you. After all, men will be men," Rachel continued in an unreasonably chipper tone.

Yeah, right! This bitch is acting entirely too civilized; she has to be up to something.

"I guess you're wondering why I'm calling."

I know why you're calling! You want to demand a paternity test so you can put a stop to that hundred grand check your husband promised me! "Yes, I am," Nivea said, suspicion coating her words.

"After thirty-two years of marriage, Bertram has never been unfaithful. That is, until his one-time encounter with you. You and my husband were together only once; am I right, Ms. Westcott?"

Nivea pondered the question. It was a Catch-22. Admitting to only a one-time fling made it seem less likely that Dr. Sandburg was Mackenzie's father. But accusing the doctor of having a full-fledged affair with her might piss his wife off, altering her sweet disposition. Instinct told Nivea that she needed the doctor's wife as an ally and not an enemy.

"Well, this is really awkward, Mrs. Sandburg...I mean, Rachel."

"I understand. I won't pry into the specifics. But please set my mind at ease—is the affair between you and my husband over?"

"Yes, it is."

"Thank goodness. I was stunned by Bertram's confession of adultery. But now that I've had time to process everything, well, I'm ready to get to the matter at hand. My husband confided that he doesn't believe that he fathered your child. He wants to spend money to get rid of you and your child, but I don't want to make a mistake we'll all regret. I told him that I want to handle the matter properly."

She wants a DNA test. I'm so screwed! Nivea placed her fingertips on her forehead and rubbed the skin circularly. "How do you propose to handle this matter properly?" she asked with dread.

"Well, Nivea...may I call you Nivea?"

"Yes, of course," Nivea responded, still wondering why Mrs. Sandburg was bothering to play nice.

"I was hoping to see the baby for myself. I'll know whether or not she's Bertram's daughter. And if she is, rest assured, my husband will do the right thing by his child."

Really? Oh, wow! A renewed sense of hope straightened Nivea's shoulders. "When would you like to see Mackenzie?"

"Is that her name...Mackenzie?"

"Yes."

"It's lovely."

"Thank you." The pleasantries were weird, but Nivea was willing to play along as long as she had a big payday coming. Getting on the wife's good side and convincing her that her husband had fathered Mackenzie might be more profitable than Dr. Sandburg's offer. *Do I dare hope for eighteen years of generous child support!*

"I'm really anxious to see her, but I don't want to interfere with your schedule..."

"Don't worry about it. Would you like to see the baby this week?"

"Yes, as soon as possible."

"How about tomorrow afternoon? You could come here or we could meet you somewhere. Uh, somewhere discreet," Nivea offered.

"You're welcome to bring the baby to our home. Bertram will be at work, of course. So there will only be us girls," Mrs. Sandburg said with a little laugh and then gave Nivea her address—her very prestigious address that was located in an area known for its luxurious, multimillion-dollar homes.

Nivea had no idea Dr. Sandburg had it like that. The cheap bastard had tried to pay her off with peanuts. But if she could convince his wife that Mackenzie was his, she and her baby would be rolling in dough.

Rachel sounded lonely, albeit a bit nutty. A childless old biddy looking for some company and a child to dote on. Nivea felt a little gush of pleasure at the idea of receiving generous support checks and her child being showered with a plethora of material things.

Nivea had intended to ask her rich friend Harlow to be Mackenzie's godmother, but she wouldn't have to be bothered taking handouts from Harlow if she was able to convince Rachel Sandburg that Mackenzie was her husband's child.

After concluding her strange call with Rachel Sandburg, Nivea crept into Mackenzie's room to check on her. She smiled down at her sleeping child and marveled at her perfection. She'd been bald at birth, but she now had a thin layer of dark hair. Her eyes were dark, too. Thank goodness, they weren't green or blue. Dr. Sandburg had dark eyes, and at this stage of Mackenzie's development, she had no glaring physical characteristics that differed from Sandburg's.

Nivea had no idea why Dr. Sandburg was allowing his wife to

believe that he could possibly be the father. Then again, maybe his measles story was a lie. At this point, it really didn't matter. Rachel seemed eager to accept Mackenzie.

Satisfied that she'd be able to pass Mackenzie off as the doctor's child, Nivea kissed her daughter and then quietly left the room.

VANGIE

Vangie wasn't happy when she looked through the peephole and spotted both Shawn and Jojina standing outside her apartment door. Jojina usually waited in the car when Shawn picked up Yuri, and that was exactly where the heifer belonged.

She opened the door, partway, but didn't allow them to enter. She observed Jojina, taking in her tiny waist, flat tummy, and perfectly round, protrusive butt. *Injections*, she thought with her lips scrunched together in disapproval. Anytime project chicks were spending money on cosmetic enhancements, it was time for Vangie to step up her game. With a little liposuction, a breast lift, and a tummy tuck, she could reclaim her banging, pre-Yuri body.

"Yuri! Your dad's here," Vangie called out.

"Okay," Yuri shouted from his bedroom.

Vangie returned her attention to Jojina. Though the woman was much prettier than she'd realized, she dressed like a complete slut with her hooker heels and skin-tight jeans. Vangie's eyes settled on Jojina's Louis Vuitton Artsy bag. Being a Louis expert, she concluded that the bag was the real deal, and wondered if Shawn had purchased it. Though Vangie had an impressive collection of Louis Vuitton bags, she still felt a stab of envy over the idea of Shawn buying this tramp such an expensive gift.

Vangie gave Jojina another long look of disdain, and then started to close the door.

"Can we talk?" Jojina suddenly asked, running her zebra-print nails through her long, wavy weave. The weave had the nerve to look really nice, and the hair was a good quality. *This fucking bitch is living good off my tax dollars!* Apparently welfare checks covered the cost of cosmetic surgery, fancy manicures, and expensive hairstyles. Vangie would have never considered receiving welfare, but maybe she had it all wrong; maybe she was a sucker for going out and earning a honest living.

Vangie turned her nose up. *"We* don't have anything to talk about. Oh, hold up, on second thought, we do need to get a few things straight. First of all, do you realize your sons troll the Internet looking at guns? You need to monitor their computer time when Yuri is at your house. Secondly—"

"What about your man?" Shawn butted in. "He's showing Yuri the real thing…that nigga put a gun in my boy's hand, and you think that's okay?"

"No, it's not. But since Alphonso is out of the country on business, I haven't had a chance to speak to him about it."

"Yeah, well, let dude know that I think he's a bad role model and I need to holla at him regarding my son."

Vangie winced. Hearing Alphonso referred to as a bad role model was disconcerting, but until she heard his explanation, she didn't want to think about the gun situation.

"Shawn told me you don't want Yuri around my brother," Jojina said.

Vangie planted a hand on her hip. "I sure don't. When Yuri visits Shawn, I expect him to be cared for by his father—not some wild teenager that I've never met."

Jojina nodded in understanding. "Man-Man was wrong. He shouldn't have put Yuri in that video. I just want you to know that I made him take the video down, and it won't happen again."

"It better not!" Vangie said, indifferent to Jojina's attempt at cooperativeness. "I don't want my son around criminal-minded thugs."

Jojina's brows drew together, suggesting she was offended. "My brother's not a criminal."

"Oh, please," Vangie muttered, rolling her eyes.

Jojina's gaze flickered upward to Shawn, imploring him to say something. Shawn placed an arm around her and glared at Vangie. "There you go, stereotyping your own people," he said, shaking his head.

"I call it like I see it." Vangie was unapologetic. Though Jojina had extended an olive branch, Vangie refused to accept it. The ghetto tramp had a lot of nerve coming to her door. She needed to stay in her place and keep her big butt inside the car. Vangie was about to express her feelings about Jojina showing up at her apartment, uninvited, when Yuri came barreling into the living room. He was struggling with his overly stuffed duffle bag, but his eyes were alight with joy as he raced toward his father, his small body awkwardly pulled to one side.

"Hey, Dad! Hi, Jojina!" he said with a big smile.

"Hey, what's up, Son?" Shawn relieved Yuri of his heavy bag and Yuri straightened upright. Jojina beamed at Yuri and affectionately tousled his hair. Vangie wanted to smack Jojina's hands away from her son's head, but when Yuri smiled up at the woman, Vangie realized he'd be upset if she cursed out his father's girlfriend.

"Your brothers and sister are in the car," Jojina told Yuri.

Is this bitch serious? "Yuri doesn't have any siblings," Vangie pointed out.

"Yes, I do. I have two brothers and a sister," Yuri insisted, wearing a hurt expression.

"Your father and I only have one child—*you!*"

"Your brothers and sister are waiting in the car," Jojina said, glancing at Vangie challengingly as she stroked Yuri's cheek.

Seething, Vangie glared at Jojina. "Get your hand off my son's face and stop telling him those lies."

"Mom, don't be mean to Jojina," Yuri pleaded.

"Shawn, you better talk to this chick," Vangie said threateningly. "She's taking too many liberties with my child."

"I think of Yuri as my fourth child," Jojina explained in a fake, sugary voice.

Vangie wanted to slap her. "Yuri's not your fourth child! And let me tell you something else…you need to stop trying to act like y'all are one big, happy family because you're not. You're nothing more than an extended booty call…believe that! I know Shawn, and he'll be on to the next one in a few months!"

"You can't speak for me," Shawn interjected. "Come on, let's go." He steered Jojina and Yuri away from the door. Vangie watched with bitter resentment as Shawn and Jojina walked along the corridor with Yuri between them. When Jojina reached for Yuri's hand, it took all of Vangie's willpower not to run behind them and punch the bitch in the back of her head. It took every ounce of restraint not to snatch Yuri's hand out of the grasp of that trifling, unemployed, welfare-fraudulent ho.

Jojina had a lot of game, but Vangie could see through her façade. Underneath Jojina's seemingly sweet surface was a ruthless chick, and she was pretending to love Yuri simply to get her hooks deeper into Shawn. Claiming another woman's son as her own was insulting as hell, and Vangie wondered why Shawn wasn't calling Jojina out on bullshit. *That project pussy must be the bomb. I know one thing, I'm going to hire a new lawyer—someone who can do a better job of keeping my child away from that conniving bitch and her ghetto-ass family.*

Vangie closed the door and immediately called Alphonso. She got his voicemail again. She realized he was busy and all, handling the opening of the London office, but couldn't he at least have called her to let her know that he'd arrived safely? She doubted if Drake treated Harlow with such a lack of regard.

Compared to most men, Alphonso was quite a catch. He was very generous, showering Vangie with expensive gifts, and he always showed her a good time when he was in town. But their relationship wasn't evolving the way she'd hoped. They were no closer to picking out rings than they were when they'd first met. Harlow had advised Vangie not to try to rush Alphonso to the altar. He was a confirmed bachelor, and if Vangie wanted him to take their relationship to the next level, she would have to be patient. But all this pretending that she was content with the unlabeled status of their relationship was starting to get her down.

She knew Alphonso carried a gun, but she'd never seen it. Frankly, she was uncomfortable about bringing up the subject. But what choice did she have? When it came to Yuri, Vangie became as protective as a mother lion. Alphonso was dead wrong; he should not have allowed Yuri to touch a gun. What the hell was he thinking?

She thought about calling Harlow to get her opinion, but nixed the idea. She and Harlow used to share intimate stories about their relationships with Drake and Alphonso, but ever since the two men had become business partners, Harlow had become tight-lipped, as if afraid of allowing some kind of top-secret information to slip out.

And with Harlow desperately trying to get pregnant, her entire conversation revolved around pregnancy and baby-related themes. Harlow was still her girl and everything, but she'd be glad when she got back to being her old self. The baby-obsessed Harlow was… well, there was no way to put it nicely—Harlow had become boring.

Maybe she could talk to Nivea. Well, not about Alphonso and the gun. Nivea was so damned opinionated and Vangie suspected Nivea was secretly envious that she'd snagged Alphonso. Nivea used to sarcastically refer to Alphonso as "the bodyguard," but now that he and Drake were partners, she didn't seem interested in talking about Alphonso at all.

Vangie wondered if Nivea had gotten Mackenzie's paternity test back. She shook her head about the whole paternity disaster. Nivea swore that her daughter had been fathered by Knox, but any fool could see that the child was mixed. Nivea needed to leave her sister's husband alone and go after the real father—whoever he was.

It was a damn shame that after being faithful and true to Alphonso, she couldn't even get a phone call when he was out of town.

It was time to break it off with Alphonso. Fuck the gifts and the fancy dinners and trips. She should hold him to the same standards that she'd held Yuri's dad. Back when she and Shawn were together, and when he'd made it clear that he expected all the perks of family life, minus the marriage certificate, Vangie had ended the relationship.

But for some reason, she was hanging on to Alphonso. In the back of her mind, she held the hope that with patience and understanding, she could change his outlook on matrimony. She *had* to change his mind. Where would she find another catch like Alphonso? He was an affluent businessman and extremely generous. Marriage to him assured her of financial security and a luxurious lifestyle like Harlow had. She didn't consider herself as a gold digger, but like anybody else, she desired the finer things in life.

She imagined Alphonso carrying her over the threshold of a dream house. She didn't expect a mansion or anything; she simply wanted a comfortable and spacious home in a good neighborhood. She could see herself as a stay-at-home mom, carpooling

Yuri to his sports events and other extracurricular activities. And of course, she'd have Alphonso's baby. She'd try to get a bun in the oven soon after they walked down the aisle. A rich man's baby was sort of an insurance policy…in case the marriage didn't work out.

Unfortunately, the odds of her acquiring the lifestyle she yearned for were as remote and farfetched as hitting the Mega Millions lottery.

Vangie would be thirty on her next birthday and was no closer to the altar than when she'd first met Alphonso at Harlow's wedding. What was it about her that caused her to always attract commitment-phobes?

Feeling sorry for herself, Vangie slumped into a chair. She checked the time. It was barely past nine in the morning, and the remainder of her weekend was free, but instead of feeling relieved and joyful, she felt neglected and lonely. While other single women her age were either at the hair salon getting glammed up for a hot date or going to the mall to buy a sexy outfit, Vangie was home alone without any plans. She could use the spa day that Harlow had offered, but her heart wasn't in it. At this point, the only thing that would put a smile on her face would be getting the green light to start planning a wedding. She wanted to look at gowns, taste test samples of cake, search for a wedding venue, and set up a bridal registry. She wanted to do all those activities with an indulgent, groom-to-be in tow.

But it wasn't going to happen. She was going to end up gray-haired and old and alone.

Maybe she should take Harlow up on her invitation. A girls' night out would help her forget her problems. Trouble was, being around happily-married Harlow was a glaring reminder of her permanently single status.

Vangie and Harlow were worlds apart. Harlow had it all. She

was a pampered lady of leisure with a wealthy husband who adored her, while Vangie was a working, single mom in an uncommitted relationship. Even worse, she had to put up with ghetto drama from an irritating baby daddy and his conniving, project chick.

Harlow had no idea that Vangie was growing more bitter by the day, and she didn't need to know. Despite her luxurious lifestyle, Harlow was the same down-to-earth person she'd always been. It was Vangie who had changed. Though she tried to fight her emotions, she couldn't help feeling resentful of dear, sweet Harlow. Jealousy was an ugly emotion and she wished she could cut it out of her heart.

She glanced at her silent phone. It would be nice if Alphonso called and checked on her, but their relationship was what it was. He probably wouldn't call until he was back in the States. Being someone's occasional lover and special friend really sucked. It was demoralizing, but she'd invested a lot of time in their "special friendship" and wasn't willing to throw in the towel.

Maybe she should reconsider visiting Harlow. If she confided her awful dilemma, perhaps the two of them could put their heads together and come up with a scheme that would motivate Alphonso to hurry up and pop the damn question.

Feeling hopeful, Vangie picked up the phone and called Harlow. "Hey, girl. Is the invitation still open?"

"Of course. You're always welcome, Vangie. You know that," Harlow replied.

"Okay, I'll catch an afternoon train and get a cab to your place."

"Fantastic. I'm so excited. Wanna see a Broadway show?"

"Sure."

"I've heard good things about *Motown: The Musical*, *Wicked*, and *Kinky Boots*. Which would you like to see?"

"Surprise me, okay?"

"All right. See you soon."

In her bedroom, Vangie opened her closet and pulled out her Louis Vuitton duffle bag. She'd trade in all her designer bags, her red bottom shoes—everything he'd bought for her—if only she could have his heart.

HARLOW

"Did you enjoy the play?" Harlow asked Vangie as they merged into the crowd of people exiting the theater.

"It was all right," Vangie said, unenthused about *Motown: The Musical*. "The chick playing Diana Ross got on my nerves."

"Really? Why?"

"She seemed to be overacting. And she didn't look or sound anything like the real Diana Ross."

"I thought she was good."

"Umph." Nivea twisted her lips, conveying her dissatisfaction.

"What's going on with you, girl? You're so grumpy and irritated, lately."

Vangie gave a little shrug. "I'm okay."

"No, you're not. Let's get something to eat and something good to drink. I have to get all my drinking in before I get pregnant," Harlow said with a smile that quickly vanished when she noticed Vangie's gaze shifting downward. She wondered if Vangie assumed that she couldn't have kids and was embarrassed for her.

Outside the theater, Harlow aggressively hailed a cab, stepping in front of several patrons of the theater who were also trying to get a cab. The two women slid into the backseat and Harlow gave the driver the address of the restaurant.

"The way you flagged down this cab was impressive," Vangie said, her mood seeming to have elevated. "You hailed this cab like a native New Yorker."

"I know, right? It took a lot of practice, but I figured it out," Harlow said in an upbeat tone.

"What's the secret?"

"Secret to what?"

"The secret to getting a cab in this chaotic city. I had to wait for a cab in a long-ass line outside Penn Station; I tried stepping off the curb and waving my arms, but each cab drove past me like I was invisible. It was so infuriating."

"There's no secret. I simply have the attitude that I'm entitled to have a cab, and drivers act accordingly and pull over."

"I guess you have to be rich to have that *entitled* feeling."

"No, it has nothing to do with money. It's an inner feeling."

"Uh-huh," Vangie said doubtfully. "I bet you didn't feel entitled before you married Drake."

"You've been making a lot of snide comments, lately. Are you upset with me about something?" Harlow scrutinized Vangie's face, her eyes, searching for the truth.

"No, I'm not mad at you. I just have a lot going on right now."

"Like what?"

Vangie blew out a long sigh. "Well…Shawn, for one thing."

"What about Shawn?"

"He and his tramp of a girlfriend ganged up on me this morning."

"You're kidding? I hope it didn't get physical."

"Hell, no. I would have whipped that skank bitch's ass if she put her hands on me."

"Well, what happened?"

"He brought her to my front door when he came to pick up Yuri, and that slut had the nerve to tell me that she thought of my son as her fourth child. And Shawn co-signed on that mess she was talking. She was deliberately trying me by tousling Yuri's hair, caressing his face, and telling him that his brothers and sister were waiting for him in the car."

"I'm glad you were able to control yourself."

"Girl, it was hard. I was two seconds from slapping the shit out of her, but the last thing I need is an assault charge. What I really need is another attorney. The one I have is too soft. I need a barracuda that can convince the judge that my son's life is endangered every time he spends time in that dangerous housing project where bullets are flying and all the kids are fascinated with guns. It's disgusting the way Shawn has Yuri spending the weekends in the damn projects with that tacky bitch and her three heathen-kids…and I can't do anything about it."

"Why don't you get another attorney?"

"It's not that simple. A good lawyer, the kind that would fight to strip Shawn of his visitation rights, costs money. A lot of money."

"Can't Alphonso help with that? Have you spoken to him about giving you the money for a new attorney?"

"No."

"Why not? He's very generous, isn't he?"

"Yeah, in his own way. He buys me what he wants me to have… treats me to nice getaways and fancy dinners, but so far, he hasn't been doling out any cash. And I don't think I'd be comfortable asking him for money."

"I know what you mean. I was the same way before Drake and I got married."

"Oh, God!" Looking disgruntled, Vangie shook her head.

"What's wrong?"

"Why do you always have to throw your marriage in my face?" Vangie asked bitterly.

Harlow looked perplexed. "I don't know what you're talking about."

"Every chance you get, you bring up the fact that you're married and I'm not."

"You can't be serious." She placed a hand on top of Vangie's.

"You're my best friend, Vangie; I would never deliberately say anything to hurt you."

"It doesn't seem that way," Vangie said with a scowl and removed her hand from beneath Harlow's.

The cab pulled up in front of a Japanese restaurant on East Forty-Seventh Street.

"This place looks expensive as hell," Vangie grumbled as she climbed out of the cab.

"It is. They serve top-notch sushi; the fish is flown in from Japan. But don't worry; dinner is on me."

"You already treated me to the play. I thought we were going to an affordable Caribbean place."

"You said you didn't care where we ate. Why are we arguing over every little thing? I'm trying to show you a good time in New York and all you're doing is complaining."

With tension in the air, the two women were silent as they were escorted to their table. The silence continued while the hot sake was being poured. Vangie wrinkled her nose when she tasted the rice wine. "Oh, hell no; I can't drink this nasty shit. I need some American alcohol."

Harlow burst out laughing, breaking the tension. "Sip it slowly. Sake is an acquired taste."

Vangie wrapped her palms around the cup and took another sip. She grimaced. "Is this your way of punishing me for having a bad attitude all night? If so, I'm sorry." She reached across the table and squeezed the top of Harlow's hand. "I have a confession, and I hope you can forgive me."

"What is it?"

Vangie took a deep breath. "I'm ashamed to admit it, but I'm envious of your perfect life. I don't want to be, but I am. I've even prayed to God, asking him to take the jealousy out of my heart, but He's not listening. Oh, Harlow, I'm so...so sorry. You're the best friend in the world, and I've allowed this evil envy to drive a wedge between us."

Harlow studied Vangie's face. "I knew something was wrong, but I had no idea you were hating on me. If I could, I'd give you a million dollars like Oprah gave Gayle back in the day. But it's not my money to give; it's Drake's."

"I know. And to be honest, it's not only your money that has me feeling inferior and insecure. It's your marriage."

"Why?"

Wearing a pained smile, Vangie said, "I'm jealous of what you and Drake have."

Harlow lowered her head, feeling hurt and disappointed in Vangie. "And..."

"There's more?"

Vangie nodded. "I've been keeping a secret from you." She sighed and shook her head. "I've been acting like it's all good between Alphonso and me, but actually, our relationship is a hot mess, girl. And I've been too ashamed to tell you that Alphonso only thinks of me as a special friend. He told me a few months ago that he's a confirmed bachelor. Not interested in marrying me or anyone— ever!"

"Are you kidding me?"

"I kid you not. The man is a commitment-phobe like Shawn. I'm so pathetic." Vangie shook her head.

"No, you're not. Don't say that."

"It's true. After he told me his views on marriage, I should have ended our relationship, but instead of moving on, I accepted his terms."

"Why?"

"I was hoping I could figure out a way to change his mind."

"But you tried that with Shawn and it didn't work. Why would you knowingly repeat the same mistake?"

"I'm a stupid ass and a glutton for punishment, I guess." Vangie laughed bitterly. "Seriously, where would I find another single black man, who doesn't have any kids and who's as sophisticated and successful as Alphonso? I don't feel like I have a choice. I have to be patient and stay the course."

"That doesn't make any sense. You both want two different things, and since he straight out told you there's no possibility of him ever getting married, what's the point in waiting around?" Harlow went quiet and thought for a few moments. "Are you in love with Alphonso?"

Vangie shrugged. "Not really. I doubt if I'll ever love anyone the way I loved Shawn. I think a lot of women feel the way I do, you know, after they have a man's child."

"Are you saying you're still in love with Shawn?"

"Hell no. I hate Shawn's guts. But I used to love him. I loved him hard, and I could never feel that way about anyone else."

"Then it shouldn't be difficult for you to break it off with Alphonso. You're wasting precious time and humiliating yourself by lingering in a relationship that isn't going anywhere."

"You're right."

The waitress, a beautiful woman dressed in traditional Japanese garb, approached their table and asked if they were ready to order. "Not yet; we need a few more minutes," Harlow said as she scanned the menu. "Can you bring my friend another drink? She doesn't like sake."

The waitress nodded in understanding. "What would you like?" she asked Vangie.

"Can I get a pomegranate martini?"

"Sorry. We only have a small wet bar. We don't serve that here. I can offer cold sake."

Vangie scrunched up her nose. "No more sake. Do you have anything sweet?"

"Plum wine?" the waitress offered.

"Great. Bring us both a glass. Hell, bring us a bottle," Harlow said and nudged a menu toward Vangie.

They both studied the menus. "I'm not feeling all this raw fish," Vangie said.

"You don't have to get sushi. Why don't you order the Russian King Crab with Special Vinegar Sauce for an appetizer? I've had it and it's really good."

"Okay, what are you having?"

"I think I'll start out with the Tuna Tartare with Beluga Caviar and Scallions."

Vangie scanned the menu, checking out Harlow's selection. "Damn, your appetizer costs a hundred and fifty dollars!"

"And it's worth it. So delicious. Wanna try it?"

"No, I'll stick with the King Crab. Hell, thirty dollars for crab meat is bad enough."

"You're not paying for it, so stop worrying about it."

"Seems wasteful," Vangie said, shaking her head.

Harlow glanced at Vangie's new handbag that was hanging on the back of the chair. "I guess that Louis Vuitton bag was cheap?"

"I get to carry my bags over and over, but this food is going in one end and out the other."

"Oh, live a little and stop being a joy snatcher."

When the waitress returned with the drinks, Harlow ordered their appetizers and main course, getting the Chef's Special Sushi and Sashimi platter for herself and Teriyaki Chicken and Tempura Shrimp and Vegetables for Vangie.

They both liked the plum wine and raised their glasses in a toast. Harlow's phone rang and she broke into a grin when she saw Drake's name on the screen. "Hello, sweetheart! How's everything working out in London? It's going good?... Oh, I'm so glad to hear that." Then she lowered her voice. "I miss you, Drake. Our bed is so big and lonely without you."

"Tell Drake I said hello," Vangie chimed in.

"Vangie says hello." She glanced at Vangie. "Drake said, hi." Then she returned her attention to her call. Vangie began taking big gulps of the wine while Harlow talked with Drake.

"We went to see that play about Motown. It was awesome. Now we're at Kurumazushi. Yes, we're having a great time...Okay, see you soon, darling. I love you, too." Wearing a pleasant smile, Harlow clicked off the phone and returned it to her bag.

"That's what I wish I had," Vangie said solemnly, and took a big sip of wine. "I wish I had someone who cared enough to check up on me. A man who loved me enough to put a ring on my damn finger."

"Your day is gonna come, Vangie. But the first thing you have to do is break it off with Alphonso."

"Why are you pushing so hard for me to dump him?"

"He won't even define your relationship; he refers to you as his *special friend!*" Harlow made a scoffing sound. "What kind of mess is that? From what you've told me, I get the feeling that you're being treated like a mistress...or worse."

"Well...to be honest, we don't spend that much quality time together, and he gives me expensive gifts every time we sleep together. So, I guess you could say I'm allowing him to treat me like a whore."

"Why, Vangie? Why would you stoop to that? Your personal integrity has to be more valuable than a pair of expensive sandals..." Harlow paused and glanced down at Vangie's metallic sandals. "You can do better than Alphonso, girl. I want you to find someone who wants the same thing you want. Even if you end up with a bus driver, so what? I mean…why these high standards now? Shawn was a barber…cutting hair in his mother's basement and you had a child by him. Alphonso was only a bodyguard when you met him at my wedding, and that didn't bother you at the time."

"Well, I've grown accustomed to the finer things in life now. Alphonso has given me so many material things, I couldn't imagine being with an average guy after being with him. I want the kind of life you're living, Harlow. Why don't you want that for me?"

"Because you're being fake and materialistic, Vangie, and I've never known you to be that way. I didn't marry Drake for his money; I married for love. Rich or poor, I'll always love him."

"Good for you, Harlow. You've always been a Miss Goody Two-Shoes. Everybody isn't like you." Vangie leaned forward and whispered, "By the way, I have another confession."

"Jesus! What now?"

"Alphonso is terrible in bed. Girl, he's the worst. I've never had an orgasm with his no-fucking self."

Harlow frowned and then giggled. "Oh, my God. I feel so embarrassed for Alphonso. What's the problem? Is he packing a mini… down there?" She nudged her chin downward.

"It's not exactly a mini, but it's short and stubby. I can't stand his fat little, sawed-off dick. But that's not the worst of it."

Harlow frowned. "There's more?"

"Uh-huh. Your boy is a five-minute man."

"Oh, no! I shouldn't be hearing this. I'm never going to look at Alphonso the same!"

"He has no finesse in bed. Doesn't bother with foreplay at all. He doesn't do shit. No kissing. No caressing. No nothing."

"He doesn't kiss you?" Harlow asked, looking astonished.

"Nope." Vangie took another sip of wine. "In the beginning, he had me thinking I had bad breath or something, but the dude simply isn't affectionate. He's a strange individual. Really cold and disconnected."

"So, I ask you again, why are you still dealing with him?"

Vangie shrugged. "He's generous. So generous that I've convinced myself that eventually our sex life will improve."

"Seems like you've been trying to convince yourself of a lot of things. I'm trying to picture this five-minute sex act that's devoid of affection. It sounds like a nightmare."

"It is. Want me to paint you a vivid picture?"

"Not really."

"Well, I insist. I suck his stumpy dick for a few moments and then he rams it in me and fucks me doggy-style."

"Only doggy-style?"

"Yup, and he's fast and furious. That bastard pounds my pussy like it did something to offend him. Thank God he's quick, otherwise, I don't think I'd be able to survive his vicious hard-fucking. It's not his dick that's hurting me; it's the way he slams his hard, muscular body against my ass. He seems to be trying to make up for that stubby dick by pounding his hard body against mine. It's a wonder my insides haven't been knocked all around."

Harlow turned up a corner of her top lip. "Does he go down on you, at least? You know, to get you in the mood."

"Nope. I have to use a lubricant before I let him ram the hell out of me. Luckily, it only takes a few strokes for him to bust. Selfish bitch doesn't give two shits whether or not I get mine."

"I don't know what to say. I'm stunned speechless. I mean…I thought you two were in love."

"What made you think that? Did he say anything about our relationship?"

"No, Alphonso never talks about his personal life with me."

"He doesn't talk about it with me, either." Vangie refilled her glass and quickly drained it.

"Don't try to drink your troubles away," Harlow cautioned. "Think about Nivea and how she practically ruined her life with all that drinking she was doing."

"My life is such a mess. I might be worse off than Niv."

"That's impossible. But speaking of Nivea, did she get the results of the baby's paternity test?"

"I don't know; I haven't talked to her in a minute. Between you and me, I don't think the baby is Knox's child. That baby belongs to a white man, trust me. I don't know who Nivea thinks she's fooling."

"I haven't seen Mackenzie since she was born, but I thought she'd darken up over time."

"She's four months old and still pale as a ghost," Vangie said and burst out laughing.

"But she's cute, though," Harlow added.

"Uh-huh, but Nivea needs to stop trying to mess up her sister's marriage and go after the real baby daddy."

"Who could it be?"

"I have no idea, but I'd bet money that it's some fly-by-night white man. Nivea probably doesn't know who the father is, her damn self. Our girl went on a sexual rampage after Eric dumped her. God only knows how many potential fathers are out there."

"For the child's sake, I hope Nivea can give her some information about her biological father."

"I doubt it." Vangie took another sip from her wineglass, and Harlow gave her a stern look. "All right. I'll slow down, but it's… I'm just so miserable, Harlow."

"I know exactly what you need."

"I need a husband!"

"But while you're waiting on Mr. Right, you need some immediate gratification. I made an appointment for us to get massages at my favorite day spa, and our appointment is tomorrow afternoon."

"Okay, that's cool. I've shared my secret, so what can you tell me about Alphonso? Like, is he seeing other chicks? Does he have a baby mama? Or God forbid, a *wife* I should know about?"

"I told you, he keeps his personal business to himself. Seriously, Vangie, after all you've told me, I think you need to let him go."

"It's not that easy. I've put in a lot of time with him."

"So, what!"

"I'm not ready to give up." Vangie turned somber and briefly drifted off in thought. Then she gazed at Harlow with a mischievous glimmer in her eyes. "I do know a little something else about my mystery man."

"What do you know?"

"I know that he keeps a gun strapped to his ankle."

"How do you know that?" Harlow asked in a whisper and looked around the restaurant, indicating that Vangie should keep her voice down.

"Yuri told me."

"How would Yuri know?"

"He saw it and asked Alphonso if he could hold it, and Alphonso actually let my son hold his gun."

Harlow gasped.

"I know, right? Awful, isn't it?" Vangie leaned in closer and spoke in a conspiratorial tone. "I was thinking about when you confided in me. Remember when you told me about that incident on that yacht, back when Alphonso was Drake's bodyguard?"

Harlow nodded. "I remember, but I don't want to talk about that. Can we please change the subject?"

Vangie ignored Harlow's request. "Since Drake and Alphonso are partners now, and since Alphonso is supposed to be a refined gentleman like Drake, I wonder why he feels the need to carry a gun. What exactly are they into—you know, besides the car dealerships?"

Harlow tried not to dwell on thoughts of Drake and his gun-toting ways. It was an uncomfortable topic, causing her palms to sweat and her heart rate to increase. "Drake doesn't tell me all the details of his business and I don't ask."

"Hmm. Has it ever occurred to you that maybe you don't know Drake as well as you think?"

Harlow glowered at Vangie. "I don't know what you're insinuating, but I don't like it."

"Don't shoot the messenger," Vangie said, holding up her hands in surrender.

The food arrived and Harlow and Vangie ate their meal in complete silence.

NIVEA

T he Sandburgs' maid admitted Nivea into an entryway that had a dramatic dual staircase. The home was even more luxurious than Nivea had imagined. Dr. Sandburg was living the life! Hopefully, Nivea and her daughter would be, too.

Mother and child were both dressed in high fashion, with Nivea wearing a Prada ensemble and Mackenzie decked out in lilac-colored Baby Dior. Her head was adorned with a headband made of a cluster of silk violets. Purple was Mackenzie's color, Nivea had decided, and the baby's wardrobe was filled with various shades of the color.

"Welcome to my home," Rachel said, smiling broadly. Rachel Sandburg wasn't the dowdy matron that Nivea had assumed she'd be. Despite the few strands of gray that threaded through her curly, dark hair, she appeared much younger than her husband. Dressed in shimmery yoga pants and a fitted T-shirt, she was trim and fit. Though she couldn't be described as beautiful, she exuded a sense of confidence and vitality that made her attractive.

"Let me have a peek at her," Rachel said, taking Mackenzie from Nivea's arms. Her brows gathered together as she trained her eyes on Mackenzie. She studied and assessed her as if searching for defects that would rule her out as her husband's child. Waiting for the verdict, Nivea anxiously nibbled at the corner of her bottom lip.

She emitted a sigh of relief when Rachel proclaimed, "She's a beautiful child, and she's the spitting image of Bertram—an exact replica of his baby pictures."

Nivea seriously doubted that her gorgeous daughter resembled the unattractive doctor when he was a child, but she smiled as if the comparison was a compliment.

"Let's have tea, shall we?"

"Sure." With dollar signs in her mind, she allowed Rachel, who was still holding Mackenzie, to guide her to the formal living room that was exquisitely furnished in Edwardian style. A tea tray and china tea set were placed at the end of a sturdy mahogany table.

Rachel cooed to Mackenzie in French and then returned her to Nivea's arms.

What a show-off! Rachel was wealthy, fit, attractive, and she had a luxurious home. Adding to her list of attributes, she spoke fluent French. Nivea was beginning to dislike the woman slightly, but she kept a smile affixed on her face as she accepted the cup of green tea that the maid poured for her.

Gazing around the room, Nivea's eyes landed on the enormous wedding portrait of Dr. Sandburg and Rachel. Old Doc Sandburg had the nerve to have been quite handsome in his younger days. In the portrait, Rachel's face was girlishly round and her hair was long and straight, but aside from a few lines at the corner of her eyes, and the strands of gray hair, Rachel hadn't changed very much.

"Well, let's get down to business," Rachel said, taking a seat in an elegant antique chair. Nivea leaned forward, eager to hear Rachel's proposition. "As you can see, Bertram and I are very well-off. But Bertram's income is only a fraction of our wealth. I inherited a large sum of money from my parents, and my money allows my dear Bertram and me to lead a luxurious lifestyle."

"I see." Nivea wondered why such a wealthy, energetic, and attractive woman would want to be saddled down with dowdy, old Dr. Sandburg. He couldn't even get it up without the help of Viagra, and with his potbelly and lumbering movements, he obviously didn't follow his wife's healthy lifestyle. Yet despite his flaws, Rachel seemed devoted to him. Then again, maybe someone else took care of her womanly needs. Someone like a strapping young gardener or a handyman who took care of the upkeep of the lovely home.

Rachel sipped her tea and then regarded Nivea intently. She stared at Nivea for an uncomfortably long period of time.

"Is something wrong?" Nivea asked.

"No. I was just thinking…"

"Yes?" Nivea said, urging her to continue.

"If you decide to sue Bertram for child support, you'll find that his income is relatively meager, but if you agree to keep this out of court and allow my attorney to discreetly draw up the paperwork, I assure you, you'll be more than pleased with the financial arrangement I have in mind."

"What do you have in mind?"

"I would like to offer you the original sum Bertram suggested."

"Only two hundred fifty thousand?" Nivea had hoped to be presented with a much larger figure.

"We'd also provide health care coverage for Mackenzie, child care costs when you return to work and—"

"Oh, Kenzie's not going to a child care center. I plan to hire a nanny to look after her in our home," Nivea interjected.

"Of course." Rachel nodded thoughtfully. "Hopefully, you'll insist upon a nanny who speaks French. It's important for children to know a second language. My former nanny was French, and I've been bilingual my entire life."

Rachel was an annoying snob, and she reminded Nivea of her mother. "And what else did you have in mind, financially?" Nivea asked, hoping there was more money on the table. Enough to provide whirlwind shopping sprees and a lifetime of financial security.

"Five thousand a month in child support, and when Mackenzie's of school age, we'll pay for the absolute best private school in the area," Rachel concluded.

"I appreciate your generosity," Nivea said calmly, while refraining from letting out a joyful yelp. She couldn't believe her luck. Rachel was willing to hand over a truckload of cash without requiring a paternity test. Things were finally looking up; Mackenzie would have everything Nivea desired for her. It was as if she'd hit the jackpot…or had given birth to a celebrity's or a star athlete's child. Life was good, and she felt herself flush with the thrill of it!

"You're welcome to stop by and see Mackenzie whenever you'd like. Or I could always bring her here for a visit if you'd like," Nivea offered with a smile.

Rachel gave Nivea a beneficent little smile. "Thank you, but that won't be necessary. This arrangement is strictly business; Bertram and I don't want to establish a relationship with your daughter." This was said through lips that were turned down in revulsion.

Insulted, Nivea recoiled. Her jaw clenched visibly. She wanted to curse Rachel out, but considering it wise to hold her tongue, she expressed her displeasure with furrowed brows and a sidelong glance. It wasn't that she desired to have the Sandburgs in her daughter's life, but Rachel's comment made it seem as if Mackenzie was scum—not good enough to socialize with. *The nerve of the bitch, bamboozling me into coming here, and pretending it was all good when she really thinks my daughter and me are trash!*

"Let's not pretend to be friends. I'm paying you to keep your mouth shut. I'm trying to prevent you from going on a smear campaign; I can't have my good name ruined, you know. Bertram told me you have connections with the local media, and I need to know that you won't be holding any press conferences or selling your story to the tabloids." Rachel grimaced. "Those rags would have a field day with this information. I can see the headlines: *Husband of Wealthy Heiress has Child out of Wedlock!* Oh, the humiliation would be unbearable, which is why I'm making sure that you're well compensated. With the money I'm willing to pay you, there's no reason for you to breathe a word of Bertram's scandalous behavior."

"I won't," Nivea murmured as thoughts swirled in her head. Since Rachel was so afraid of negative press, Nivea wondered if the $250,000 she'd offered was enough for her silence. Maybe she was cutting herself short. She and Mackenzie needed something a lot bigger than their tiny townhouse; they needed a home with land around it. A home that had a big playroom for Mackenzie, a huge master bedroom, and lots and lots of bathrooms. Something in the million-dollar range would suit their needs. Nivea was about to bring up the subject of their housing situation when Rachel cleared her throat, drawing Nivea away from her thoughts.

"My attorney will draw up the paperwork. I'll schedule an appointment for you to meet with him and sign off on all my conditions."

"Well, I think I should have my own attorney present before I sign anything. Two hundred fifty thousand might not be enough."

Rachel smirked and shook her head. "Do you suppose your attorney could negotiate a better deal? If so, we can haggle for months. We could also involve the court system and perhaps clear Bertram's good name with a DNA test." She gave Nivea a long and significant look, which prompted Nivea to guiltily drop her gaze.

"I'll sign the papers," Nivea acquiesced.

"Good. My attorney will be in touch." Rachel stood, indicating the meeting was over.

As Nivea gathered Mackenzie, the baby began to cry. "I have to feed her before we leave."

"Take your time. It was nice meeting you and Mackenzie." She gazed down at her watch. "I have a meeting with my yoga instructor; the maid will see you out."

Rachel exited the living room, without giving Nivea and Mackenzie a second glance. The rude, arrogant bitch really grated on Nivea's nerves.

She placed a blanket over her shoulder and began to nurse Mackenzie. As Mackenzie suckled, Nivea felt a shiver of dread. Rachel Sandburg was a shrewd and ruthless woman. Not someone you wanted as an enemy, and Nivea intended to sign the papers, keep her mouth shut, and make sure she and Mackenzie stayed far away from Rachel Sandburg.

VANGIE

After she'd suggested that Drake and Alphonso might be into something shady, Harlow became quiet and pensive. On Sunday, they had appointments at Harlow's favorite spa, but Harlow complained of having a headache and urged Vangie to keep her appointment, which Harlow had already paid for in advance.

"Since the spa is close to Penn Station, there's no point in me coming back to the Upper East Side. I guess I'll go back to Philly after my massage," Vangie said.

"That's a good idea."

It was clear that Vangie had upset Harlow when she'd suggested that Drake was shady, but it was too late to take back the hurtful words. Normally, Harlow would try to keep Vangie in New York for as long as possible, coming up with a number of ways to keep Vangie entertained, but not today.

Harlow retired to her bedroom and didn't come out to walk Vangie to the elevator or down to the lobby when Vangie hollered, "I'm leaving!"

She's pissed—and I have to figure out a way to fix this rift I've caused.

A massage was exactly what Vangie needed to take her mind off Yuri hanging in the projects, Alphonso…his gun and his unwillingness to commit, and now a hurt and angry Harlow. In all their years of friendship, Harlow had never been upset with Vangie. But Vangie had crossed a line when she'd suggested that Drake might not be the upstanding man he appeared to be. Maybe she should give Harlow some time to cool down and then call her and offer an apology.

The moment Vangie stepped inside the day spa, she felt her troubles begin to melt away. The comingled scents of citrus and flowers had a soothing effect, giving her a feeling of complete calm. While lying on the massage table, Vangie came up with an idea. She'd send Harlow some flowers with a note expressing how sorry she was for making such an unkind comment about Drake. Yes, that would work. Harlow was a sweetheart; she wasn't the type to hold a grudge.

The woman who was kneading her back and getting out the kinks in Vangie's neck had introduced herself as Frieda. She was somewhat heavy-handed, hurting Vangie as she dug her thumbs into her shoulder blades, causing her to groan in pain. Frieda was a large and obviously strong woman, and she wasn't exactly feminine. Vangie was trying not to hold her mannishness against her, but damn, didn't the big bitch know her own strength? She was damn near crushing Vangie's bones.

"Can you take it easy?" Vangie asked, trying to keep the annoyance out of her voice.

"Pain is good. Your muscles are tense—tight and knotted up," Frieda explained, speaking with a heavy accent that sounded like German. Then again, it might have been Swedish. Hell if Vangie knew or cared.

"I don't care how knotted up I am…you're hurting me. I didn't come here to be tortured; you need to lighten up."

"Do you want something gentler?"

"Yes, please," Vangie said with irritation. *This rough bitch was trying to break the bones in my damn back.*

Frieda's large hands now glided over Vangie's body, gently rubbing her neck and her back with scented oil. It was so pleasant, Vangie dozed off briefly and when she awakened the masseuse's hands were traveling up and down her thighs and over her butt, lightly squeezing each cheek. *A butt massage?* She supposed there was a first time for everything, and instead of protesting, she simply went with the flow, relaxing under the expert hands of the massage therapist. Using the pads of her fingers, Frieda conducted a deep tissue massage on Vangie's derriere. It felt surprisingly good. And since it was therapeutic and nothing inappropriate, Vangie uttered sounds of pleasure as she felt the stress being kneaded out of her buttocks.

Then those thick fingers began to inch toward a more intimate part, brushing softly and tickling at her labia. *A pussy massage? Oh, hell no. I'm not with this perverted shit!* Vangie bristled, her muscles clenching in alarm. She lifted her torso and glanced over her shoulder. "What the hell do you think you're doing?"

The big German…Swede…or whatever she was, gave her a sneaky smile. "Relax. Let yourself go," she said in that thick accent of hers.

Before Vangie could protest further, manly-looking Frieda slid her other hand beneath her and quickly clasped her inner lips between her sturdy thumbs and index fingers, massaging the plump flesh, while the knuckles of her thumbs brushed against Vangie's sensitive clit. Sensations coursed through her, overwhelming her, and the feeling was unlike anything she had ever experienced. Every fiber of her being screamed that this behavior was wrong. She wanted to flip over on her back and scoot off the table, and cuss the big dyke out for taking such a liberty with her pussy.

But the only sound Vangie emitted was a soft moan. The shit felt good, and after so many months of bad sex with Alphonso, her pussy was yearning for release. She couldn't control it—couldn't stop her body from undulating, writhing, and acting on its own accord.

"Do you want me to explore?"

"What?" The word came out in a squeaky gasp.

"Do you want me to explore inside?"

"Do whatever you want," she answered breathlessly, and then buried her face in the pillow to stifle her loud moaning as the masseuse wriggled and corkscrewed her finger into the confines of her soft interior.

On the brink of climaxing, Vangie gasped in objection when Frieda suddenly withdrew her finger. "Don't stop, please," she murmured.

"You paid for deluxe treatment. Turnover, and I'll finish you off."

Deluxe treatment? What the hell kind of massage had Harlow paid for? Too wound up to think rationally, Vangie did as she was told and turned over. Too ashamed to look the foreign woman in the eye, she covered her face with the pillow. Unable to see what was being done to her, she shivered in anticipation.

She flinched as she felt her legs being gently pulled apart, and then began to tremble violently when Frieda's short hair brushed against her inner thighs. "Oh, God!" she cried out as a warm tongue delved between her silken folds. Bolting upright, she bit into the pillow and screamed as a powerful orgasm nearly knocked her unconscious.

"You can get dressed now," the masseuse said, giving Vangie's pussy a final pat.

"Okay," Vangie muttered, still covering her face with the pillow. She couldn't bring herself to face the lesbian who had brought her to a climax with her tongue. She felt like a fool hiding behind the pillow, but she was too embarrassed to look the masseuse in the face.

She'd sunk about as low as she could go. *I'm straight as an arrow; I can't believe I let this dyke bitch take advantage of me. If that fuckin' Alphonso had been handling his business, this depraved bullshit would have never happened.*

Frieda pulled the pillow away from Vangie's face, forcing her to meet her gaze. Her eyes were brown and seemed kind. "No reason to be ashamed. Plenty of women come to me to get their needs satisfied."

"Really?" Vangie wondered if Harlow was one of those women. *Nah, I can't even imagine Harlow coming here for some down-low freakishness.*

"By the way, I make house calls," Frieda said and handed Vangie a business card.

Wanting to forget this day ever happened, Vangie declined the card. "No, thanks; I don't need it."

"Take it; you never know when you'll have another stressful day."

With Frieda urging her to accept the card, she grudgingly stuffed it her handbag with the intention of ripping it into shreds the moment she exited the building.

NIVEA

Carrying her daughter, Nivea entered Rachel Sandburg's lawyer's well-appointed sanctum and settled into the visitor's chair across from Andrew Brackman's executive desk. She offered a smile in greeting, but the arrogant attorney turned down his mouth and acknowledged her presence with a terse thrust of his chin before glancing down at the papers on his desk. It was a deliberate snub…haughty disregard. The ill-mannered attorney was the perfect representative for obnoxious Rachel Sandburg.

No sooner had she sat down when he began pushing papers toward her. He didn't bother to make small talk, and he sighed with irritation whenever Nivea tried to speed-read the legal jargon before affixing her signature.

"I'm scheduled to appear in court in an hour, and so if you could hurry along, I'd appreciate it," Andrew Brackman said, tapping his fingertips together impatiently. As if to motivate her to sign quickly, he eased the $250,000 check to the center of the glossy desktop.

After she signed all the papers, Brackman sat back and regarded Nivea with a challenging look in his eyes.

What now? Nivea wondered nervously if there were more hoops to jump through before she was handed the money. Through sheer will she maintained a passive expression as she met the attorney's piercing stare.

Toying with her, Brackman didn't speak for a few moments. He rested his elbows on the armrests of his chair, steepled his fingers and finally said, "My secretary is going to have to get a DNA sample from the baby."

"You can't be serious!"

Rachel Sandburg was aware that Mackenzie wasn't her husband's biological daughter, but she wanted scientific evidence for some unknown reason. What a conniving bitch!

"I'm very serious." His thin lips twisted into a scornful smile. "Mrs. Sandburg ordered the test to satisfy her own curiosity. The arrangement she made with you won't change either way. As for the test, it's very simple…a quick swab of the baby's mouth. My secretary will use a sterile Q-tip to—"

"I know how it's done! But Rachel told me that we didn't have to be bothered with the test; she said she knew by looking at Mackenzie that she was her husband's child."

Brackman didn't respond. Not with words. He snorted and raised an eyebrow, and his mocking sound and expression spoke volumes. He picked up the phone on his desk. "Can you please come in my office, Laurie? To administer the test."

Laurie, a mature woman with thick, brown hair that was worn in a bob, entered the office carrying a small packet, which contained a sterile swab that was encased in paper packaging.

Nivea sneered at the packet and then glanced at Laurie, who had a fabulous figure and was very pretty despite the lines on her face. In an odd way, the cracks of age that usually marred a woman's beauty seemed to enhance Laurie's. Gave her something undefinable that probably turned men's heads—both young and old. Nivea looked from silver-haired Brackman to his secretary and wondered if the two were banging each other. *More than likely.*

After Mackenzie's mouth was swabbed, Nivea sat across from Brackman, rocking her fretful daughter in her arms.

Brackman double-checked the pages with her signature and then told her he'd send copies after Dr. and Mrs. Sandburg had both countersigned. Finally, he slid the check across the desk, placing it directly in front of Nivea.

Nivea snatched it up before he could think of another reason to delay handing over the money. With the check tucked inside a Gucci handbag from last year, Nivea floated out of the lawyer's office, imagining all the handbags, shoes, and clothes she could buy from all her favorite designers' current collections.

❤ ❤ ❤

Finding the right nanny took an entire week of screening applicants. She finally decided on a forty-something woman named Odette, who was from the Bahamas. Odette came with sparkling recommendations and possessed a winning smile that encouraged Mackenzie to gurgle happily and coo while in her arms.

In addition to shopping for a new wardrobe, Nivea needed to hit the gym hard. The residual baby fat had to go! Wanting something a lot more posh than the overcrowded chain establishments, she joined an exclusive fitness center in St. Davids, Pennsylvania. The drive was rather long, but the amenities the gym offered were well worth it. The spacious club had multiple levels, giving its elite clientele what they paid for: state-of-the-art equipment, a pool, a full-on café and a spa. The locker rooms had comfortable lounging chairs and a flat-screen TV, and friendly staff that kept the place impeccably clean.

At the gym, while powering through her elliptical routine, Nivea felt a pair of eyes on her. She looked to her right and noticed a dreamy-looking, caramel-toffee-colored brother who was a few yards away from her. Too far away to talk without shouting, but close enough to notice his light-brown eyes and curly brown hair. Nivea hadn't noticed any other African Americans at the club and so she nodded her head in acknowledgment. He revealed a confident smile that was partly amused and partly flirtatious and then greeted her with a sort of quick salute.

He was distractingly handsome. And tall and fit. Perspiration molded his blue T-shirt to his well-defined torso, revealing side abs of steel. Something about that smile of his and the mischief in those light-brown eyes made him appear entirely too self-assured. Like he'd led a charmed life with everything coming easily to him—especially women. After giving him a brief but thorough looking over, Nivea noticed he didn't have on a wedding band. *Single. Hmm. I bet when he does get married, it won't be to a sister. I know his type; he won't settle for anything other than a white girl—a spaghetti-thin blonde.*

Throwing herself back into her workout, Nivea dismissed the hunky dude from her thoughts. She was focused on getting back in tiptop shape before returning to her job. She refused to give any of her coworkers the satisfaction of thinking she couldn't get rid of the baby weight.

After a half-hour on the elliptical, Nivea whizzed past Mr. Handsome without making eye contact.

"Hey! Have a good day. Hope to see you soon," he called out brazenly.

What a cocky, shameless flirt! She waved her hand behind her in his general direction, but she didn't turn around or slow her stride. Eager to try out the Aerial Yoga class that was being held on a lower level in less than ten minutes, she stopped at the water cooler, filled her water bottle, and then hurried down the stairs.

She marveled at her new attitude and felt proud of herself. The old Nivea would have flirted back with the hunk. Would have wondered about his profession and if he was marriage material. That old and emotionally unstable Nivea, whom after being dumped by her ex-fiancé, had gone out on a sex binge with multiple partners and had gotten pregnant in the process, no longer existed. The new Nivea was whole and healed. She didn't need a ring on her finger to feel secure. She and her daughter were doing just fine by themselves, and the only thing a man could do was complicate her life and drive her crazy—like her ex-fiancé, Eric, had.

She shook her head as she recalled her downward spiral after being dumped by Eric. But in retrospect, Eric had actually done her a huge favor. Being married to his trifling ass would have been a living hell. Like Beyoncé said in her song, Eric was the *Best Thing I Never Had!*

Aerial Yoga was a form of the practice where participants stretch and exercise, while suspended a few feet above the ground by a silky, hammock-like device. The soft fabric trapeze hung from the ceiling like a swing, and Nivea thought the class was interesting and sort of fun, but afterward, she was left bone-tired and muscle sore.

With Odette at home caring for Mackenzie, Nivea had plenty of time to indulge in an hour-long, Hot Stone massage. After the massage, feeling soothed and relaxed, she leisurely walked to her car. Though she was weaning Mackenzie, a tightening in her breasts told her she needed to hurry home before her breasts became engorged.

"We meet again; it must be kismet," said a male voice that was filled with playful laughter.

Nivea glanced over her shoulder and groaned a little when she spotted the handsome guy from the elliptical room. He was too fine for his own good, and he knew it, and Nivea had no intention of feeding his already inflated ego by bantering back and forth with him. She turned around and crinkled her nose as if detecting a foul odor. "You're starting to become a pest."

"Wow, that's a low blow. What did I do to deserve that?"

"Excuse me, I'm sort of in a rush; I have a child at home waiting for me." She expected a reaction when she mentioned her child, but his expression didn't change.

"I won't take up much of your time; I'm just trying to get to know you, pretty lady."

"Flattery won't get you anywhere," she retorted, aiming the remote at her car. She was angry with men—all men. Didn't want anything to do with them. The way she felt, she'd be well into her forties before she regained the mental strength to get entangled with another no-good man.

He held his hands up in surrender. "Okay, I'll back off. But I want you to know, I'm not the bad guy you seem to think I am." He offered a seductive smile that would have had her panting for him in the past. But she was so bitter toward the entire male species, it would take a lot more than a handsome face to get her juices flowing.

Nivea sucked her teeth. "Bad guy or nice guy, it doesn't matter to me. I chose this gym for its unique workouts, pleasant ambience, and other amenities. I didn't come here to get hit on, so please leave me alone."

His smug smile vanished; disappointment flickered across his face. "Sorry I bothered you. It won't happen again." He stuck a hand in his pocket and jostled his keys, and then turned away in defeat. Satisfied that she'd put him in his place, Nivea slid into her car and watched through the rearview mirror as he walked across the lot. He moved with a sort of strut, betraying no sign that he'd been knocked down a peg. He paced toward a dark-colored SUV and disarmed it. The trill of his cell phone went off before he opened the door. With the phone held to his ear, he laughed and talked. His languid posture—the sensual way he leaned against his vehicle—announced that he wasn't talking to one of the boys.

He probably received numerous offers for sex every day. She was relieved she hadn't taken his flirtatiousness seriously. He was simply another no-good dog.

Thank God for Mackenzie. Her beautiful baby was all she needed in the world. And she needed money, of course. Anxious to see her daughter—to hold her and inhale her sweet scent—Nivea exited the parking lot with a sense of urgency.

HARLOW

S ince returning from London, Drake had been spending more time than usual with Harlow. Today, he left his office for a few hours to have a lunch date with her, and instead of rushing back to work, he accompanied her back to their apartment building for a little afternoon delight.

The average wife would be flattered if her husband took time out of his busy day to wine and dine and make love to her, but Harlow found it increasingly difficult to spark up her libido for anything other than conceiving a child. Sex for the sake of sex didn't interest her much. But Drake was trying hard to reignite the passion in their marriage and she did love him. And for love's sake, she intended to go through the motions and pretend that making love was still fun.

As they strolled into their apartment building, hand in hand, they were the image of a glamorous, happy couple. But Harlow was desperately unhappy. She loved Drake with all her heart, but there was something going on with him—something dark and dangerous. A baby would fill her life and take her mind off the unpleasant thoughts about Drake and the questions that plagued her.

The concierge greeted the couple with a smile. "Good afternoon, Mr. and Mrs. Morgan. These are for you, Mrs. Morgan," he said to Harlow, producing from behind the desk, an array of light and dark pink lilies and a spray of pink roses in a clear vase.

Harlow beamed up at Drake. "Oh, this is too much. You're so sweet. Thank you, darling," she said sincerely. She decided then and there that it was time to let go of her foolish doubt. Drake was a good man, and he loved her deeply. He'd saved Harlow's life after their wedding, and instead of mistrusting him, she should be grateful.

"I didn't send those," Drake said, raising a brow as he gazed at Harlow.

"Does Mrs. Morgan have a secret admirer?" asked the concierge.

"Not that I know of." Laughing, Harlow opened the card while both Drake and the concierge waited in suspense.

"Oh, these are from Vangie, thanking me for her mini-vacation last weekend," Harlow said, leaving out the apology that Vangie had expressed in the note. She tossed the note inside her clutch bag and slipped her arm inside her husband's as they headed for the elevator.

Inside the lofty apartment, Drake's phone rang. He glanced at the screen. "It's Alphonso. Give me a few minutes," he said and began moving in the direction of his study to speak with him in private.

Harlow carried the flowers to the kitchen and set them on the counter. She stood back and observed the arrangement. Though it was a thoughtful gesture, it was too little too late. Vangie had crossed a line when she'd slandered Drake's name. A flower bouquet couldn't make up for Vangie's unkind words.

Hearing Drake's footsteps approaching, she turned around.

Drake gave Harlow an odd look. "Is something wrong, sweetheart?"

"No. Why do you ask?"

He studied her with his intense dark-brown gaze. "You look sad...you seem sort of tense."

"I'm fine, Drake." She managed a faint smile.

Drake made long strides toward her and then banded his arms around her. "Whatever's bothering you, Daddy's gonna make it all better," he murmured, his lips gliding briefly against hers. A tiny shiver moved through Harlow as she inhaled his unique, manly scent and felt the heat of his body.

Like old times, a tiny shiver moved through her and with a soft groan, Harlow pressed her body into his, clutching at his lapels as she buried her face into the curve of his shoulder, breathing him in deeply.

"Baby," he moaned, pulling her closer and cupping her buttocks possessively. "I need you so bad."

She gazed at him. Struck by his gorgeousness and his massive sex appeal, she must have been out of her mind to have treated him as if he were nothing more than a sperm donor. "I need you, too," she whispered, lifting her mouth to his and parting her lips invitingly.

His tongue stroked against hers, and it was literally, the sweetest kiss. His mouth tasted delicious. Like the wine he'd drunk during lunch. A charge went through her, quickening her pulse, and she was hit with an overwhelming desire to feel his flesh next to hers. She was married to the hottest man on earth and yet she'd been foolishly going through the motions of lovemaking. Her desire to conceive had been so powerful, she'd denied herself the sexual pleasure that no one in the world except her insanely sexy husband could give her.

Her shaky hands yanked off his tie and grabbed at his expensive shirt, ripping it open. Buttons popped off, scattering and rolling around the marble kitchen floor. With the ferocity of a wild animal, she clawed at his undershirt, slitting it open with her fingernails. With a primal yearning, she licked the flesh of his chest, moaning at the firm texture and the salty-sweetness of his rich velvet skin.

"Damn, babe," Drake rasped in an appreciative tone as Harlow's busy hands worked to undo his belt. His breathing became harsh and audible as he surrendered to his wife's uncharacteristic aggression. Knowing Drake as she did, she figured he had probably planned a slow seduction—candlelight, soft music, and wine before luring her to their bedroom. But in this moment with heat spreading from her cheeks down to her loins, her need was baser and she didn't require ambience. All she needed was his thick shaft plunging into her depths.

Their hungry eyes locked and they both realized they'd never make it out of the kitchen.

With swift and steady hands, Drake deftly separated Harlow from her clothing, flinging her top in one direction and her skirt in another. Stripped down to her underwear, she fumbled with the hooks of her bra while he wedged off his shoes and shed his pants.

"You get more beautiful every day," he gasped, taking in her lovely face and then gazing at the ripe swell of her breasts as she freed them from the confines of the pink, satin bra. Under the heat of his gaze, Harlow's chest heaved with excitement and her nipples tightened into hard knots of desire. He nuzzled the fragrant valley between her breasts and nipped at the hardened peaks before backing away and discarding his briefs.

Naked, now, Drake was a magnificent specimen. The sight of him took her breath away. She swallowed hard as it dawned on her that her handsome husband with his hard and muscular body resembled a gladiator or some type of immortal sex god. Enraptured, Harlow released a sigh as she reached for his burgeoning manhood with one hand and caressed his bulging bicep with the other.

She wanted him in her mouth and inside her body at the same time, but that was an impossible desire. Selecting to satisfy her oral craving, first, Harlow dropped to her knees and clasped Drake's rigid dick with both hands. She held it for a moment, admiring it almost prayerfully before pressing the smooth helmet against her lips.

Unable to wait any longer, Drake entered her mouth with a forceful thrust. He clamped his hands on the sides of her head. With driving thrusts that rammed her throat and threatened to choke her, Drake revealed how long he'd been denied this pleasure.

Harlow pulled back. "Slow down, darling. Let's enjoy this."

"I'm sorry, babe. Really sorry," he uttered while guiding his swollen dick back to the warmth inside her mouth.

With his eyes clenched shut and while gritting his teeth, Drake appeared to be in sexual agony as Harlow sucked in his length.

"Baby. Please. That's enough. I'm ready for you. Let me get in it," he pleaded, breathing so harshly he could hardly speak.

"Not yet; you taste so good, Drake. Let me suck it a little while longer."

"But, babe, I'm ready for you," he said in a voice that sounded tortured.

She shook her head and continued to leisurely tug on the hard and slippery member, pulling it in and out at an agonizingly slow pace. Drake entwined his fingers in her hair, gripping and pulling much harder than he intended.

The sharp flash of pain in her scalp didn't deter Harlow; it aroused and intensified her sexual pleasure. She couldn't recall the last time she'd sucked Drake's dick. No doubt, she had to have been a little crazy to have denied herself such pleasure.

"You gotta stop! I'm about to come, babe," Drake warned.

Begrudgingly, she released him, and Drake took her hand helping her to her feet. "What was that all about?" he asked, still breathing hard as he looked at her quizzically.

"I guess I missed you," she said with a sneaky smile.

"Is that right?" He backed up, bracing himself against the island. He held out his arms. "Come here, baby, let me hold you for a moment while I catch my breath." Harlow fell into Drake's arms and he kissed the top of her head and then lowered his mouth to her ear.

"If I were you, I'd be gathering my strength right now," he warned.

She looked at him questioningly.

"I'm about to beat that pussy up, and I don't want you passing out on me before I'm finished with you."

She smiled. "I can take it; I like it rough."

NIVEA

"Now that Kenzie is getting strolled around the neighborhood, I thought she should roll around in style," Nivea said, gesturing with a grand flourish toward the $2,000 pram carriage that was delivered earlier in the day.

"It's so elegant, like something the royal baby would ride in," Odette replied, stroking the chrome handle that was padded in the center with soft leather.

"She won't outgrow her new pram until she's thirty-six months old. Look inside, Odette—see how plush it is." Nivea stroked the soft interior.

Odette peeked inside, patted the fluffy pillow and pressed the cushioned lining. "Mackenzie is going to have many sweet dreams in her new buggy."

"Don't call it a buggy," Nivea corrected. "It's a pram. Inspired by nineteenth-century British aristocracy."

"Yes, I know. English ladies who vacation on my island are fond of these big contraptions," Odette said with a generous smile. "Of course, the nannies are the only ones who cart the children around in these cumbersome things," she added.

"You're going to be the envy of the neighborhood when you take Kenzie out for her daily stroll," Nivea said, oblivious to Odette's thinly veiled sarcasm.

Odette placed Mackenzie in the carriage. "Well, let's try out your new Cadillac, Kenzie, my girl. And let's pray we don't get carjacked or robbed of those shiny chrome wheels." Odette gave Nivea a mischievous smile as she tucked Mackenzie inside.

Nivea scowled.

"I'm only joking, Miss Nivea."

"I didn't find that joke funny at all."

"Okay, I'll be mindful of the jokes I tell." She steered the grandiose carriage out the front door. Nivea hovered in the doorway as Odette struggled getting the pram down the steps. She watched as the nanny pushed the pram down the street, pleased with the extravagant purchase and mentally plotting on a designer high chair.

Odette's comment about the baby riding around in a Cadillac got the wheels turning in Nivea's mind. Her six-year-old Acura was in good condition, but it was time for an upgrade. With the enormous amount of money in her bank account, and all the extra cash that would be pouring in for the next eighteen years, she could afford something more luxurious to get around in. Besides, now that she had a child, she needed a vehicle with a little more room. An elegant "Mommy-type SUV." Maybe a BMW X6 or a new Cadillac SRX.

She went online and checked out the prices. The brand-new SRX with all the extras cost around $57,000, which was only a drop in the bucket and wouldn't put much of a dent in the hush-money she'd gotten from Rachel Sandburg.

Nivea left the Cadillac dealership driving a new white-on-white SRX and feeling smugly content. Looking and acting affluent and important, she had sneered when the salesman had offered a variety of loan options. Declining the loan offers, she haughtily pulled out her checkbook and her Montblanc pen.

That purchase triggered an urge to spend more money. She and Mackenzie needed a new all-white wardrobe to match the car. Instead of heading for home, she got on the expressway, her hands clutching the steering wheel excitedly as she headed in the direction of the King of Prussia Mall, where high-end brands were housed under one roof.

Gucci was the first stop. She spent $350 on a white tulle dress for Mackenzie and $200 on an adorable, tiny pair of white patent leather ballet flats. Her daughter would look like a dream in all white. After leaving the Kids Department, she spent another $900 on white sandals and a pair of white sunglasses with the Gucci logo for herself. Unable to find a white dress, she paid a visit to Hermes and found the perfect, whimsical white dress crafted from luxurious Egyptian cotton and blended with silk and cashmere.

After splurging on additional, all-white clothing items in other exclusive shops, the mall trip was completed after a jewelry shopping excursion at Bailey, Banks, and Biddle as well as Tiffany & Co.

All total, she'd spent $60,000 at the Cadillac dealership and $11,000 at the mall. But Nivea wasn't worried about the money; she was rolling in dough with lots more to be deposited into her bank account each and every month.

Later that night, after the baby was asleep and Odette had gone for the evening, Nivea had yet to open the bags that contained her new purchases, yet she powered on her laptop and went online to continue her compulsive shopping spree. She wanted her little girl to have a doll collection, and once she started looking, she wanted every doll she saw. She not only purchased five insanely expensive dolls, but she also bought their exclusive little wardrobes and adorable accessories.

While browsing doll furniture, she happened upon a site that featured custom-made clothes hangers that were made of satin with pearl handles. Nivea's heart began to pound when she realized she could get Mackenzie's name hand-sewn in glittery thread in the center of each hanger. She immediately ordered two dozen of the personalized hangers.

Kenzie really needs a bigger room with a walk-in closet. Her small bedroom is already beginning to overflow with her numerous toys and extensive wardrobe. The moment I have an extra minute, I'm going to have to start looking at houses. We're outgrowing this townhouse at a rapid pace.

HARLOW

Harlow let out a gasp of surprise when the positive sign appeared on the test stick. Impulsively, she picked up the phone to call Drake and share the good news. But exactly how reliable were home pregnancy tests? She'd be distraught if the test result turned out to be a mistake, and so she decided against sharing the news with Drake.

She poised her finger to call Vangie, and then remembered they were no longer friends. She called Nivea instead. She hardly ever called Nivea, but she had to talk to someone.

"Hey, Niv, this is Harlow. How're you doing and how's the baby?"

"Hi, Harlow, what a pleasant surprise. Mackenzie's doing great. She's putting on some weight, has cute lil' chubby cheeks, and her hair is finally starting to come in."

"I can't wait to see her again. Maybe we can do lunch or go shopping the next time I'm in town."

"That sounds like fun. Lunch will be my treat."

"Oh, you don't have to—"

"I insist."

"Okay, that's really sweet, Niv. Thanks."

"So, when do you think you'll be coming to Philly?"

"Drake has a charity function at the Art Museum next Friday. Maybe I'll join him and get together with you the next day. Is next Saturday good for you?"

"It's perfect. I guess Vangie will be joining us, but I'm not picking up the check for her, and you shouldn't, either. That heifer always gets a free ride when she's with you," Nivea said with a chuckle.

"Actually, Vangie won't be joining us. She and I have sort of parted ways—"

"What happened?"

"I really don't want to talk about it."

"Okay, well, I won't pry, then. On the bright side, I hope you and I can become closer friends. I blame Vangie; she always stood in the way of our getting closer. She enjoyed being the link between us, and frankly, I don't think she wanted us to get too close."

"You could be right," Harlow said, though she really didn't agree with Nivea. Vangie didn't have anything to do with Harlow's and Nivea's lack of closeness. Due to Harlow's upbringing in the foster care system, Nivea had always looked down on her. Now that Harlow had a wealthy husband, she was finally good enough for Nivea. Nivea seemed to have matured since having the baby, and Harlow was willing to let bygones be bygones.

"I don't know what Vangie did to you, but it had to be horrible. You rode hard for that girl, and I can't imagine what she did to piss you off to the point where you've ended a lifelong friendship."

"I thought you weren't going to pry."

"That's right; I forgot." Nivea laughed embarrassedly. "Moving on to a different topic, did you know that things are finally looking up in my life? I'll tell you all about my good fortune over lunch."

"Great. You sound really happy."

"Happier than I've ever been."

"Now I'm curious."

"My lips are sealed; I'll tell you all about it when we get together."

"Okay. Listen, Niv, I wanted to get your opinion on something…"

"Sure. What is it?"

"I took a home pregnancy test and it came out positive. Since you're in the pharmaceuticals business and you've been pregnant, I was wondering if you could tell me how reliable those home kits are."

"Pregnancy tests work by detecting hCG, a special hormone that's found in the blood and urine, and it's only there when a woman is pregnant. Home pregnancy tests are pretty reliable but you can get a false negative if you take it too soon. You'll get a more accurate reading if you wait a week after your missed period."

"That's the thing—my periods are irregular."

"It's rare to get a false positive, but if you want to be a hundred percent certain and if you're anxious to know, then go to your doctor and get a blood test. A blood test can detect hCG levels much earlier in a pregnancy than a urine test."

"I've been to my gynecologist three times in the past six months and it's getting a little embarrassing."

"Don't be embarrassed; I'm sure your doctor understands your anxiousness. But if you're that embarrassed, then go see a different doctor. After you find out you're really pregnant, start seeing an obstetrician so you can begin your prenatal care as soon as possible. I'm sure your gynecologist can recommend a good baby doctor," Nivea said.

"Good advice! I don't know why I didn't think of that."

"You're all wound up and under a lot of stress right now."

"That's true. Anyway, thanks again for listening to my troubles. I love your positive attitude, Niv. You make it sound like I'll be popping prenatal vitamins in a matter of days."

"I have a good feeling about it, but you need to see a doctor ASAP, for your own peace of mind."

Feeling hopeful, Harlow said, "You're right."

"If it turns out you're pregnant, we'll have to celebrate when you come to town. Do a little shopping for baby things."

"I'd love that!"

"I'm a pregnancy pro. I know all the basic necessities you'll need for yourself and your newborn."

"My newborn. God, I love the sound of that!"

"Kenzie wasn't planned, as you know, but I took to motherhood like a duck to water. Due to the situation, with my family being against me and all, my mom didn't offer any kind of assistance or advice. I took a training class for mothers-to-be and it was really helpful. Other than that, I had to rely on my own motherly instincts. But you're lucky; you won't have to figure it all out on your own because you have me. Honestly, Harlow, being a mother is my greatest accomplishment. It's not all about me anymore; Kenzie comes first. I honestly love my daughter more than I could ever tell you."

"I can hear that love in your voice. You really have changed; motherhood becomes you."

"You're going to be a great mom, too. Our kids will be like siblings!"

"Oh, my God; I'm so excited. Do you really think I'm going to have a baby?"

"Yes, I do. You can't argue with that positive sign."

"I hope you're right. I'm so glad we had this conversation."

"Me, too."

"Oh, one more thing before we hang up. How soon can the gender of a baby be determined?"

"Generally between the eighteenth and twenty-sixth week of pregnancy, but there's newer ultrasound technology that determine the baby's sex around the twelfth or thirteenth week."

"That's exciting. I'm definitely going for the newer technology. I want to know my baby's sex as soon as possible."

"What do you want, a boy or girl?"

"I'd prefer a girl, but I don't care as long as it's healthy."

"What about Drake?"

"He'd be ecstatic if we had a son and I want to give him whatever he wants. Maybe I'll luck up and have twins!"

"A doting father is the only thing Kenzie's missing, but between her nanny and me, we try to fill that void by giving her plenty of love and affection."

"You have a nanny!"

"Full time. But you have to wait until our lunch date before I tell you the whole, fantastic story of my sudden windfall."

"Okay, well, I'm going to get off the phone and look for an OB/GYN. I'll talk to you, soon, Niv."

VANGIE

Vangie pulled her earring off and pressed the phone against her ear. "Hey, Niv. Haven't heard from you in a while...how are you?"

"Fabulous, girl. I'm absolutely fabulous."

"Gone with the wind fabulous?" Vangie said, borrowing a line from reality star, Kenya Moore.

"Gone with the wind, what?" Nivea asked.

"Oh, nothing." Apparently Nivea didn't watch *The Real Housewives of Atlanta*, which wasn't surprising given Nivea's bourgeoisie status. "Did you get the paternity test back?"

"Sure did," she said casually.

"Really? Is Knox the father?"

"Hell, no!"

"Didn't you want him to be?"

"Things have changed and I don't need that deadbeat anymore."

"Forgive me for sounding confused, but how is it that you're feeling so fabulous? You had your heart set on destroying your sister's marriage, and I thought you'd be distraught if it turned out Knox wasn't the baby's father."

"Girl, Knox and Courtney can both kiss my ass. I found a much better father for my daughter. Someone who's not only wealthy, but also extremely generous. I have a full-time nanny for Mackenzie, a hefty monthly child support check, and a lot of money in the bank. Oh, yeah, and I recently paid cash for a brand-new Cadillac SRX. It's gorgeous, girl. White on white. After I bought it, I had to run out and get Kenzie and me a white wardrobe to match the new ride. And I didn't shop at The Children's Place for my baby. No, girl, it's all about Gucci, Prada, Marc Jacobs, and Hermes around here."

Nivea sounded delusional and Vangie wondered if her friend was suffering from yet another emotional breakdown. "Whoa. Whoa. How is all that possible? When I talked to you about two weeks ago, you were biting your nails, worrying about going back to work and waiting around to get the results of the paternity test."

"I'm still going back to work because I don't want to dip into Kenzie's inheritance, you know what I mean?"

"Her inheritance?"

"That's what I call the lump sum of money I got from Kenzie's father. So much has changed in our lives."

"Who is her father?"

"A rich doctor. One of my clients."

"Are you serious? You had sex with one of your clients?"

"I had sex with several clients, but who cares. The right one stepped up to the plate and that's all that matters. Now that I'm financially secure, I'm going to start hanging out with Harlow. Since she and I are pretty much on the same level now, I bet she'll be thrilled to have a friend that can pay for her own dinner."

Vangie gulped. "What are you implying? Are you trying to say that I've been mooching off Harlow?"

"I'm not implying anything, but if the shoe fits…well, you know the rest."

"I'm insulted."

"Didn't mean to offend you, but I'm only speaking the truth."

"Have you spoken with Harlow? Did she say anything about me?" Vangie felt particularly paranoid in light of the fact that

Harlow hadn't been returning her calls. She'd sent her flowers over a week ago, and hadn't heard a word from Harlow. Additionally, she'd been calling Harlow for the past few days, but her calls either went to voicemail or weren't answered at all. It wasn't like Harlow to hold a grudge, and Vangie was starting to feel sick to her stomach with worry.

"As a matter of fact, Harlow and I have been talking—a couple times a day."

Vangie was stunned. Harlow and Nivea didn't have anything in common. They didn't care for each other, and Vangie had always been the glue that kept them together. It was hard to imagine Harlow and Nivea sharing a friendship without her. "Did she say anything about me?"

"No. We don't talk about you at all. Our conversations tend to focus on matters of high finance. Stuff you wouldn't know much about. Like hot vacation spots, summer homes, nannies and house-keepers. Shit like that."

"That's interesting." Vangie had an attitude. How dare Harlow and Nivea shut her out?

"We also talk about pregnancy."

"What's there to talk about when Harlow isn't even pregnant," Vangie said in a surly tone.

"Well, she's working on it and I'm sure she'll be pregnant very soon. She appreciates the way I encourage her. She says she never knew that I was such a positive person."

"Since when? I've never known you to be anything but negative and all about yourself."

"People change. And I'm being a very good friend to Harlow, listening to her pregnancy concerns and giving her sound advice. Unlike a certain someone who acted bored whenever she brought up the subject of her desire to have a baby."

"Did she tell you that?"

"No, you told me."

"I did not!"

"Think about it. During our last conversation, you sort of confided that Harlow was becoming a bore and that all she wanted to talk about was getting pregnant. Remember, Vangie?"

Vangie swallowed guiltily. "I didn't put it that way. I hope you didn't carry that malicious gossip back to Harlow."

"As I said, your name hasn't come up during any of our conversations."

"Good. So, tell me some more about your rich baby daddy. Is he crazy about Mackenzie? She's such a cutie; I know he fell head over heels in love."

"He's not interested in having a relationship with her and I couldn't care less. He's going to pay for European vacations, private school, and I'm going to talk him into buying us a new home. Something lavish that's sitting on several acres. I want Kenzie to have lots of room to play."

"That's great, Nivea," Vangie said, sounding good-natured, though a part of her hoped that Nivea was experiencing illusions of grandeur and hadn't actually struck it rich. Everything Nivea claimed the doctor had given her was what Vangie wanted for Yuri and herself. Needing to investigate the matter further, she asked, "What are you doing next Saturday? I haven't seen Mackenzie in a while... wanna meet for lunch?"

"Next Saturday? Sorry, I can't. Harlow's coming to Philly with Drake for a fund-raiser at the Art Museum on Friday night. She and I are getting together Saturday for lunch and shopping. She hasn't seen Kenzie in a while, so I may bring her along...and her nanny, of course. Harlow is going to be so shocked at how much Kenzie has grown. And how gorgeous she is," Nivea added boastfully.

Vangie groaned inwardly. Nivea was such a braggart. She complained about her mother being pretentious, but she failed to realize she was exactly like Denise Westcott.

"I hope Harlow has a girl," Nivea went on, oblivious that she was being totally obnoxious. "She and Drake would make a beautiful little girl. Of course, Kenzie and Harlow's daughter will be the best of friends. Two pretty little rich girls, accustomed to living in the lap of luxury. Like Paris Hilton and Nicole Richie. Isn't that an adorable thought?"

Ugh! "If you say so." Vangie couldn't deal with the conversation much longer. Vangie thought Nivea had been humbled when her family had abandoned her, but she was as sickening as ever. Apparently the "nice" Nivea routine had only been an act.

"I want to buy Kenzie a pair of diamond studs, but I'm afraid to get her ears pierced. She's so young, you know. What do you think?"

"Uh, I don't know. Listen, I have to help Yuri with his homework. Have fun with Harlow on Saturday."

Instead of getting off the phone, Nivea kept talking. "Harlow and I are going to have a ball. She's going to be so relieved when I pick up the tab for lunch. Can you imagine how she must feel, having to put up with underprivileged friends that always expect her to pay for everything?"

"It must suck," Vangie said ashamedly.

"Hanging with me is going to be a welcome change for Harlow."

"Listen, I really have to get off the phone; I'll talk to you later, Niv."

After hanging up, Vangie had to sit down and collect herself. Was Harlow really kicking her to the curb in favor of Nivea? She couldn't wrap her mind around that. Nivea was lying, deliberately trying to get under Vangie's skin. Harlow couldn't stand Nivea and her phoniness. There was no way Harlow would willingly spend an entire day with Nivea if Vangie wasn't around.

An uneasy feeling came over her. Harlow had been avoiding her ever since she'd made the snide comment about Drake. It was time for Vangie to let Harlow know how sorry she was for hurting her feelings.

She pressed a button and entered Harlow's number. Harlow didn't pick up until the fourth ring.

"Hi. Did you get the flowers I sent?"

"Yes, I did." Harlow didn't sound enthused.

"Why didn't you call and let me know? Actually, I know the answer to that. You've been avoiding me because you're upset over the remark I made about Drake, and I want to formally apologize."

"Oh, really?" Harlow said, sounding uncharacteristically sarcastic. "I'm not interested in your apology, Vangie. There's been friction between us for months. I didn't understand it, and I allowed you to be rude and impatient with me. I had no idea what was bugging you, so I held my tongue, hoping you'd get over whatever was wrong with you. Now that I know about your resentment toward me—"

"It's not that serious, Harlow."

"Don't tell me what's serious. It's very serious that a so-called friend shuts me down every time I talked about my desire to get pregnant. And it's very fucking serious when you start insinuating that my husband is involved in something illegal."

"Don't put words in my mouth; I didn't say that."

"You insinuated."

"Harlow, I was drunk. You know I had too much wine that night."

"That's no excuse. Drunk or sober…friends don't deliberately say hurtful things to each other. And frankly, Vangie, I don't need a friend who's envious of me."

"I'm sorry I shared my feelings. I honestly thought you'd understand."

"There's nothing to understand. Your snotty attitude toward me was becoming unbearable, but I had hoped you'd get over whatever was bugging you. I took your shit for too long, Vangie. The more I took, the meaner you got. It was as if you wanted to punish me for living a charmed life."

"That's not true."

"It is true. You resented me because of your own deficiencies."

"What deficiencies?" Vangie asked in a wary tone.

"Hell if I know. You have to ask Alphonso and Shawn about your deficiencies. They should be able to clue you in on what makes you so damn unlovable that neither one of them were willing to wife you."

Vangie's mouth fell open. She dropped her hand downward and clutched her stomach, feeling kicked in the gut by Harlow's harsh words. "How could you say something so cruel?"

"I'm keeping it real."

"I've been mean to you Harlow—for no reason—and I'm woman enough to admit it. But I hope you're not ending our friendship over something I said when I had too much to drink."

"Unfortunately, I am. I think it's best that we part ways, Vangie."

"I said I'm sorry," Vangie whined.

But Harlow wasn't accepting Vangie's apology; the low scornful sound she made announced as much.

"Can't we talk this through? We've been through thick and thin together; how can you allow one incident to destroy a lifelong friendship?"

"I don't trust you, Vangie. You treated me like shit for no reason and I allowed it. But you took it too far when you went in on my husband."

Resigned to the fact that their friendship had been fractured, Vangie said, "All right, well, you don't have to worry about me bothering you again." She tried to sound nonchalant, but her voice cracked, betraying her emotions.

"You need to delete my number because I'm definitely deleting yours."

"Okay," Vangie muttered weakly, and then the phone went dead after Harlow terminated the call. She gazed at her phone in disbelief and realized her hand was shaking. In all the years she'd known Harlow, she'd never heard her sound so bitter and cold.

Vangie would have given anything to take back what she'd said about Drake. She'd allowed the green-eyed monster to destroy a friendship that had endured both good times and bad. Being rejected by Harlow felt oddly similar to the way she'd felt when Shawn had walked out on her soon after she'd given birth to Yuri. Once again, she felt the pain of abandonment. The pain of being misunderstood. Why had she driven away the best friend she'd ever had?

A low moan turned into sobbing. Vangie began to weep and gasp, crying loud and uninhibited as if she were home alone.

Yuri heard her and came running into the living room. "What's wrong, Mom?" He stared at her posture, which was bent at the waist with her hands clutching her stomach. "Are you sick? Does your stomach hurt?" He chewed nervously on his bottom lip and his eyes were filled with fear.

She hadn't meant for her son to see her so helpless and broken. She'd always been strong in his presence. "I'm okay, Yuri." She straightened herself up and wiped the tears from her face with both hands. Dry-eyed, she gave him a faint smile, proving she was all right.

Yuri continued to stare at her. "Why were you crying?"

"A friend gave me some bad news."

"Who? Auntie Harlow?"

"No. Someone from work." She couldn't bear to tell Yuri that she and Harlow had parted ways. "Don't worry about me, Yuri; I'm okay, now." Trying to convince him, she forced another weak smile.

"I have some good news for you." Yuri grinned at his mother.

"What's the good news, sweetheart?"

"My dad is going to open his own barbershop, and he's going to let my brothers and me work with him on the weekend."

"That's real good news, Yuri," Vangie said, though she didn't like the idea of Shawn starting his own business and moving up in the world. And she absolutely hated hearing Yuri referring to those little project hooligans as his goddamned brothers.

"Wanna know something else?"

"What else?" Vangie smiled in earnest. Her sweet little man was actually worried about her and was doing his best to come up with news that he hoped would cheer her up.

"I'm going to be my dad's best man at his wedding!"

Vangie gasped. "What wedding?"

"His wedding with Jojina. I'm going to be my dad's best man. Devontay is going to walk Jojina down the aisle and give her away. Guess what Javarious has to do?"

In a state of shock, Vangie couldn't believe what Yuri had told her. Shawn was getting married to that gaudy, project chick? Oh, God! Vangie was hurt and mortified. Could her life get any worse? Everybody was moving forward except her. "Mom!" Yuri blurted, snapping her out of her reverie.

"What!" Vangie said in annoyance.

"Guess what Javarious and Starlet are doing at the wedding?"

"I don't care what they're doing," she snapped. "Go do your homework or watch TV or something."

"Okay, but I have to tell you about Javarious and Starlet." He broke out into a fit of giggles. "Starlet was bragging about being a dumb flower girl, but Javarious is mad that he has to be the ring boy. The ring boy has to walk down the aisle carrying a fruity-looking pillow with the ring on it."

Vangie was too hurt and weak to correct Yuri and tell him the proper term was *ring bearer*.

"I bet Devontay five dollars that Javarious is gonna drop the ring. It's gonna roll around the floor and get lost and Javarious is gonna be in so much trouble." Yuri broke into more titters of childish laughter.

"Your father's getting married in church?" Vangie asked incredulously. Shawn, the man who was so against marriage, was trying to turn a hooker into a housewife? It was un-fucking-believable! Vangie wondered if her day could get any worse. "Yuri, please start your homework."

"I can't."

"What do you mean, you can't?"

"I can't think when I'm hungry. What's for dinner, Mom?"

Vangie had completely forgotten about fixing Yuri a nutritious dinner. The idea of trying to pull together a meal made her head throb. "Call Domino's and order two medium pan pizzas."

"Yay! We haven't had pizza in a long time. Thanks, Mom!"

"Welcome," she yelled in forced cheerfulness.

For Yuri's sake, she was attempting to keep up the façade that she was okay with the news of Shawn's upcoming marriage. In truth, she was pissed-off, shocked, and felt betrayed. Her mind raced with bitter thoughts: *We'll be eating a lot of take-out from now on. I'm not slaving over the stove after working all day. Why should I waste my time preparing nutritious meals when no one appreciates anything I do? Not Yuri, not his damn father, and not Alphonso. All the men in my life take me for granted and treat me like crap. Shawn re-*

fused to marry me, the mother of his child, and now he's planning a big wedding with a tramp that has three kids that aren't even his!

Suffering two harsh blows in one day left Vangie feeling nauseous. "Yuri, I have to lie down for a few minutes. Let me know when the delivery guy gets here," she said as she dragged herself down the hall toward her bedroom.

NIVEA

For the first time in her adult life, Nivea felt a sense of calm. Not stressing over a relationship or money was a welcome relief. And Odette was a godsend. The woman was amazing with Mackenzie, singing Caribbean songs to her while she rocked her to sleep, and taking her for long carriage rides in her elegant pram. Prior to Odette coming into their lives, Mackenzie had never been exposed to so much fresh air and sunshine. Nivea had always strapped her in her car seat and driven her wherever they needed to go.

Due to Odette's influence, Mackenzie was finally starting to sleep through most of the night. With so much free time on her hands, Nivea was practically living at the gym, and her toned body was proof of her effort.

Nivea kissed Mackenzie goodbye, handed her to Odette, and then breezed out the front door. Her hair was piled on her head in an artful top knot and she was dressed in top-of-the-line fitness attire. Continuing the all-white theme, she wore white designer yoga pants, white sneakers, a fitted white tank top, and a soft-as-butter, white leather gym bag was slung over her shoulder. She looked and felt like a million bucks. Money sure made a difference; life was beautiful.

Windows rolled down and the sunroof slid open, she inhaled the fresh air and blasted the radio as she made the trip to St. Davids.

She arrived at the fitness center at ten in the morning and was relieved to see only a few parked cars.

The gym was a ghost town with only a few employees and a handful of club members. It was thrilling to have the place practically to herself. Good fortune seemed to be coming to Nivea in leaps and bounds, lately. After going through the worst year of her life, it was about time that her luck finally had changed.

She started off with a half hour of cardio, and then an hour of Pilates. By eleven-forty, she headed to the weight room to get in another half hour of strength training before calling it quits and relaxing in the hot tub.

A couple of guys were in the weight room, announcing their presence by grunting and groaning like Neanderthals as they bench pressed enormous weight. Nivea sucked her teeth in disgust as she moved to the far side of the room and began working her back muscles. After ten relatively easy repetitions, she added more weight. Sweat poured down her face, confirming that she was pushing herself to the maximum.

She squeezed her eyes shut and scrunched her face in an unattractive grimace as she went through the painful repetitions.

"Maybe you should use lighter weights; you don't want to pull a muscle," said a male voice, taking her off-guard. Feeling somewhat embarrassed at being caught with her face scrunched in such an unappealing way, she relaxed her facial muscles and opened her eyes, expecting to see a helpful staff member. To her surprise she was looking in the face of the obnoxious Mr. Handsome. He was holding a container of orange juice.

"Not you again!" Nivea frowned in irritation.

"Hey, I was only trying to prevent you from straining your muscles," he said with that cocky smile that made her want to slap him.

"Did I ask for your help? Why don't you go pester someone else?"

Unfazed by her negative reaction to him, his brow arched in amusement. "Suit yourself, but if you get hurt, don't say I didn't warn you." With a shrug, he turned away. Chugging down orange juice, he sauntered toward the racks of free weights and barbells.

She caught a glimpse of his arrogant strut, and thought, *He irks the shit out of me. Acting like I was supposed to swoon over his offer to help me. His conceited ass must think he's God's gift to women!* Every fiber of her being tensed and stiffened, objecting to his cocky demeanor and air of entitlement. Even though he was no longer invading her personal space, she was completely rattled by the intrusion. With her workout officially ruined, she let go of the bar, allowing the loud clang of steel against steel to express her disgust. Head held high and with an angry sway to her hips, Nivea exited the weight room and hit the shower.

After showering, she considered getting another massage, but decided to try another spa experience. Selecting to unwind in the hot tub, she put on a lime-colored, one-piece swimsuit. A glance in the mirror told her she looked hot and curvaceous and the little bit of baby fat that had accumulated in her lower abs was completely concealed.

Nivea smiled at her image. If she continued working on her abs, in another month or so, her tummy would be flat enough to show off in a bikini.

She swept into the hot tub area and was grateful that the area was vacant. The hot, swirling water instantly relaxed her. Reclining with her head resting on a neck pillow, she closed her eyes as the powerful warm jets of water gave her a neck-to-toe massage. The water was incredibly soothing and soon she was in a tranquil state, hovering somewhere between sleep and wakefulness. A slight shift in her position and the jets of water shot between her legs, jolting her with pleasurable sensations that shot directly to her core.

She hadn't thought about sex since giving birth; it was as if her libido had completely shut down. Now it was awakened and she felt a familiar throb. Her hand meandered downward, settling between her legs. Using the pads of four fingers, she gently pressed against the distressed area, attempting to soothe the dull ache.

But the throbbing persisted, growing more urgent as her middle finger unconsciously fondled her clit. The tempo of her finger strokes increased along with her breathing. Resting her head on the ledge, she closed her eyes, enjoying the warmth and the feeling of anticipation that coursed through her.

The goal was to give herself an enormous orgasm. She could get there quickly by fingering her pussy with her longest finger while pressing on her clit with the heel of her palm. Or she could take her time and savor the journey as she thought about scenes from her kinky past. The more vivid her imaginings, the more intensely she would climax. She thought about her various sex escapades and decided to relive the threesome she'd had with two anonymous bartenders last year. Getting fucked by one man while sucking off the other had been one of the freakiest situations she'd ever been involved in. It wasn't something she'd ever do again now that she was a respectable parent, but it was a convenient memory she could rely on to get her juices flowing.

Mmm. The pressure was building. It had been so long since she'd had any sexual release, she couldn't control the soft murmurings or the gentle thrusts of her pelvis as her mind drifted from the ménage to the time Knox performed oral sex on her while her sister was in the next room making drinks to celebrate her and Knox's upcoming wedding.

Mmm. Oh, yeah. Her hand moved more urgently and perspiration beads popped over her forehead. That memory of Knox eating her pussy with Courtney only a few feet away really had her going. So much so that she bit down on her lip, grimacing as mounting pressure accumulated in her core. Soft moans escaped her lips and her heart raced. As if a switch had been turned on inside her, Nivea's flesh was buzzing and vibrating; she could tell it was going to be a massive orgasm. She could tell by the uncontrollable movement of her hips. And the way her groin jutted upward, welcoming the contact with her caressing fingers as well as the heated pressure from the water jets.

"Maybe I can help you with that," someone whispered close to her ear.

Startled, Nivea gasped; her eyes popped open. Water splashed as she snatched her hand from beneath the crotch of her swimsuit. Pulling herself upright, she twisted around to face the intruder.

It was *him!* Mr. Handsome was crouched behind her, so close she could feel his breath on the back of her neck.

Recoiling, she frowned at him. "Why would you sneak up on me like that? The way you keep following me around is ridiculous. Your stalker behavior is scary, and if you keep it up, I'm gonna be forced to get a restraining order on you."

"Didn't mean to startle you." He gave her a smile that didn't seem sorry at all. Then he gazed at her for a few beats with those gorgeous light-brown eyes. Momentarily dazzled by his striking looks and his enviable thick, long lashes, Nivea studied his face.

In the split seconds that she was mesmerized, Mr. Handsome quickly kicked off his sneakers and socks and whipped off his shirt, revealing a mouthwatering display of musculature and caramel-toffee-colored skin.

"Seems like you're in a little distress and I thought I might be able to help you," he said as he boldly came out of his shorts. With his workout gear tossed in a heap, he was stripped down to only a pair of briefs as he lowered himself in the water.

"What do you think you're doing? How dare you invade my privacy?"

"Let me help you out."

Nivea wrinkled her nose and recoiled. "Get away from me. I'm not in distress and I don't need your help. Just leave me alone… please!" Ordinarily, it would have been extremely embarrassing to be caught masturbating, particularly in a public place, but Nivea was too furious by the audacity of the conceited, pretty boy to feel anything except indignation.

"Hey, I'm not looking for anything in return." He softened his tone. "Just relax and let me suck your pussy. Would you let me do that?"

Whoa! Had she heard him right? Little jolts of electricity instantly began shooting through her coochie.

His pretty eyes gazed downward. His laser-sharp gaze seemed to penetrate the water, zooming in on her most intimate part, prompting it to involuntarily contract. Nivea had a weakness for getting her pussy eaten in unexpected places.

"I want you to cum in my mouth," he stated with a stoic expression.

Oh, God! Such crude words never sounded so sweet. But Nivea was noncommittal, glancing around the room as she gave the freaky offer some thought. *I'm not like that anymore; I don't have sex with random partners,* she reminded herself. *On the other hand, I'd be a fool to turn down oral sex from this kinky-ass, pretty boy.*

While Nivea struggled with her the moral dilemma, he gripped her by the waist, lifting her up and placing her rump on the ledge. *I guess one last hoorah won't hurt,* she concluded.

He rested his forearms on either side of her, palming her ass as he pulled her closer. "Open up," he gently prodded.

Uncertain if she should slip back into the ways of her slutty past, Nivea sat quietly for a moment, pondering his request.

"You know I want you," he said. "Been wanting to taste you from the moment I first saw you."

She was aware that he wasn't confessing any sincere emotions or even admitting to a physical attraction. He was bluntly stating that he hungered for her pussy; he wanted to dine between her legs. During her sex binges last year, Nivea had developed a taste for impromptu, freaky sex. She glanced at him, wondering what his story was. Did he select the pussy he wanted to eat based on a specific body type or did her pussy throw off a certain, alluring scent?

"Just this once," she said firmly, and then looked around. "But suppose someone comes in and catches us?"

"Nobody's coming in here." He shook his head and widened his eyes, striving to convince her. Those beautiful, light-brown eyes, clearly his defining characteristic, were so bright and vibrant, they seemed to give off a glow.

Feeling a pinch of worry, she tilted her head toward the door.

"Seriously, it's okay. I wanted to be alone with you for a few minutes…you know, to talk to you and find out why you keep giving me the brush-off, so I locked the door. And I'm glad I did." He smiled and this time his smile didn't seem arrogant.

Not sure if she should trust the guy, Nivea gave a grudging smile.

"Are you going to let me eat your pussy?"

The question was so unnervingly provocative, she winced as a flash of heat blazed through her, melting away her resolve. Somewhat breathless and unable to speak, she responded by slowly spreading her legs.

Standing before her in the hot tub, he began the sweet seduction by rubbing the stretch of fabric that concealed her mons pubis. He stood there, caressing and fondling her pussy with large hands that possessed a slow and gentle touch. His hands didn't wander to her breasts. His eyes didn't steal glances at her face. He concentrated on her crotch, tracing circles on her hardening clit, and sliding a finger up and down the crease of her pouty, inner lips. He stroked and massaged until honeyed moisture dampened his fingertip.

"Take this off," he urged, tugging at the strap of her swimsuit.

"I can't get naked in here." Her eyes darted about nervously.

"Yes, you can. Nobody's gonna bother us."

"I don't think—"

"Let me see that beautiful body you've been working so hard on." He cracked a sexy smile. "And stop trying to hide that pussy from me."

Still feeling uneasy but definitely aroused, Nivea pulled down the top of the swimsuit. Her full breasts spilled out and jiggled free. He groaned in approval. Before she could finish peeling off the swimsuit, he gravitated toward her bared skin. His eager hands pushed her luscious mounds together. He lowered his head, covering her nipples with soft kisses before puckered lips gently tugged on a nipple.

Nivea could feel the last dregs of breast milk being siphoned from her body and she was mortified. Her face aflame, she pulled away, crossing her arms over the breasts that had betrayed her. "I'm sorry. I didn't know there was any milk…" She dropped her gaze and stammered, "I…I recently weaned my baby."

"Shh. It's okay; I think it's sexy." He unclasped her arms, revealing her plump, lush breasts.

It was weird—in a good way—that he thought her leaking tits were sexy. Leaning in, his eager mouth closed around one nipple and then the other, his suckling lips giving Nivea tingling sensations that were strangely sensual.

After he'd had his fill, he raised his head and kissed her deeply. His tongue tasted sweet and tangy, an oddly pleasant combination—a milk and orange juice flavor.

She arched upward, assisting, as his busy hands peeled the bottom portion of her swimsuit from her body. He broke the kiss and observed her nakedness, and Nivea wasn't the least bit self-conscious about her pudgy tummy or any bodily flaws that lingered after giving birth. Oddly, she felt completely flawless and absolutely beautiful beneath his heated gaze.

And when he stooped down, pressing his mouth against the triangle of pulsing flesh between her legs, Nivea practically convulsed. She'd been sex-deprived for so long, her pussy was leaking profusely as if crying tears of joy.

Releasing a blissful sigh, she opened her legs wider, urging him to penetrate her pussy with his tongue. But he had other ideas. His head turned back and forth as he brushed his soft lips across her lower region, and then teased her clit with the tip of his tongue.

Oh, God, this is torture. Eat my pussy; eat my pussy, eat my pussy… please, she chanted over and over in her mind. But neither her secret mantra nor her desperately winding hips persuaded him to give her what she wanted.

Frustration soon turned into aggression. Succumbing to a burst of rage, she grabbed the back of his neck and demanded in a coarse voice, "Eat my fuckin' pussy!"

Apparently, he wasn't the sort of man that did what he was told. As if he hadn't heard her, he continued the leisure licking, with the tip of his tongue alternately circling and flicking her clit until the nubby appendage emerged from beneath its fleshy hood, throbbing with ardent desire.

Delirious with passion, Nivea dug her nails into the side of his neck, moaning pitifully and muttering incomprehensibly.

Showing a little mercy, he let up on the clit-licking. His tongue slid along the seam of her labia and then teased the sensitive lips apart. At last, he stabbed into the exposed and needy orifice, driving Nivea wild. Anxious little pussy muscles tried to clutch around his tongue, but he didn't linger in one area long enough for her pussy to get a good grip.

The things he did with his mouth were scandalous. Soft pussy kissing was followed by sudden tongue-thrusts and tongue-twists, a sort of oral gymnastics that caused Nivea to whimper, made her toes curl up tightly.

Sensing that she was dangerously close to releasing a long, scary, half-crazed-sounding howl, his long arm reached upward and muted her by clamping a hand over her mouth. For some odd reason, she was further aroused by his palm pressed against her lips, and couldn't suppress the urge to taste him.

While he slurped at her nether regions, she licked and sucked the center of his palm. It made no sense, but she couldn't help herself. And judging from the way he began to ravage her pussy, delving deeper and sucking more ardently, he was apparently turned on by what she was doing.

So turned on, he came out of the water, slid off his briefs and stretched her out on the wet, tiled floor. Growling softly, he climbed on top of her and plunged inside her warm depths. He fucked her without tenderness; his thrusts were rough, brutal, savage-like as he strived to enliven a pussy that had been unattended for far too long. It was as if he knew exactly what Nivea needed.

Teeth gritted, Nivea struggled to hold back a shriek that was rising in her throat. This time, she took the initiative, groping around until her hand clenched his wrist. On her own volition, she drew his hand to her face and sealed his palm against her mouth. And when his dick pushed against her special spot, her strident scream was muffled inside his cupped hand.

❤ ❤ ❤

"That was crazy," he said, sticking a leg into his shorts and shaking his head in pleasant bewilderment.

"Real crazy," she agreed with a wistful smile, though already regretting having lost control of her morals. Nivea struggled into her wet bathing suit and wondered how this sex slip-up would affect her. Now that she'd reverted back to her old ways, were more adventures in whoredom waiting right around the corner? For her daughter's sake, she hoped not. Her child deserved a mother with sound judgment and moral integrity.

She also wondered if Mr. Handsome would start avoiding her at the gym, now that he'd had his way with her. It didn't matter. Although he was a damn good fuck, it was highly unlikely that she'd turn into a dick-whipped stalker. The next time she bumped into him, she'd make it a point to ignore him and act like absolutely nothing had happened between them.

"We'll have to get together again. Soon, I hope," he added with what Nivea interpreted as a patronizing smile.

"Well, I guess I'll be seeing you." She wrapped a towel around her waist and took a few steps toward the door. Feeling ashamed of her lack of self-control, she was more than ready to get out of there.

"Oh, it's like that?"

She stopped walking and turned around. "Like what?"

"You're just gonna use me and leave without even offering your number." A shadow fell across his face. He looked sad. Almost forlorn. But Nivea wasn't falling for his pitiful act. For a hottie like him, women came a dime a dozen. Nivea didn't know who he thought he was fooling.

She put a hand on her hip and arched a brow. "We both got we wanted, didn't we?" she asked challengingly. She didn't appreciate him pretending that he wanted to take things further. Why did men always feel the need to play games? It was their egos. They couldn't stand it when a woman could get her sexual needs met and then walk away, without appearing the least bit needy.

"I was hoping to get to know you better." He did something pouty with his mouth that was sinfully sexy, and she glanced away from his face, refusing to fall into his trap.

"You just finished fucking me; you can't know me much better than that," she said with a wry smile.

"Why're you being so hard on me?"

Nivea shrugged and turned away, leaving him to wonder. She'd won the battle and it felt good. Before she reached the door, she heard the rattle of keys and the door suddenly opened.

A young, skinny blonde entered the room, holding a binder. She blinked in surprise at Nivea, and when she spotted him, her eyes widened and her face reddened as if she'd caught her man cheating on her. Squaring her shoulders, she visibly pulled herself together.

"There you are, Malcolm," the blonde said in a perky voice and rushed to him. "I've been calling your cell and looking everywhere for you. Something's up with the delivery of the new equipment— some sort of delay. I tried to handle it, but the manufacturer's rep won't talk to anyone but you," the blonde said.

"Thanks, Heidi."

"I'm only doing my job," she replied and patted Malcolm's arm and then slid her hand downward in a sneaky sort of caress. She opened the binder and began speaking softly, showing him some- thing that was work-related, something that made him furrow his brows and give his full attention to.

While Malcolm frowned and turned pages, no longer concerned about getting to know Nivea better, the blonde moved closer to him and made an *oh, you poor baby* overture, patting his bicep and shaking her head, commiserating with him over the bad news.

She cut an eye at Nivea, making sure she'd gotten the message: *He's mine; stay away!*

Nivea was sorry she'd witnessed the exchange between Malcolm and the skinny employee. Before the blonde opened the door, Nivea had no idea what his first name was and didn't know he was affiliated with the gym in some capacity. If only she'd kept walking, she would have won the battle between the sexes. But now, a twinge of jealousy squeezed at her heart. And that was followed by a surge of anger that propelled her furiously toward the door. Instead of the victorious exit she'd intended, she walked out the room feeling like a woman scorned.

VANGIE

"What's good, ma?" Alphonso asked over the phone in a lustful tone.

"I'm good," she said drearily.

"You sound a little down, but don't worry; I got the cure for whatever's ailing you." His words were thick with sexual innuendo, as if he could really back them up.

Nigga, please! Vangie could use an hour-long dick-down, but Alphonso sure as hell couldn't deliver it.

"I'm in town—at the Ritz-Carlton. Why don't you put on something sexy and come through?"

It was a damn shame the way Alphonso popped up on her whenever he got good and ready and expected her to jump, but if she wanted to continue enjoying some of the finer things in life, she had no choice. It was also a damn shame that she didn't have the heart to confront him about the gun he'd placed in her son's hand. Cussing him out the way she wanted to could possibly end their special friendship. The best she could do was to make sure that Yuri was at her mom's house whenever Alphonso visited.

Vangie took a deep breath, and then another. She was furious with Alphonso, and blamed him for her plight in life. Harlow was living like royalty, and even Nivea had had a life-changing come-up. And worse, that ratchet project queen, Jojina, was planning a wedding with the love of Vangie's life. While everyone else was making major strides, Vangie was caught in limbo—still living in the same apartment building she'd been in for the past three years, still driving the same car, and it seemed she'd be single forever.

Fucking around with Alphonso and assuming he was her Prince Charming had been a huge mistake. She had nothing except shoes and handbags to show for the time she'd put in with him. Now he was summoning her so he could literally bang her. Foolishly clinging to the hope that she might one day become his wife, she was afraid to refuse his request.

"What's your room number?" Vangie asked through clenched teeth.

"Same as usual," he replied.

Vangie glanced at the clock. It was too late to go shopping, and she hoped he didn't assume that their last shopping trip was still good for another roll in the hay. Shit, her pussy wasn't on retainer; she needed a steady stream of gifts to be able to fuck him. One thing about Alphonso, he wasn't cheap. Most likely, he'd brought her something exquisite from London. She brightened up imagining him handing her a shopping bag from Harrods department store.

"Okay, I'll be there in about an hour."

"See you soon, ma," he said and hung up. He hardly ever called Vangie by her name. Always referred to her as Ma, which was impersonal and a reflection of how emotionally detached he was from her.

Vangie shouldn't have been upset with Alphonso; she only had herself to blame. From jump, she'd acted docile, accepting his bad sex and disrespect in the hopes that being patient and understanding would encourage him to marry her. She'd obviously played herself. Alphonso spent money on her like water because he had it like that, not because he gave a damn about her. She was nothing more than his personal fuck-piece.

And since he wanted to treat her like a damn whore, then he was going to have to start coming off some cash instead of giving her what he wanted her to have. If he wanted to keep her as a *special friend*, then tonight he needed to open up that safe in his hotel room and lay some cold, hard cash across her palm! Fuck if she was going to continue living from paycheck to paycheck while Harlow and Nivea were enjoying the good life.

Dressed in a short, sparkly skirt, heavy makeup, a pair of fuck-me heels, and a blonde wig she'd worn on Halloween, Vangie arrived at Alphonso's hotel suite looking like a hooker.

"Damn, ma!" he said, looking at her with a horny gleam in his eyes.

"Hey, baby," she greeted in a sultry tone of voice. "I missed you while you were in London. Both of us did."

"Both of y'all? Who…you and Yuri?" He gave her a baffled look.

Vangie licked her lips and shook her head. "Me and she," she responded, brushing her fingers against her crotch. "We missed all of that." Boldly, she gave his dick a quick squeeze.

"Oh, damn. I like your freaky side. You need to let me see this side of you a lot more, ma."

"Don't call me ma."

"Why not?"

"I want you to call me by my slut name."

"Your *what* name?"

"My slut name—Venus—that's what I want you to call me." She wrapped her arms around his neck and kissed him deeply, snaking her tongue inside his mouth, aggressively licking his tongue and his inner cheeks.

"Damn, I kinda like Venus. Why am I just now meeting her?"

Vangie ran her hands over Alphonso's shoulders and arms. "Venus is aggressive; the kind of woman that takes control. I wasn't sure how you'd respond to a female that likes to take charge."

"I'm cool with it." Excitement gleamed in his eyes. "I'm yours; do whatever you want with me, ma."

"You need to get my name right, nigga," Vangie said with disdain.

"I meant, Venus," he corrected with uncomfortable laughter.

"Is something funny?" she asked in a no-nonsense tone.

"Whoa. What are we doing, here?" There was a note of concern in Alphonso's voice.

Fully in character, Vangie squeezed her breasts and gyrated as if overcome with uncontrollable desire. "You're about to give me some dick and show me how much you missed *her!*" She shoved her skirt up and caressed her pussy.

"You on fire, ma…I mean, Venus," he quickly corrected.

Vangie pulled her thong down and moaned as she fingered herself. "Come get this hot pussy," she coaxed. "Fuck getting in bed… I want you to do me right here, on the floor." She stuck her middle finger in her pussy and slid it in and out. Transfixed, Alphonso stood with his tongue practically hanging out and with his eyes glued to the masturbation scene unfolding before him.

He undid his belt, ready to get in on the action.

"Hold up," Vangie said. "Venus needs to get paid first."

"Huh?"

"You gotta pay before you start pounding and beating up on this delicate pussy."

"All right, I'll pay you," he said, breathlessly as he unzipped his fly and yanked his pants down.

"Ain't no fuck now and pay later; Venus needs her money now," Vangie insisted.

"Tell Venus, I got her," he said, suddenly all over Vangie, kissing and licking her neck while groping her breasts and grinding on her like a dog in heat. It was the first time he'd ever lifted a finger to do more than take his dick out of his drawers.

"Stop being cheap and give me some fucking money," Vangie said roughly, pushing Alphonso away.

"Okay, okay." He dug in his pocket and extracted several hundred-dollar bills. She put the money in her purse and then frowned. "Is that all you think Venus is worth?"

"Naw, she's worth a whole lot more; I'll give it to her later."

Vangie pulled her thong up. "Venus don't fuck on credit."

"What's the problem; how much more do you want, ma?"

"Don't call me ma…my name is Venus, muthafucka!" In an act of extreme disrespect, she poked him in the middle of his forehead and gave him a nasty look. Vangie was feeling her alter ego. Venus, the sassy prostitute, was taking out all her pent-up frustration on Alphonso.

"I like Venus's feisty ass. How much you want, baby?"

"Five thousand."

"Fuck that," Alphonso scoffed. "You're taking this game too far. How I look paying that much money for some pussy?"

"Whatever, nigga. I guess you gon' give yourself a hand job because Venus is out!" Vangie pulled her sparkly skirt down.

"Are you seriously leaving?"

"Fuck yeah, you cheap bastard. Call an escort service!" She strode toward the door.

"Hold up. I was only kidding. I got the money in the safe," he said, sounding desperate and horny. He walked over to the closet where the safe was located.

Vangie smiled in triumph as she listened to the beeps coming from the safe as he pushed in the combination numbers. He returned with two stacks of crisp bills. Vangie accepted the money with a smile.

"What about those hundreds I already gave you?"

"You're not getting that back. That's my tip, cheap ass."

Alphonso bit down on his bottom lip and pushed on the lump of dick that suddenly sprang up. "I like all that tough talk. You got my dick rock-hard." He took off his pants and Vangie stripped out of her clothes.

Assuming her regular position, she got down on her hands and knees and waited for Alphonso to mount her. Oddly, she didn't feel degraded. With $5,000 tucked in her purse, she felt empowered and could easily withstand his hard thrusts.

"Get up. I don't want to fuck you in that position," Alphonso said, surprising the hell out of Vangie.

"Really?"

"You're bringing out a freakier side of me and I like it." He began stroking his erection. "While I'm jerking myself off, I want you to do something for me."

"Whatever your heart desires," she said in a sweet tone, slipping out of character as she imagined getting herself a good lawyer that would strip Shawn of his visitation rights. *I'll show that bastard that he can't get away with disgracing me by getting engaged to that tramp. He can marry her all he wants, but Yuri won't be participating in that circus!*

"I want you to talk dirty, Venus," Alphonso requested, drawing her away from her reverie. "Curse at me and call me names…you know what I mean? And uh…you can spit on my dick if you want to. That'll make me nut like crazy." Hunched over, Alphonso stroked faster and was breathing heavy, while murmuring, "Talk dirty, baby."

Vangie couldn't believe her ears! Bad-ass Alphonso—Drake's former die-hard bodyguard and protector—wanted to be humiliated and spat upon. Not knowing what to say or do, she was momentarily stunned silent. She felt as if she'd been shoved to center stage and handed a microphone without having a speech prepared. *What the fuck does this pervert want me to say?*

"Come on, Venus, don't hold back. Throw shade; get reckless with it."

She thought briefly, but couldn't think of anything to say. Somewhat panicked and feeling compelled to uphold her end of the bargain, she decided to simply say whatever came off the top of her head. And since her head was swimming with furious thoughts toward both Shawn and Alphonso, it was going to be easy to curse out Alphonso.

"Do you like the way I fuck you?" he inquired in a throaty voice as he jerked his dick.

"Hell, no, bitch. You can't fuck for shit," she blurted with hostility, grateful for the opportunity to let him know what she thought about his sex game.

"Aaaah, yeah. That's what I'm talkin' about," he moaned as if in ecstasy. "Do I have a big dick?"

She released a burst of malicious laughter. "Nigga, please you don't even have a dick; you working with nothing but a clit, you fuckin' pussy."

"Oh, baby, that's the kind of shit I want to hear." His voice was thick with lust as he frantically yanked on his dick—a dick that resembled a fat stump.

"You're nothing but scum, Alphonso. You're worse than the dirt on the bottom of my shoes. I hate you, you filthy, trick-ass bitch. Punk muthafucka gotta carry a weapon to feel like a man. Does that gun represent the dick you don't have?"

"Yes," he admitted as he shuddered with ecstasy. It was shocking the way Alphonso had done a one-eighty and was no longer the intimidating, scowling man whom she had allowed to treat her like a second-class citizen. He was downright pitiful, a sick puppy with low self-esteem and self-loathing.

"Call me a bitch, again," he moaned.

"Shut the hell up, dirty bitch! You don't run shit, so don't tell me what the fuck to say." Infuriated when she thought about how he'd revealed a weapon to Yuri, she pushed his hand away and roughly seized his dick. She gathered up as much saliva as she could, spat on his shaft, deriving a tremendous amount of satisfaction as she regarded the revolting sight of saliva oozing over his stump of a dick.

Alphonso gripped his dick inside his fist, and using Vangie's saliva as a freaky lubricant, he stroked fast and frantically. Sperm shot out forcefully, spraying high in the air, curving into a thick, white arc.

HARLOW

Harlow cried tears of joy when the doctor confirmed her pregnancy. Then she thought about her other child. Though years had passed, she'd never stopped loving and yearning to mother her stillborn infant. *My poor baby, my poor little innocent baby never had a chance.* Consumed suddenly with overwhelming sorrow, the trickle of tears that she attempted to wipe away soon turned into a torrential downpour.

The female doctor gazed at Harlow, perplexed. "I thought you were happy about the pregnancy. I can make a referral for abortion counseling if you're considering terminating."

It was as if a switch had been flipped. Hearing the word *abortion* sent Harlow into a rage. In a sudden outburst, she knocked a box of tissues off a nearby metal table, sending the box flying clear across the room. "How could you say something like that to me—are you crazy? I'm not a baby killer; I would never terminate my pregnancy. Never!" she shouted, glaring at the doctor and feeling unhinged enough to attack the woman for making such a despicable suggestion.

The doctor looked at Harlow skeptically. With her brow wrinkled, she gazed at the wall-mounted phone as if considering calling someone for assistance.

And then, as quickly as she'd flipped, Harlow pulled herself together, taking calming breaths as she straightened her shoulders and produced an apologetic smile. Looking utterly embarrassed, she retrieved the box of tissues and returned it to its place. "Excuse me, I'm a little overwhelmed by the news. I apologize for yelling at you."

Not easily placated, the doctor frowned and pursed her lips in irritation. Sighing, she ran a hand through her hair as if smoothing it into place after a physical altercation. Perched on a stool, the doctor began typing on her laptop. "I'm writing a prescription for prenatal vitamins, and I'd like to see you back in a month. Stop at the reception desk on your way out to pick up your appointment card," she said crisply, with her head lowered, apparently too offended to look at Harlow after her angry flare-up.

Harlow gathered her bag and stood. "Thank you, doctor." She tried to manufacture another smile, but her attempt failed.

Harlow didn't wait for the prescription nor did she stop at the reception desk. She walked out of the medical suite, realizing she needed an emergency visit with her therapist.

"The way I acted in the doctor's office was crazy. I completely freaked out when she brought up the subject of terminating the pregnancy. I'm afraid I may be more unstable than I realized. Suppose I flip out like that after I have the baby? Do you think I could unintentionally harm my child?"

"Have you ever harmed anyone, Harlow?" Dr. Wagner asked.

"No, not intentionally."

"What do you mean?"

"I allowed that lady to give me an abortion."

"That was your mother's decision. You were only a child yourself. What choice did you have?"

"I could have run away or something. I should have protected my baby."

"We've been through this. Why do you think these feelings of guilt are resurfacing?"

"Because I'm pregnant, again."

"Yes, and this is a time to celebrate, wouldn't you say?"

"It is. But I'm a little scared."

"It's not unusual for a mother-to-be to feel anxious and afraid. What do you think triggered your outburst at the obstetrician's office today?"

"The very suggestion of terminating another pregnancy caused me to fly off the handle. I never act that way. I don't have tantrums and I don't lose control. That's why I'm here. My behavior frightened me. "

"The idea of you or anyone else doing harm to your child brought out all your motherly instincts."

"Exactly."

"The same instincts that you weren't allowed to express when you lost your first child."

"That's right," Harlow agreed, her eyes filling with tears.

"You're going to be okay, Harlow, and I know you're going to be a fantastic parent."

"Do you really believe that? Do you really think I'm stable enough to be a parent?"

"Absolutely. And you're going to protect that child in a way that you were never protected."

"Yes, I am," Harlow said with conviction as she wiped away tears.

Tomorrow, she'd make an appointment with her regular gynecologist. And after her doctor confirmed the pregnancy and recommended an obstetrician, Harlow would share the good news with Drake.

NIVEA

Where the hell was her necklace? Nivea had been cranky for several days and discovering her necklace was missing didn't improve her mood. That good licking and dicking she'd received from Malcolm had her craving for more. The sexy bastard! As much as she loved the fitness club, she'd have to find another one. Bumping into Malcolm and possibly getting a terse hello or a curt head nod would be mortifying. *Why'd I fuck him? Now I have to find another gym, dammit!*

Frowning, she searched her jewelry boxes, her drawers, between the cushions of the sofa, beneath the baby's mattress. She'd turned her Gucci, Prada, and Chanel bags inside out and still couldn't find it.

She should have known that Odette, with her island songs and perpetual smile, was too good to be true. Nothing had ever gone missing until Odette had appeared on the scene, and Nivea had to face the facts: Odette was a thief!

The gold seashell pendant that hung from a delicate eighteen-karat gold chain had only cost $800, but that wasn't the point. If Odette got away with taking inexpensive pieces, she'd soon work her way up to the pricier items. Nivea did not want to live in a household where she had to lock down the silverware.

She hated the idea of having to look for another nanny, but Odette's kleptomaniacal ass had to go. Mackenzie had grown attached to her, but she was only a baby. She'd fall in love with the next nanny, forgetting Odette ever existed.

Nivea sighed. Replacing Odette would be so inconvenient. She'd be returning to work soon; how in the world would she have the time to break in a new nanny? Maybe Odette didn't take the necklace, she thought hopefully. Before jumping to conclusions, she decided to interrogate the nanny, and if she seemed the least bit guilty, she'd give her walking papers, and insist that she vacate the premises immediately.

But she needed Odette. Desperately. No other nanny would do. Upon that realization, she searched her mind, tried to imagine where the necklace was hiding. A light bulb clicked in her mind. *My gym bag!* Nivea searched through the bag but only found toiletries, sneakers, socks, stretch pants, a workout bra, and a business card.

Momentarily forgetting about her problem with Odette, Nivea stared at the name embossed on the card.

Malcolm Armstrong.

The name had such a nice ring. Sounded so masculine. Strong and upstanding. But Malcolm with his freaky self was anything but upstanding. But Nivea was no saint, either. The scam she was pulling on the Sandburgs attested to that. Not to mention how she'd tried to destroy her sister's marriage. And the bad thing about it…she felt no remorse for her misdeeds. Why should she? Her bratty sister had gotten what she deserved for trying to upstage Nivea's wedding back when she was planning to marry Eric.

It didn't bother her in the least to take money from a man who couldn't have possibly fathered her child. The way she saw it, if it hadn't been for his bout with the measles and his sterility issues, he could very well have been Mackenzie's father. Therefore, Nivea was perfectly okay with blackmailing him and his uppity wife into paying a lifetime of child support.

She looked at the number that Malcolm had printed neatly on the back of the club's business card the last time they'd bumped into each other. He'd handed her the card and said, "This is my personal number. Call me if you feel like talking. You know, about anything. We don't have to discuss what happened between us— pretend like it never happened. We can start all over again and get to know each other. I'd love to take you out…no strings attached. We could do something totally innocent, like go out and get an ice cream cone or something."

Nivea smiled, recalling the laughter in Malcolm's voice. She was tempted to call him.

But her smile vanished when she thought about the skinny blonde who came to collect him from the spa area. Everything about the girl's voice and body language suggested that she and Malcolm were fucking. Malcolm was probably sleeping with all the female staff. Club members, too. A man like Malcolm Armstrong was nothing but trouble and Nivea was pretty sure she was simply another notch in his belt. Fuck him! It would be a snowy day in hell before she picked up the phone to call him.

Their impromptu encounter wasn't anything special, she told herself. It was strictly a one-time thing. Anyone that had drifted into the hot tub while she was pleasuring herself could have given her the powerful orgasm she needed. She'd used Malcolm like a human dildo, but he was too smug and full of himself to realize she wasn't interested in taking things any further. Her life was perfect the way it was. She tossed the card bearing his number in the waste bin. *Don't hold your breath, waiting to hear from me, pretty boy!*

Taking her mind off Malcolm, she thought about her budding friendship with Harlow. She was looking forward to girls' day and couldn't wait to show off Mackenzie. Wondering if Harlow had taken her advice and visited an OB/GYN, she picked up her crystal-encased phone and sent Harlow a text: *Did you go to the doctor's?*

Harlow responded right away: *Yes, I'm pregnant! Keep it to yourself; I haven't told Drake yet. See you Saturday.*

Nivea felt honored that Harlow had shared her good news with her before telling her husband. She'd love to rub that in Vangie's face, and perhaps hint that Harlow had asked her to be the baby's godmother. As tempted as she was to taunt Vangie, she couldn't risk betraying a confidence and ending up on Harlow's shit list.

She wondered for the hundredth time what Vangie had done to piss Harlow off so badly that Harlow decided to cut all ties with her. The suspense was killing Nivea, and she thought about calling Vangie to pry the information out of her, but changed her mind. Harlow was a socialite and a friendship with her could help Nivea maneuver her way into high society—for Mackenzie's sake, of course. Vangie, on the other hand, was a loser, who couldn't do a thing for Nivea. Vangie wasn't worth the time of day.

The sudden peal of her phone intruded on her thoughts. She eyed the screen through narrowed eyes and was prepared to let the call go to voicemail if Vangie was calling. An unfamiliar number appeared on the screen. Out of curiosity, she answered on the second ring.

"Hello."

"Hey, Nivea. Hope I didn't catch you at a bad time."

"Who is this?" she asked, though she recognized the voice.

"It's Malcolm."

"How'd you get my number?" She managed to sound offended despite feeling flattered.

"I have access to all the members' records."

"That's stalker behavior."

"It could be interpreted that way, but I have something that belongs to you."

"Oh, yeah? What might that be?"

"Someone turned in a gold, seashell necklace to our Lost and Found department. I recognized it and decided to give you a call. Hey, I'm just doing my job, and I'm not looking for a reward… that is unless you want to reward me by going out with me."

Nivea was so relieved that she didn't have to fire Odette, she wanted to jump up and shout with glee. "Okay, I'll go out with you," she said, surprising herself.

"Really? Wow, I wasn't expecting you to accept. Uh, are you free Saturday?"

"No, I have plans Saturday but Sunday afternoon is good—you know—for getting ice cream."

"That works for me. But I had something else in mind."

"Oh, yeah?" Nivea said suspiciously. Malcolm was a typical man and she wasn't the least bit surprised that he would try to finagle his way into her panties again. But she had news for him. Any sexual acts that happened between them would be strictly on her terms.

"I had plans to go skydiving Sunday and I was thinking maybe you'd like to join me."

"Are you out of your mind? I'm not risking my life, jumping out of an airplane."

"Calm down, I was only inviting you to accompany me. Free falling through the clouds at a hundred and twenty miles per hour is not for the faint-hearted. Afterward, we'll go get that ice cream."

"I don't know about ice cream; I'm watching my weight."

"Then, how about a salad?"

"All right," she agreed.

"I knew I'd find a way to your heart. I guess I'm going to have to load up on romaine, arugula, endive, escarole and all types of leafy greens to keep you satisfied." Malcolm laughed and Nivea couldn't suppress a smile. Malcolm certainly knew his varieties of lettuce, and there was something about the sound of his laughter that warmed her inside.

"So, I take it, you're an alpha male—a daredevil type that won't be satisfied until you wind up breaking every bone in your body."

"I'm an adrenaline junkie, I admit it. But skydiving gives you a rush like nothing else can. When you face the power of terminal velocity and walk away victorious, you'll discover that all your typical daily challenges pale in comparison."

"Hmm." She couldn't think of any kind of response to what he'd said.

"I don't fear much of anything, and I welcome challenges...like you," he said in a lowered tone that was filled with masculine sensuality.

Nivea blushed and fiddled with her hair. She was grateful Malcolm couldn't see her. She'd have to learn to keep a straight face around him, and be on guard for his unexpected flirtatiousness.

HARLOW

Her gynecologist confirmed her pregnancy and recommended Dr. Carmen Talbert, one of the top obstetricians in Manhattan. Harlow quickly made an appointment and didn't blink at the astronomical cost of a first visit with the celebrated doctor. She would spare no expense to make sure she and her child received the best possible care.

And now, Harlow was finally ready to share the wonderful news with Drake. Filled with a sense of wonder and immense joy, it seemed she would literally burst if she didn't hurry and tell Drake they were going to be parents. The problem was, she couldn't locate her husband. She'd been calling and texting him all day, trying to get an idea of what time he planned to come home. Drake kept odd hours, coming home anywhere from seven in the evening until after midnight. But he almost always gave her updates, phoning or texting if a business dinner or a meeting with a client was taking longer than anticipated. But today, the most important day since their wedding, Drake was uncharacteristically missing in action. She told herself not to worry, but she couldn't help it; it wasn't like Drake to allow hours to elapse without checking in with her.

Suppose he had a car accident. He could be lying in a hospital, unidentified and clinging to life. Suppose he'd gotten robbed and shot—it happened every day on the cruel streets of New York. The terrifying thoughts that crowded her mind were too scary to dwell on and so she focused on her pregnancy.

Harlow lifted the lace camisole and stared at her abdomen in the mirror, looking forward to the day when she had a baby bump to show off. She ran a hand over the flat surface of her tummy and lovingly caressed the area that showed no outward signs of the beautiful life that was forming within. *Hello, sweetheart. Thank you for finally coming into my life; I feel so complete now. You have no idea how much I love you.*

The door chime sounded followed by the computerized voice from the alarm system, which announced, "Front door, open."

She lowered her camisole and gave a quick prayer of thanks that Drake was safe and sound and finally home. Tonight had been the first time she could recall ever being concerned about Drake's well-being while he was away from home. Although she needed her husband like never before, she hoped being pregnant and having raging hormones didn't turn her into a constant worrier.

Harlow assessed her appearance in the mirror, fluffing her hair, and giving it a sultry, tousled look. A few sprays of her favorite fragrance, and she was ready to greet her man with a tight hug and a kiss. This was one of the happiest days of her life and she couldn't stop smiling as she waited to hear Drake's footsteps.

But he was taking a long time to come to their bedroom and greet her. Impatient to share the good news, she swept along the corridor and peered into the living room. The expansive room was semi-dark and Drake wasn't anywhere to be found. "Drake?" she called, heading for the kitchen. She clicked on the light switch in the massive chef's kitchen and then ambled in the direction of his study. The door was closed but she heard movement inside. "Drake?" she said again, tapping softly before opening the door.

She uttered a startled sound and then covered her mouth in

shock. Drake had filled his silver-plated briefcase with stacks of money. He froze when Harlow opened the door. For a moment, he stood there unmoving, with a guilty look on his face.

Her stunned gaze roved from Drake's face to the safe that was set inside the wall with its door wide open. This safe that she had no knowledge of had been camouflaged by a large oil painting of a Caribbean seascape. The painting was on the floor, leaning against the wall.

Harlow felt immediately ill. "What's going on, Drake? Are you leaving me?"

"No, of course not."

"Then, what are you doing?"

"I, uh…" A glint of annoyance flickered in his eyes, and his jaw tightened. "Why are you still up? I thought you'd be asleep by now." His words came out in an accusing tone.

"I was waiting up for you…I was worried."

"I'm a big boy, no reason to worry about me."

"Answer me, Drake. What're you planning to do with all that money?" She cast a wary glance in the direction of the safe and gestured toward it. "And how long has that been here?"

"Long before we were married." He closed the lid on the briefcase, closed the door to the safe and rehung the painting on the wall. "I have to go back out and take care of some important business." He took steps toward her and kissed her on the forehead. "Babe, this has nothing to do with us. You have to trust me on that. Now, go back to bed…get some sleep."

"How could I possibly go to sleep after this? Drake, I'm your wife and I deserve to know what you plan to do with that money."

"Please don't question me about matters that don't concern you." His tone was icy, reminding her of the brusque way he spoke to her right after their wedding when she'd questioned him about shooting Ronica. This callous version of Drake was disturbing, causing Harlow to question whether she knew him at all. She searched his face, hoping for an assuring smile…a spark of love in his eyes. But his eyes were devoid of emotion. It was amazing that the person she was looking at didn't seem to be her husband. She squinted, trying to find something familiar in his eyes, but it was like staring into the eyes of a stranger.

His gaze flickered down to his Rolex. "I don't have time for this; I have to go," he said, brushing past her clutching the briefcase that was filled with stacks of hundred-dollar bills.

"Drake!" She clasped his arm. "Don't you think I'm entitled to some kind of explanation?"

"No, I don't," he said calmly as he eased his arm from her grasp.

"But this is totally crazy! I haven't heard a word from you all day. Do you realize how upsetting it was for me to not be able to get in touch with you?" She turned her gaze on the briefcase and frowned. "Where are you taking all that money?" On the verge of crying, Harlow shuddered involuntarily.

Drake put down the briefcase and hugged Harlow. He pulled her close and gave her a tight squeeze. "I'm sorry, babe. I'm in a tight spot right now. I need you to trust me. Please. I promise, we're going to get past this."

"Get past what, Drake? Talk to me," Harlow pleaded.

"I can't," he said and released her.

"Drake," she said in a shrill voice. "Tell me what's going on."

As if steeling himself for combat, his expression hardened and his eyes went cold again. "It's best that I don't discuss business with you, Harlow."

"Under these circumstances, I feel I deserve an explanation."

"Just enjoy the benefits of my labor, and don't ask questions." He picked up the briefcase and strode past her.

Harlow dropped her head in defeat. Sniffling, her shoulders shook from the effort of fighting back tears. The door chimed, announcing that Drake had exited the apartment. He was off into the night with a briefcase stacked with money. Anxiously, she padded through the sprawling apartment, going from one luxurious room to the next, taking in the exquisite furniture, plush Persian rugs, sculptures, and gilt-framed artwork. To the people who knew her, her life appeared to be a success story—a fairy tale. Former foster child and daughter of a crack addict had grown up and married well. But her picture-perfect life wasn't as idyllic as it appeared to others.

Feeling a tremor working down from her shoulders and traveling through her body, she hugged herself, struggling to hold it together and contain the storm of emotions that were bottled up inside. For the baby's sake, she couldn't feed into the panic, the fear, and the overwhelming suspicion that threatened to knock her off her feet. In the living room, she gripped the arm of a chair that faced the picturesque view of Central Park and carefully lowered herself into it. Staring out the window usually brought her peace, but not tonight.

Drake was in some kind of trouble. She could feel it. And tonight… the park, the sky, the bright moon, the stars, and the silhouettes of the towering buildings in the background didn't provide the usual comfort. She was finally pregnant, but with her marriage on the rocks, she couldn't bask in the joy. Repelled by the idea of bringing an innocent child into a world filled with turmoil and uncertainty, Harlow dropped her face in her hands and cried.

VANGIE

With her attorney by her side, Vangie left the courtroom, infuriated with the outcome of her attempt to strip Shawn of visitation rights.

"You were recommended as the best, and I paid you twenty-five-hundred dollars to represent me, but I might as well have flushed that money down the toilet," Vangie spat as she and her attorney, Clyde Wortham, walked to the bank of elevators. She groaned when she saw the crowd of people that were already waiting. "God, we're never going to get out of here," she complained.

"I presented your case to the best of my ability, but you gave me inadequate information."

"I gave you the information I had."

"I based my motion on the fact that you didn't want your son spending weekends in a dangerous housing project. You never mentioned that your son's father and his girlfriend are cohabitating in a lovely home, outside Philadelphia, in a safe, suburban neighborhood."

"I can't believe those two morons were even capable of blindsiding me like that. Quite frankly, I don't believe it. I think they're lying. Anyone with half a brain can print documents off the Internet. Neither one of them has a real job with pay stubs! He cuts hair and gets paid under the table and she's on welfare. You tell me how those two derelicts could possibly have a high enough credit score and enough money to make a down payment on a decent home?" Vangie waved her hands around in frustration. "I mean… Shawn is a bum! A well-dressed, handsome, bum! He's been living in his mother's basement since the day I met him! He's a hood rat and hardly ever leaves North Philly. I simply can't imagine him having the wherewithal to make a major move to Thornbury, Pennsylvania. Hell, I never even heard of Thornbury, Pennsylvania. Sounds like a fictitious town from a fairy tale."

"It's in Delaware County. A beautiful area with great schools," Wortham added as if he represented Shawn.

Vangie sucked her teeth. "Whatever. I still don't believe it."

"He provided the court with documentation that proves his new address is in Thornbury, and in my legal opinion—"

"Your legal opinion sucks!"

The attorney cleared his throat and continued. "I suggest you find a way to get along with your child's father."

"Why should I?"

"He alluded that your home was an unsafe place."

"That's bullshit!" Vangie blurted, her outburst drawing attention to her and the attorney.

"Please try to compose yourself," Wortham said with his eyes darting around in embarrassment.

"If Shawn can afford to buy a nice home, then he can afford to pay more child support. He gives the court bogus pay stubs, pretending to only make minimum wage. I'm sick of him and his tricks." She pointed a finger at Wortham. "You need to do your job and get me a decent support check from that deadbeat!"

"We weren't in court for child support," he reminded. "That's a totally different case. If you want to file for more child support, you'll need to pay—"

"Are you serious? You want more money out of me?" She sucked her teeth. "I'm not paying you another dime!"

An elevator arrived and the throng of people squeezed inside, packing it. Left to wait for the next one, Nivea sighed and shifted her weight from one foot to the other.

"As your attorney, I think you should quit while you're ahead."

"What do you mean by that?"

"Asking the judge to increase your child support payments is only asking for trouble. Your ex's attorney gave me a heads-up. He told me if you bring his client back into court, he's going to have your son testify against you."

"Against me?"

"According to your ex, your son has told him that he's being exposed to guns and allowed to handle them while in your care."

"Shawn is such a liar! I can explain that. My son asked a friend of mine, who's licensed to carry a gun, if he could hold it. My friend removed the clip before he let Yuri touch it. And it only happened on one occasion. I realize that allowing a young kid to touch a gun wasn't a very wise thing to do, but Shawn is blowing this thing way out of proportion."

"If the judge deems your environment as unsafe, you could lose custody of your child."

"That is the most ridiculous thing I've ever heard; my environment is totally safe. Shawn and his ghetto tramp are trying to get under my skin, that's all." Vangie folded her arms and turned her back to Wortham, but she quickly whirled back around when she saw Shawn and Jojina approaching. Vangie seethed silently while Shawn and Jojina joined them in front of the elevators. Wearing a gloating smile, Jojina entwined her hand with Shawn's.

"Can we finally end this, Vangie?" Shawn asked. "Don't you get tired of dragging me to court? All we're doing is lining the pockets of our attorneys. I don't know about you, but I'm tired of throwing away money."

Vangie stared at the screen of her phone, ignoring Shawn as if were invisible.

"Seriously, Vangie…why can't we handle this like two adults?" he said, releasing Jojina's hand as he moved closer, violating Vangie's personal space.

"Get out my face, Shawn, all right? I don't have anything to say to you—not now—not ever. If you have anything to say to me, then have your attorney call mine!"

Jojina tugged on Shawn's arm. "Forget about that low-budget bitch; you can't reason with her dumb ass."

"Who are you calling low-budget and dumb? You're nothing but ignorant, welfare-receiving, ghetto trash!"

"*You're* the one who lives in the ghetto. I live in a big, beautiful home sitting on a bunch of acres, baby. I got the picket fence, kids, the dog, and I'm planning a big wedding. You better step up your game and getcha life, wench!" Jojina held up her ring hand and then flung her long and flowing weave with the other.

"Excuse me," Vangie's lawyer said, looking embarrassed. "I have to speak to a few of my colleagues." He pointed to a group of suit-and-tie-wearing men who were chatting outside one of the courtrooms. "I'll give you a call later this week," he said with a sheepish smile as he fled the scene where tempers were flaring and harsh words were being exchanged.

"Whatever," Vangie muttered. *Your ass is fired, anyway.*

Jojina flashed her ring again. Vangie walked to the far end of the elevator bank, unable to bear the sight of that ring. It was such a slap in the face that Shawn had refused to make an honest woman out of her—the mother of his child—yet he was ready to settle down with the unemployed, project queen.

"What's the problem? Is my bling too bright? Maybe you need to put on a pair of shades to protect your sensitive eyes," Jojina said mockingly.

"Oh, she went there! She dead wrong for that," an onlooker remarked in a laughing tone that encouraged Jojina to continue taunting Vangie.

"You're really selfish. Yuri would get a much better education if he lived with us in our nice neighborhood." Jojina looked over at the group of people waiting for the elevator and directed her next comment to them. "Seriously, though…wouldn't you think a mother would want what's best for her child? I swear…some women are so spiteful, they don't care about what's best for their kids."

There were murmurs of agreement from people whose own domestic squabbles had brought them to Family Court.

Vangie was sick of listening to Jojina's mouth. "Why don't you stop worrying about my son and worry about your own wild-heathen kids?"

"I'm not worrying about nothing you have to say, hater. You're just mad because I got everything you want. I got Shawn, a nice home, and in a few months, I'm gonna have a big wedding. Whatchu got? Nothing! Your own son doesn't even want to be with you. He tells me all the time, that he wishes I was his mother!"

Vangie couldn't tolerate any more of Jojina's insults. It was true that the bitch had Shawn's nose wide open for some unknown reason, but hearing that Yuri was also under the heifer's spell pushed Vangie over the edge. "My son would never say any shit like that!"

"Tell her Shawn; tell her how much Yuri hates going back to her cramped, little apartment!"

"Shut your lying mouth, bitch!" Raging mad, Vangie stormed toward Jojina.

It wasn't that she planned on assaulting Jojina; she was simply acting on impulse. Her feet decided to move in Jojina's direction, and Vangie didn't have any control over herself. Within split seconds, she was in Jojina's face, cursing her out and calling her every raunchy name she could think of. But Vangie was momentarily silenced when a wad of slimy spit landed on her nose and trickled down the side of her face.

It took a second or two for her to process that Jojina had spit in her face. Incensed, Vangie grabbed a handful of weave-hair and tried her best to rip it out of Jojina's head, but the hair was sewn in and unyielding. She yanked on the stubborn weave with one hand, causing Jojina to wail. With her other hand, she peppered the woman's face with a series of blows. "You could never be my son's mother, you ratchet, welfare bitch!"

"Get off her, Vangie. Let her hair go," Shawn shouted, trying to get between the two women. Excitement twinkled in the eyes of the onlookers as they gaped at the unlikely spectacle of a brawl taking place inside the courthouse.

As if something wild and vicious had taken over her body, Vangie pummeled, scratched and bit her nemesis while Shawn struggled with her to no avail. He couldn't get Vangie off of his fiancée, and with her hair being pulled out by the roots, Jojina was in too much pain to fight back.

It took two police officers who happened to step off the elevator to subdue Vangie. Handcuffed and yelling obscenities, Vangie was carted off to jail.

NIVEA

An unexpected phone call from her mother had Nivea rattled, and she was at a loss for words.

"I think it's time we attempt to repair our broken family," Denise Westcott said.

"My family is intact," Nivea replied petulantly.

"I want to get to know my grandchild. You can't deny me that."

"You weren't interested in knowing Mackenzie when you thought Knox might be the father."

"We were all under a great deal of duress while waiting for the results of the paternity test, but now that it's been established that Knox is not the father, I'd like to see this family heal and try to move forward."

"How does Courtney feel?"

"Your sister forgives you."

"Does she forgive her husband, too?" Nivea asked snippily.

"Don't be crass, Nivea. I'm extending an olive branch. It's bad enough that I wasn't there for the birth of my grandbaby…" Denise sighed. "I don't want to miss out on her entire childhood."

"Mother, you're acting as if I refused to allow you to see my daughter. Dad came to see her; he sees her regularly."

"He does? That's news to me."

"He didn't want you to know that he went against your mandate to ostracize Mackenzie and me—to pretend that we don't exist."

"That's ridiculous. You were never ostracized, but for the survival of your sister's marriage, I thought it best that we all kept a distance from you. You know, until we knew for certain whether or not Knox had fathered your child." Denise paused for a beat and then cleared her throat. "Who is the baby's father, Nivea? Do you know?"

"He's a physician, Mother. A well-off physician."

"Is it possible that he'll make an honest woman of you?" Denise asked, her voice filled with hope.

Nivea knew her pretentious mother would love the idea of having another doctor for a son-in-law. And it brought a smirk to her lips when she replied, "I'm afraid not. He's already taken."

"I don't understand."

"He's happily married, Mother, and doesn't care to be involved in Mackenzie's life."

"Oh. Well, that's his loss, isn't it?" Denise said, surprising Nivea. Nivea had expected a lecture or a snide comment regarding the perils of dallying with married men. "I'm so anxious to hold my grandbaby. Why don't you bring her over on Sunday? Dinner's at five—as usual."

"Sorry, I have plans. How about next Sunday?"

"Our door is always open to you and Mackenzie. I hope to see two very soon."

"We'll be there." Nivea hung up feeling both devilish and victorious. Bratty Courtney wouldn't be the center of attention once Mackenzie was introduced to the family. And it would be great fun being around Knox and making him uncomfortable. After she'd exposed her affair with Knox, she'd been treated like a pariah while her family rallied around Knox as if he were a rape victim.

Her life was steadily improving. She hated to admit it, but it would be nice to see Mackenzie surrounded by and doted on by her grandparents. It probably had taken a lot for her proud mother to swallow her pride and practically beg to see her granddaughter. Perhaps it was time to forgive and forget. As dysfunctional as her family was, Nivea missed them—even spoiled-rotten Courtney.

VANGIE

Jail was a scary place. Inside the Police Administration Building, also known as "The Roundhouse," at Eighth and Race Streets, Vangie was deprived of comforts and basic human needs. She felt dehumanized and disoriented as she waited in the holding cell. Time dragged on and she hadn't been given a phone call. She desperately wanted to get in touch with her mother to inform her of the outlandish predicament she was in. She repeatedly asked the guards to grant her a phone call, but her requests were ignored.

While the other women in the holding cell chowed down on the dry cheese sandwiches and guzzled the ice tea that was offered, Vangie pushed the food aside. To her amazement, two women fought over her discarded meal.

Jail was purgatory, and she had never wanted anything as badly as she wanted to get out of there, go home and hug her son.

Since the guards wouldn't give her any information regarding how long she'd be locked up, she began questioning a prostitute who seemed saner than many of the others and seemed to know the ropes. "Do you know how long it takes to get out of here?"

"Depends on what you're in for?"

"Fighting." Deep shame washed over Vangie. "Fighting my son's father's fiancée."

"As long as you didn't stab or shoot her, or do any major damage, you should get a light bail and be out of here sometime tomorrow."

"Tomorrow! You mean, I'll have to stay here overnight?"

"Hell, yeah. You won't get to speak to the bail magistrate until sometime tomorrow, and you'll be talking to him via closed-circuit TV."

"Oh, my God. This nightmare just won't end. Aren't we supposed to get a phone call?"

"You'll get it, eventually. You're on their time, so you might as well take your shoes off, get comfortable, and find a corner to sleep in."

Vangie looked down at the concrete floor. "You're kidding. They expect us to sleep on the floor?"

"You'll get a hard cot in the Philadelphia Prison System if you don't make bail."

"How much is bail…you know, usually?" Vangie didn't know anything about the prison system.

"Depends on what the DA asks for. If you don't have any priors—"

"I don't!"

"Well, you should be all right. Fighting is a simple assault— only a misdemeanor. Your bail will probably be about a couple thousand—maybe less," said the knowledgeable prostitute. "You only have to post ten percent. But you better get somebody to pay it as soon as your bail is granted. Otherwise, you'll be put on the next van that's headed for State Road."

State Road was in the far Northeast section of Philadelphia and contained five major prison facilities. Vangie had no intention of going anywhere near State Road. She had a couple thousand left over from the money she'd gotten from Alphonso. All her mother had to do was go to her apartment, get the money, and pay her bail. Vangie wanted to see a light of hope in this tragedy, but couldn't. She pictured Yuri's face and was close to tears. Knowing ignorant-ass Shawn, he wouldn't protect their son's innocence; he'd allow Jojina to callously tell Yuri that his mother was in jail. Oh, God.

Yuri would be traumatized by that information. He'd probably cry himself to sleep and she wouldn't be there to comfort him.

Vangie was angry with herself for allowing Jojina to provoke her. That bitch knew exactly how to push her buttons. She should have been arrested, too, though. Spitting in someone's face could be deadly. For all Vangie knew, Jojina could have HIV. Hmph! She was acting in self-defense when she whipped that bitch's ass and that's what she planned on telling the judge. On second thought, she needed to keep quiet and have a lawyer speak for her. She wondered if Clyde Wortham could represent her in this matter. She'd already paid him for absolutely nothing; maybe he could be persuaded to show up for her bail hearing out of a sense of decency and fair play. She'd ask her mother to contact him after she got her phone call.

When her phone call was finally granted, she could barely keep her emotions together when she heard the familiar sound of her mother's voice.

"Mom!" Vangie wailed. "Oh, Mom, I can't believe they locked me up for defending myself against Shawn's crazy girlfriend! When they set bail, I'm going to need you to bring a couple hundred dollars, so I can get out. I don't know what time I'll have a hearing, but I want you to come down here as soon as possible and pay the money immediately after I see the Magistrate."

"Two hundred dollars is a lot of money for a woman who's living on a fixed income."

"Don't worry about the money, Mom. I have some stashed at my apartment, hidden inside a box of Tampons in my bathroom closet."

"I can't go to your apartment right now, Vangie. I finally got Yuri to go to sleep. He's been crying for his father for hours."

Crying for his father instead of me? "Mom, how did Yuri end up at your house? He's supposed to be with Shawn."

"Shawn called me and told me what happened. He asked me if I could pick Yuri up from school while he went to the hospital with that girl whose tail you decided to whip in court—of all places. What were you thinking, Evangeline?"

Barbara only used her full name when she was pissed, and Vangie would have tried to placate her if she'd had more time. *Hold up; did my mom say Jojina was in the hospital? That dramatic heifer is faking injuries and trying to build a stronger case against me.* "Mom, I only have a few minutes—"

"This is serious," Barbara cut in. "That girl is getting her head stitched up in several places."

"Why!"

"You ripped out tracks of hair and tore up her scalp. And she's undergoing a series of shots for all the bite wounds she sustained. What the hell was wrong with you—were you temporarily insane?"

"Yeah, I guess," Vangie said, feeling suddenly terrified about the charges she might be facing. "Mom, please go get the money; I want to get out of here as soon as possible."

"I'll get the money in the morning, after I take Yuri to school. You need to sit your behind in jail overnight and get your thoughts together and your priorities in order. You've been fighting women over Shawn since you were nineteen years old. It's time to let go."

"I have let go! That fight in court had nothing to do with Shawn. His girlfriend spit in my face. What would you have done if somebody did something that nasty to you?"

"I would have pressed charges."

"That's bull. You would have reacted exactly as I did. I didn't plan to fight her, but I snapped when she spit on me. Look, I was only acting in self-defense."

"Self-defense or not, I'm too old for all this drama. Do you hear me? You can fight and carry on and act crazy all you want, but you have to leave me out of it!"

"Okay, Mom, listen…I need a few more favors. I need you to call my job in the morning and tell them I'm sick."

"What kind of sick? Should I tell them you have a common cold or are you lying up in the hospital with something serious?"

"I don't know. Make up something. After you call my job, can you contact my attorney, Clyde Wortham, and tell him to come to the Roundhouse and represent me at my bail hearing."

Vangie's mother let out a groan. "I can't believe the requests that are coming out of your mouth. My daughter, whom I know I raised right, is behind bars and needs bail money and a lawyer! Umph, umph, umph! This is pitiful."

"Your snide comments aren't helping the situation. Stay focused, Mom. Please. My attorney's name is Clyde Wortham, and his office is on Walnut Street. You can find his phone number online."

"Hold on while I get a pen," Barbara said with a heavy sigh.

To Vangie's dismay, she was charged with aggravated assault. Wortham didn't show up, which infuriated her, but giving him benefit of the doubt, he was a Family Law attorney and probably wasn't comfortable handling a criminal case. She figured since the matter occurred in family court, and he'd personally witnessed the fight, he could explain her side of the story better than someone else. But, oh well…

She was assigned a disinterested public defender who looked

unkempt and disheveled. Her bail was set at $20,000, which meant she had to cough up $2,000. Luckily, she had $2,500 left from the money Alphonso had given her.

The crowded van ride to State Road was filled with hardcore women. Life had dealt some of the women a bad hand, while others, like Vangie, had made poor choices in the heat of the moment. Handcuffed to a foul-smelling prisoner, Vangie couldn't sink any lower. She felt trapped in a bad dream that kept getting progressively worse.

Being locked up at the Philadelphia Industrial Correctional Center was beyond humbling. Thrown in another type of holding tank with a lot of hostile, funky women, she was in a daze. As time passed, the various foul odors that clung to the women began to have the effect of smelling salts, bringing Vangie out of her stupor and making her painfully aware of her terrible circumstances.

Several hours later, she was issued a wristband with her name, a thumbnail picture of her mug shot, and a PID number. Jesus! Where was her mother? If she didn't hurry up, Vangie would be decked out in an orange jumpsuit and marched to a cell and locked inside with some big, dyke bitch who could have her way with her throughout the day and all night long. *Oh, God, help me!*

After about twelve hours, she was allowed to make a collect call. "What's going on; why haven't you bailed me out of here, Mom? It's not like you have to spend your own money! I don't understand why I'm still in here!"

"Who do you think you're yelling at? Don't raise your voice to me, Evangeline. I took the money down to the courthouse on Filbert Street, and they said you weren't processed yet. I waited for six hours, and after that, I couldn't stand around in that horrible place any longer."

"So you just walked out and left me in here to rot?"

"Did you expect me to spend the night at the courthouse, waiting for you to be processed?"

"Yes! You have no idea what I'm going through."

"I understand what *I* was going through. I was standing on my bad feet in a crowded room full of all sorts of lowlife heathens for hours and hours. I had the best of intentions, but I'm not a martyr, Vangie. Once I saw people starting to find spaces on the floor to camp out, I knew it was time to take my ass on home. I'll go back first thing in the morning, but you can't expect me to wait through the night."

"Mom, you can't leave me in here any longer. Please! You have to go back and pay the bail."

"I'm in my bed, where I belong, and there's not a chance in hell I'm going back to that hellish place—not tonight."

Realizing that Barbara wasn't going to budge, Vangie asked how Yuri was holding up.

"He's was grinning from ear to ear when his father came and picked him up."

Vangie sighed audibly. "After you post bail, I'm going to need you to drive up to State Road and pick me up. My car is still at the parking lot near Family Court."

"Can't you call one of your friends for that? I don't know anything about State Road, Vangie. Aren't there five or six prisons up there? I don't know which one you're in and I'm not in the mood for driving around in circles, traipsing in and out of prisons, trying to locate my daughter. It's disgraceful and embarrassing. I can't do it."

"Mom, what are you saying?"

"I'm saying, I can't do it. Call whatshisname…you know, that man with all the fancy cars."

"Alphonso," Vangie murmured, feeling disgust that she couldn't rely on her *special friend*. Calling him would have been a waste of a phone call since he only responded to her calls when he wanted to get together for his perverted fetish.

"Yeah, let Alphonso handle things from here. My nerves are on edge, and I can't deal with any more prison bureaucracy. All that waiting around and being spoken to any ol' kind of way by those rude clerks down at the courthouse is too much for a woman of my age."

"You're only fifty-one, Mom. You're making it seem like you're a feeble senior citizen. Geez!"

"Well, I'm at the end of my threshold for this kind of foolishness. I'm going to go back downtown tomorrow morning and pay the bail, but I'm not driving all the way up to the Northeast, trying to find State Road. I refuse to willingly subject myself to more mistreatment by prison personnel. I need a break from all that nonsense. You done put me in a position where people are treating me like I'm a damn criminal."

"How do you think they're treating me?"

"I can't even imagine, but you brought it on yourself. Ain't nobody tell you to go and get yourself locked up!"

"All right, Mom. I have to go. I guess I'll have to take the bus home after they let me out of here," she said, trying to illicit sympathy from her mother.

"Either that or call one of your friends."

"Okay," Vangie said, dropping her head in defeat after she hung up the phone. With no shower or even a wash-up for the past few days, she looked a hot mess and probably smelled like rotting fish. She wasn't about to get on a bus, but she'd rather catch a cab home than call Nivea or Alphonso and have them find out that she'd been imprisoned. Alphonso would pass the information on to Drake and he'd tell Harlow. And Nivea would spread the juicy gossip directly to Harlow, quicker than she could blink.

NIVEA

Mackenzie was a little fashion plate in her navy and white, Armani Junior tennis dress. Nivea was seriously high-fashion in a $15,000 Jason Wu dress. She'd gone overboard on the price of the dress, but she hadn't seen her family in ages, and it was important that she and her baby looked like money.

From the glimmer in her mother's eyes, she could tell she'd accomplished her goal.

"Nivea! Darling, you look amazing! Give me my grandbaby," Denise said, taking Mackenzie from Nivea's arms. She shot her husband a look that Nivea interpreted as: *Why didn't you tell me our grandchild was half-white?*

Nivea's father stuffed his hands in his pockets and shrugged in response to the unspoken question.

"She's a beauty!" Denise went on. "And I'm going to spoil her rotten."

Courtney and Knox arrived shortly after Nivea. "Hi, Niv," Courtney said, giving Nivea an air kiss.

Knox nodded his head curtly as if a verbal greeting would be interpreted as overly flirtatious.

"Take a look at your gorgeous niece," Denise said to Courtney.

Courtney gave the baby a quick glance. "She's cute," she mumbled, frowning as if it pained her to look too closely at Mackenzie.

Courtney appeared to have picked up a little weight, Nivea noted. About fifteen pounds. Stubbornly squeezed into a size eight when she clearly needed a ten, her ill-fitting, too-tight clothes gave her a slightly unkempt appearance. Knox was as corny as ever in his preppy attire—blue seersucker pants, white shirt, blazer, and brown loafers.

The family convened in the dining room and when Nivea attempted to retrieve her daughter, Denise said, "Oh, no. You can't have her back. Have a seat, dear. I've missed out on the first four months of this baby's life and I'm making up for lost time."

Paul Westcott hovered over his wife, smiling down at the baby. Denise squinted at her husband in annoyance. "A little birdie told me you've already spent time with Mackenzie, so you can have a seat, too."

Accustomed to being chastised by his wife, Paul smiled sheepishly and immediately did as he was told, but he pulled his chair close to his wife's, refusing to sit too far away from his granddaughter.

Nivea was amused that Courtney sat between her and Knox, distancing the former illicit lovers and ensuring there'd be no hanky-panky at the dinner table.

Denise kissed the baby and inhaled her fragrance. "You smell so good, Mackenzie, like you were bathed in sunshine and flowers." She looked at Nivea. "I would have never thought it, but motherhood becomes you, dear. Your daughter is clearly well cared for and loved, and she's going to get a lot more love from all of us." She made a sweeping gesture, intending for the broadness of her hand wave to include everyone at the table, but Courtney ducked her head down, excluding herself from the circle of love.

"Thank you, Mother." Nivea wasn't accustomed to getting compliments from her mother, and she felt a surge of pride. Denise was clearly in love with Mackenzie and Nivea felt as if her status had been elevated from prodigal daughter to family hero.

Unhappy with the tiny newcomer getting so much attention, Courtney sucked her teeth, as if personally insulted. Nivea had expected as much, and could only shake her head over the fact that her sister was envious of an innocent baby. Turning the spotlight on Courtney, Nivea asked, "What's been going on with you, Courtney? Still doing temp jobs or have you found something permanent?"

"I'm a stay-at-home wife," Courtney replied, emphasizing the word, *wife*.

"Oh, that's nice. Are you planning to start a family anytime soon?"

Courtney flinched as if reacting to a physical assault. She jumped up and threw her cloth napkin onto her dinner plate filled with food that had barely been touched. "I'm so sick of everyone harassing me about getting pregnant. Can I please get a break from the topic?" she exploded and then fled the dining room in tears.

"What did I say?" Nivea inquired, perplexed.

"Oh, she's in one of her moods," Denise explained.

Prepared to go after Courtney, Knox stood up abruptly.

"Give her some space, Knox," Denise suggested, gesturing for Knox to sit down. "She'll be okay in a few minutes. Her father and I always allowed Courtney to work through her anger when she threw tantrums as a child."

Somewhat reluctantly, Knox sat down and poured himself a glass of wine. With Courtney removing herself as a human barrier, Nivea could see Knox from her peripheral vision. She could also feel the heat of his gaze. Cutting an eye at him, she noticed his leering expression.

Her parents' attention was focused on Mackenzie, giving Knox an opportunity to get Nivea's attention. First, he ventured a smile and closely gauged her reaction. She returned the gesture, which prompted him to take it up a notch. A shameless flirt, he winked at her, and next, he licked his lips, crudely allowing his tongue to slither outside his mouth as he simulated giving oral sex.

Nivea blotted her mouth with her napkin, leaving a bright red lipstick stain. Stealthily, she dropped the napkin, and when Knox bent down to pick it up, she whispered, "Meet me in the den. I want you to pretend like you're fucking my lips while you get that dick hard for me. I'll be there in a few minutes."

Knox nodded with satisfaction, pleased to know that Nivea was still as deceitful and horny as he. He stuffed the napkin into his pants pocket and rose to his feet. "Excuse me, Mom and Dad," he said politely to the Westcotts. "I have to check on Courtney; she hasn't been feeling well today and I don't think she should be left alone."

"Go ahead, son, check on your wife," Paul permitted, scooting his chair closer to Denise and his new granddaughter. Talking baby talk to Mackenzie, he made funny faces, trying to get her to smile.

Under the pretense of being concerned about his wife, Knox left the dining room.

Five minutes later, Courtney returned. "Where's Knox?" she asked, looking around.

"He went to check on you," Paul said.

"Well, he didn't. No one checked on me," Courtney said in an accusing tone.

"He's probably in Daddy's den, you know…hitting the liquor," Nivea said with a little laugh.

"Why would he shut himself off in the den to have a drink?" Courtney rolled her eyes at Nivea for making such a foolish statement and then marched away, in search of her missing husband.

Moments later, a loud shriek announced that Courtney had found Knox.

Denise shook her head. "What could be wrong with Courtney, now? Could you go check on them, Paul?"

"No, let them deal with their personal issues, privately."

"I'm beginning to think that marriage was a huge mistake." Denise frowned, shaking her head.

"They've only been married a short while. After they work through the kinks, they'll be just fine," Paul offered as he shook a rattle in front of Mackenzie, drawing a happy gurgle from the child.

Courtney could be heard shouting something unintelligible. Then her voice carried to the dining room—her words emerging loud and clear. "That is not my napkin. I don't wear that shade of lipstick!"

Nivea smiled to herself. Courtney had caught her husband masturbating while staring at a napkin stained with the image of Nivea's kiss. Feigning innocence, she gazed at her parents and shrugged as if totally baffled by the couple's inability to get along. "Maybe they should get marriage counseling or something."

Back at home, Nivea placed Mackenzie in her crib and surprisingly, she didn't fuss. Nivea had Odette to thank for that miracle. She had no idea what the nanny had done to change the baby's feelings about sleeping in her crib, but whatever her method was, it worked.

Nivea smiled, thinking about how her parents had doted on Mackenzie. She was glad she'd made peace with them. Her daughter deserved a loving, extended family. She deserved to be treated like a little princess.

And it was high time that Courtney was dethroned.

VANGIE

S he didn't know whether to blame her mother for slow-poking around with the bail money or the prison system for detaining her longer than necessary simply for the thrill of exercising its authority. Instead of being released in the morning as she had expected, Vangie didn't get sprung until after eight o'clock at night. With fifty dollars in cash and two credit cards, she could have called a cab to take her to the parking lot in Center City, but she stood outside the prison and waited for the bus as a form of penance.

Losing her temper had cost her a lot and only God knew what else was in store for her. She was only out on bail; a court appearance loomed, making it difficult to enjoy the sweet smell of freedom as she stood waiting for the bus and inhaling the mild evening breeze.

If things didn't work out for her in court, it was possible she'd be returned to State Road, maybe sent upstate. Oh, God; she couldn't go through that again. The idea of being handcuffed and incarcerated again sent a shiver up her spine.

If she could turn back the hands of time, she would have listened to Shawn and dropped the entire matter. But now it was too late. There was no getting around it; she was going to have to spend a lot of money on yet another attorney. There wasn't a chance in hell she was going to leave her fate up to that slovenly and incompetent public defender that had represented her at the bail hearing.

Maybe it was time to play nice with Shawn. Have a friendly chat with him and try to convince him to get Jojina to drop the charges. She wondered if a so-called victim could go to court and retract her statement.

Surely Shawn would be reasonable and realize that a child Yuri's age needed his mother to be home. He'd be teased cruelly by other kids if word got out that his mother was in jail. Shawn wouldn't want Yuri to suffer for their mistakes, would he?

She heaved a sigh as she thought about all the debt she was going to be in after spending all her earnings on attorney fees. Her meager paycheck barely covered her monthly expenses. She might have to get a part-time job, which meant paying for additional child care. Damn, she simply couldn't get ahead.

Shawn should have been ashamed of himself for bringing so much trouble to her life. She was the mother of his child, and he should have been trying to ensure her peace of mind instead of keeping her stressed out.

We used to love each other, Shawn…how did things get this bad between us? She bit the inside of her lip in an effort to keep from crying.

In the distance, she saw the headlights of the bus. If my friends could see me now. She envisioned Harlow in her lavish apartment, eating caviar without a care in the world. And Nivea, deliriously happy with her new baby and the prospect of eighteen years of financial security.

Vangie felt like such a loser. Her life had turned to crap and was growing more sordid with each passing day. The way she saw it, her swift decline had begun at the day spa when she had sleazy lesbian sex with the masseuse, followed by a paid BDSM session with Alphonso, and finally a courthouse brawl that had led to her arrest and with a prison sentence hanging over her head. Things couldn't get any worse.

Unable to mask her pain, she boarded the bus with tears cascading down her cheeks. Deep in her feelings, she didn't care what anyone thought of her. She cried openly. Uninhibited, as if she was alone in the privacy of her bedroom with the door closed.

❤ ❤ ❤

"Good thing you showed up. We were about to have your car towed," said a rude parking attendant with dark brown skin and an African accent. If Vangie had been her regular, feisty self, she would have retaliated with a biting retort, but she was too beaten down to fight back. The fee for leaving her car for three days was astonishingly high, and she was glad she hadn't wasted money on a cab.

She steered with one hand and pressed Shawn's phone number with the other. Vangie was aching to kiss Yuri's face. Wrap her arms around him and hug him tight. She couldn't wait until tomorrow; Shawn needed to bring her child home tonight!

Shawn answered in the typical grumpy voice he reserved for Vangie.

"Hey," she said, her voice pleasant and non-combative.

"What do you want?" he growled.

"I was wondering if you'd mind bringing Yuri home tonight. But if you're, you know, working or if you're not up to it, I could come and get him, but I need your new address."

"Are you crazy?"

"No."

"You're not getting Yuri back. After you got arrested, my lawyer filed an emergency custody order. He's living with me and Jojina now. He's enrolled in school here in Thornbury."

A jolt went through Vangie that was so severe, she had to grip the steering wheel to keep from losing control of the car. "Yuri belongs with me—his mother. Don't do this Shawn, I'm serious. I really need to see my son!"

"I'm not stopping you from trying to get visitation. Like you told me in court, don't talk to me; have your attorney get in touch with mine." Shawn hung up.

Vangie called him right back. "Shawn. Please don't do this to me," she pleaded.

"This is harassment, Vangie. Read the restraining order!"

"What restraining order?"

"We filed a restraining order against you and you're not supposed to call us or come anywhere near us."

"Are you serious?"

"Tell that bitch she's gonna get tossed back in jail if she rings your phone one more goddamn time," Jojina shouted in the background.

"Contact your lawyer, Vangie. That's all I can tell you," Shawn said before hanging up again.

I've lost custody of my son. This can't be happening. Vangie started shaking so badly, she had to pull over in the parking lane before she caused an accident. She sat behind the wheel with the engine idling, and her whole body trembling as if she'd been suddenly stricken with an advanced case of Parkinson's disease. She took deep breaths, trying to pull herself together—trying to get to a calm place, but the breathing technique wasn't working.

She envisioned Jojina pretending to be Yuri's mother and a fire rose inside her. Her now steadied hand began searching through her wallet looking for Clyde Wortham's card. Helping her regain custody of Yuri was something her attorney should be able to handle. But when she thought about his lackluster performance in court the other day, she tossed the useless card inside her purse.

Wortham couldn't be trusted with a matter of such extreme importance. He was too detached; he didn't seem to care what happened, one way or the other. She needed a strong female attorney. Someone with kids. Someone who could empathize with the heartbreak and anguish of a mother whose child has been...stolen. Ripped from her arms by a pair of thieves.

Vangie finally got herself together and pulled back into traffic. She proceeded toward home, journeying slowly; there was no reason to rush now that Yuri wouldn't be coming home.

In the foyer of her apartment building, the door to her mailbox was bulging from the amount of mail that had accumulated in the past few days. She turned the key in the lock and various-sized envelopes spilled out, but a fat large envelope with a return address that contained the official-looking words, *Magistrate* and *City of Philadelphia* was tucked securely inside the mailbox. She pulled it out the mailbox, ripped open the envelope, and perused the document that bore the heading, "Temporary Restraining Order."

With great agitation, she read the lies that Shawn and Jojina had woven together. They claimed that she had not only brutally attacked Jojina, but assaulted Shawn as well. Of course, there was no mention of the fact that she'd been defending herself against a glob of disgusting saliva.

Scanning the four-page document, she came upon a court date. She had to appear in court two weeks from today, and a judge would decide whether to throw the matter out of court or change the order from temporary to permanent. Losing Yuri permanently was unthinkable. She'd never be able to survive the loss.

It was as if a dark cloud was hovering over her. She'd lost her child, had to make three separate court appearances, and there was a possibility that she might have to do some hard time. Vangie had to get right with God. She needed His strength and mercy. She hadn't been to church in over a year, but she'd be sitting in the front pew this coming Sunday. Singing, clapping, shouting, and praying. Whatever it took to get back in God's good graces.

Holding the assortment of bills, junk mail, and the envelope that swelled from the bulky restraining order, she entered her apartment. It should have felt good to get home and finally take a shower, but the apartment was quiet as a tomb and she felt so lonely being separated from Yuri.

She took small, hesitant steps toward her son's bedroom. The door was open and though she dreaded seeing his empty bed, she clicked on the light and allowed her eyes to wander around the room. His silent Xbox seemed to mock her. So many times she'd yelled at Yuri to turn down the volume. She'd give anything to hear those computerized sound effects and voices. She'd give anything to have her child back home tonight, asleep in his own bed.

She missed Yuri so much, every part of her body ached—her face, her arms, her legs, her back. She felt like she was covered with whip lashes and open wounds as she gazed around her son's silent bedroom.

What she needed to rectify this travesty of justice was money. And lots of it. And the only people she knew who had an excess of cash were Harlow and Alphonso. Harlow wasn't speaking to her, and so it looked like Alphonso was her man.

She'd do whatever he wanted. She was willing to fulfill whatever depraved and despicable sex act his perverted heart desired, as long as he paid the price.

She turned off the light in Yuri's bedroom. As if preserving the room until his return, she closed the door.

In the living room, she squeezed her eyes tightly shut, trying to keep from crying. A sudden sharp pain in her stomach bent her over, and she sank heavily into a puffy armchair. With her face buried in her hands, tears dampening her fingers and her hands, Vangie cried heart-wrenching, guttural sobs. She cried so loud and hard, her throat felt raw and burned. She cried and cried until she couldn't shed any more tears.

VANGIE

Basic chicks like Jojina made Vangie's blood boil. Vangie had to work to pay her bills while women like Jojina expected the government to hand them everything on a silver platter.

Less than an hour's worth of online research revealed that Jojina's lovely home in the upscale neighborhood of Thornbury, Pennsylvania was provided by Section Eight. And Shawn's name wasn't on the lease. There had to be some kind of law that prohibited the kind of scam that Jojina was running. Section Eight housing was for women and their children—not for an able-bodied man who would have been able to get credit and buy a decent home if he wasn't trying to beat the system by working under the table.

Shawn and Jojina were two of a kind—both were scam artists and they deserved each other. But in the meantime, Vangie had to get her son out of their clutches. Paying attorneys could put her into a lot of debt—force her into bankruptcy and worse. She imagined being kicked out of her apartment and having to live with her mother and Mr. Harold. The thought of moving in with Barbara Boyd and being bossed around like a little kid, motivated her to place the call she'd been dreading.

"Hey, Alphonso."

"What's up, Vangie?"

"Well, I was wondering when I'm gonna see you again," she

said in her best version of a sultry voice, though she wasn't feeling sexy at all.

There was a short contemplative pause. "I could probably make the trip tomorrow night if you make it worth my while."

"I'll make it worth your while," she replied in the breathy voice of a phone-sex operator.

"Nah, I don't think you want to see me."

You're right; I don't. "Why would you say that?" Anxiety over money caused her voice to climb an octave.

"I can tell by the way you're talking to me—all nice and soft. You know how I like it."

"Get your ass to Philly tomorrow night, you piece of shit!" she growled.

"All right, ma. That's what I'm talking about?"

"Don't call me, ma!" she said sharply.

"Oh, yeah," he said, chuckling. "What's that name you go by?"

"Venus."

"Right, Venus. I hope you don't try to charge me an arm and a leg this time."

"You can afford it, you cheap fuck. You better bring me my damn money."

"Five stacks?"

"Exactly."

"For that kind of money, I expect you to go hard. Put in some work and handle some equipment."

"What kind of equipment?"

"I got that covered. What size are you—a twelve, right?"

"Right and don't forget it," she barked, assuming the severe personality of her alter ego, Venus. For all her feigned outward bravado, she was nervous on the inside, wondering what Alphonso expected of her. She could deal with getting into character and wearing a leather dominatrix dress, if that's what he had in mind. She could also handle cursing him out and calling him degrading names. But that's where she drew the line. Vangie doubted if she was capable of causing him physical harm. Sure, she'd beat the crap out of Jojina, but fighting someone in self-defense was one thing, while cruelly whipping someone's ass with a flogging device was an entirely different matter. She wasn't a sadist and hoped Alphonso didn't show up toting an assortment of whips and chains and other instruments of torture.

❤ ❤ ❤

"Put your hands up!"

Wearing a three-piece suit and burnished gold tie, the suspect gave the cop a disdainful look and kept moving.

"Show me your hands, asshole!" The cop grabbed the suspect. "Up against the wall and spread 'em."

"I didn't do anything," the suspect said, looking over his shoulder as the cop patted him down. The cop yanked the suspect's wallet out of his back pocket and rifled through it. Finding nothing of importance, the cop's hand roved up higher and retrieved a thick envelope from inside the suspect's jacket.

The cop gave a grunt of satisfaction.

"Hey, you can't take my shit; this is harassment!"

The cop tore open the envelope and broke into a broad grin. "Your shit is mine, now. Get on the ground! Face down. Now!" With a knee planted in the suspect's back, the cop cuffed him. "Alphonso Givens, you're under arrest!"

"For what?" Alphonso asked, scowling and cursing under his breath.

"For being a pussy!" Vangie grabbed Alphonso by the back of

the collar and jerked him to his feet and shoved him into a chair. Dressed in a police uniform, replete with a shiny badge, she paced in front of him. "Start talking or you're going to spend the night in lockup."

Alphonso was playing his part as a criminal suspect, and at his request, she was assuming the role of a police officer and wearing the uniform that he provided. She didn't require a script to know her dialogue; her recent run-in with the law had prepared her for the part.

She whistled at the thick stack of hundred-dollar bills inside the envelope. "Where'd you get all this money…dealing drugs?"

Alphonso smirked. "Do I look like a drug dealer?" he asked snidely.

Unable to resist the urge of doing him bodily harm, Vangie smacked Alphonso with the wad of bills. "Watch your mouth and wipe that disrespectful look off your face." She narrowed her eyes at Alphonso as she stuffed the money—her payment for participating in Alphonso's fantasy—inside her pocket.

"I'll hold on to this cash—you know—for evidence." Sneering, she patted the bulge in her pocket.

He wanted corporal punishment and she hadn't believed herself capable, but thinking about the brutal way he used to fuck her, using his dick like a hammer and treating her pussy like it was something offensive that required punishment, infuriated her. The way she'd tiptoed around the subject of marriage, hoping her patience would endear her to him had been a waste of time. He didn't think she was worthy of marriage. She was nothing more than his personal cum hole and he kept her pacified with shoes and handbags.

Vangie glowered at Alphonso.

"Can't you let me off with just a warning, officer," he said with his head lowered in contrition. He was behaving as if he were really inside a police precinct instead of his posh hotel suite. Alphonso was beyond kinky; he was one sick puppy, she realized. The twisted bastard wanted her to get rough with him while he was restrained. Smiling cruelly, she wrapped a hand around the handle of the riding crop he had provided and began to flog her prisoner.

Alphonso cowered and flinched with each blow from the cane. All the while the fingers of his cuffed hands worked frantically, rubbing and squeezing his growing erection.

Vangie thrashed his hands with the riding crop. "Did I say you could touch yourself, slime ball?" Tormenting Alphonso wasn't as difficult as she'd imagined. Thinking of the way he'd used her pussy as if she was nothing more than a blow-up doll, caused her to see red and made it easy to dispense punishment. Her combined anger toward both Alphonso and Shawn was strong enough for her to flog Alphonso with wild abandon.

Astonishingly, the harder she hit him, the more he seemed to enjoy it.

"Please, Venus. Take the cuffs off. Let me jerk my dick for a few minutes," he begged wearing a pitiful expression and speaking in a whiny voice she'd never heard him use before.

"Fuck you!" Vangie bellowed. "I'll let you touch your disgusting dick when I feel like it, you premature-ejaculating, no-fucking bitch."

She expected Alphonso to flinch in shame, but instead, his breathing quickened and he groaned as he began grinding and humping while handcuffed and sitting in a chair. For a moment, Vangie was stunned by the sight of Alphonso humping the air like a dog in heat. Then she became incensed. "Ugh! Look at you, you nasty dog. You're so disgusting and fake. You drive around in expensive cars and wear designer suits and try to act like you're the man. But you ain't shit! You hide behind all those luxuries, and when they're stripped away, any fool can see that you're nothing but filth. And I despise you," she exploded, flogging him until he toppled to the floor.

A red streak appeared on the shoulder of his white shirt and Vangie paused before thrashing him again. Through narrowed eyes, she examined the red streak and realized it was blood. Appalled, she gasped and covered her mouth and took a step backward. She hadn't intended on drawing blood. She'd gone too far. It was time to end this game.

She retrieved the key to the handcuffs and bent over Alphonso as she hurriedly stuck the key into the lock.

"What are you doing?" Alphonso asked.

"You're bleeding; I'm taking the cuffs off so you can take care of that wound."

"No. Don't take 'em off."

"What?"

"Whip me again."

"You're bleeding, dammit; I can't hit you anymore."

"Then kick me. Kick me and call me names. You know I get off on that freaky shit."

Alphonso was crazier than she'd imagined, and Vangie wanted desperately for their freak session to be over. But she needed him to be satisfied. She couldn't afford to give him any of his money back. "Look, I'm gonna take the cuffs off so you can…" Realizing that she was speaking in a soft, caring tone, her voice trailed off and she cleared her throat.

"I'm running this show, vermin," she hissed. "You don't tell me what to do." She yanked his bound hands upward and unlocked the cuffs. "Take out that short little dick of yours, so I can have a good laugh." What she actually wanted was for him to start masturbating. Once he shot a load, this pathetic session would be over and she could take her ass home, five thousand dollars richer.

Alphonso sat up and fumbled with his fly.

"Hurry up, piece of shit," Vangie barked and smacked the side of his head. He released his dick and commenced to jerking the squat, hardened flesh. "Yeah, jerk yourself off, bitch-ass. I hope you stored away in your memory bank all the times I let you run up in me, doggy-style, because you'll never get inside this pussy again…unless you're fucking me in your dreams, muthafucka!"

All of a sudden, Alphonso's dick went soft. As if the idea of fucking Vangie was a turnoff. Insulted, she felt like whipping his ass again, but controlled the urge.

"I'm thirsty, officer."

Are we back to this shit again? The cuffs were off, and Vangie had thought they were through pretending that she was a cop and that Alphonso was being detained in jail. She was weary of his cop fantasy, but she felt obligated to hold up her end of the bargain.

"You can die of thirst for all I care," she said and spat at him.

He moaned in sexual ecstasy and uttered, "Do it again."

Disgusted, she spat at him again and this time he opened his mouth while simultaneously fondling his hardening dick. Spitting in his face over and over was a disgusting way to try and get him off. Desperate to get out of the Ritz-Carlton and go home, Vangie kept spitting and Alphonso kept opening his mouth, attempting to quench his thirst.

When he finally exploded into his hands, Vangie gave a sigh of relief and muttered, "At last!"

NIVEA

Malcolm received his tandem skydiving instructor's license and invited Nivea to celebrate with him at Bleu Martini, a trendy bar/restaurant in the heart of Old City's bustling nightlife strip that was known for its incredible martinis. It had been quite a while since Nivea had partaken in the club scene and she was slightly off-kilter. Seeming to sense her discomfort, Malcolm requested seats in the VIP lounge, where they could see and enjoy the party atmosphere without actually participating.

"This is so good," she said with a little moan, referring to the scrumptious appetizers—a combo of American, Asian, and French cuisine. "Try this," Malcolm said, holding a piece of dim sum with a pair of chopsticks, and bringing the bite-size Cantonese dumpling close to Nivea's lips.

Overcome by a bout of sudden embarrassment, she hesitated before opening her mouth. Being hand-fed by a man was not something she was accustomed to. During her engagement with Eric, she'd been the dominant partner and was so very much in charge of things, Eric never perceived her as the kind of delicate damsel who needed to be cared for. Looking back on all her previous relationships, she'd always been too busy trying to get the guy to the altar, she'd forgotten how to simply have fun.

Realizing she had finally begun to enjoy life, she opened her mouth and allowed Malcolm to feed her. Discarding the chopsticks, he picked up something from the tray of French cuisine that was so beautiful, it looked like food art. Motioning for her to open her mouth, he fed her the next tasty morsel. She moaned from the scrumptious flavors that seemed to dance on her tongue, and a quick shiver rushed through her when he used a finger to brush a crumb from her top lip. That sudden skin-to-skin contact had taken her off-guard, and had the impact of a French kiss.

She wanted to fling off her clothes and straddle Malcolm right there at their table.

Forcing her mind off sex, she asked, "How many classes were required to become a skydiving instructor?"

He thought about it, drew a breath and then gazed at her, prepared to respond. But his damned eyes were so beautiful and sexy, she couldn't look at them for long without yearning to devour him, and so she focused on his hands.

"Years ago, I took an Accelerated Free Fall course that consisted of seven jumps while being hooked up with an instructor. After completing seven jumps, you get to jump by yourself. And believe me, nothing compares to that first solo jump," Malcolm said with a wistful expression.

"Wow," she exclaimed. Though her mind was far from jumping out of planes, she was imagining jumping his bones.

"I got my Class-A license after that. I was required to do twenty-five jumps to be eligible for that. Then there was Class B, C, and then D. You only need a Class C license to become an instructor, and that involves two hundred jumps among other requirements. To become a tandem instructor, which I am now…" In a self-congratulatory manner, he thumped his chest. "You're required to have a USPA D license. Getting that involves passing a written exam, completing five hundred jumps, night jump training—solo and group jumps—a lot of stuff," he said with a boyish grin.

"Sounds intense and expensive."

"It can be a costly habit. Especially when you own your own equipment, as I do."

"You own a plane?"

He laughed. "Everything except a plane, but that's on my bucket list along with getting a pilot's license, market my own signature health drink, and turning the fitness center into a national franchise."

Being a co-owner of a successful fitness center at twenty-eight years old was nothing to sneeze about, but Malcolm was such a goal-oriented and success-driven alpha male, he wouldn't be satisfied unless he'd ticked everything off his bucket list before he turned thirty.

"Well, let's toast to the man of the hour," Nivea said, holding up her martini glass. They clinked glasses and beamed at each other.

"If you really want to make me happy, you'll…" He trailed off and gave her a bashful smile.

Anything! You sexy daredevil. You juicy slab of delicious man-meat! In her mind, she was already coming out of her clothes, ready to accommodate any freakish craving that popped in his mind. Nivea had never been sexually inhibited, and with Malcolm, she was willing to explore anything and everything. There were no boundaries at all.

"What do you want?"

"Well, now that I'm a licensed instructor, I'd love it if you'd do a tandem jump with me."

Nivea gulped and frowned in disappointment. She was braced to hear an appeal for something extremely kinky and was caught off-guard by his request for something as life-threatening as jumping out of a freaking airplane. "Oh, Malcolm, I don't know about that."

"Think about it. Promise me you'll think about it."

"I'll think about it."

"But before you respond, I want you to come out and watch me in action."

"Sure," she said halfheartedly. The thought of free falling through the sky was terrifying and made her nauseous. She hated giving Malcolm false hope, but it would be a snowy day in hell before she would even consider skydiving. She'd had such a negative response to Malcolm when they'd first met; it was surprising that they got along so well. After the way they'd started off, fucking in the hot tub without knowing each other's names, it was surprising they weren't strictly fuck buddies. Amazingly, they were so much more than that. When they weren't out on a date or spending time at his apartment (she hadn't invited him to her place or introduced him to Mackenzie yet; it seemed too soon for that), they had lengthy phone conversations. She confided a lot about herself, excluding her nervous breakdown and the fact that she didn't know who her daughter's father was. She didn't see the point in divulging unpleasant details of her past. For now, she wanted to live in the moment and continue having fun with Malcolm.

They were in a wonderful space right now—two people enjoying each other's company and having a good time.

As hot as he was, Malcolm wasn't conceited in the least and he wasn't the player she'd imagined him to be. She'd had him all wrong. So far, he seemed to be a good guy—kind, considerate, funny, and fun-loving.

It was a shame she didn't have anyone to talk to about her new-found happiness. Whenever she reached out to Vangie, she was given the brush-off. She supposed Vangie held a grudge over Nivea's friendship with Harlow.

Meanwhile, Harlow had pulled a disappearing act and wasn't answering her phone at all. Nivea wanted to talk about Malcolm to someone so badly; she was on the verge of calling her mother, of all people.

Since reconnecting with Nivea, Denise Westcott had started phoning her regularly; checking on Mackenzie and asking Nivea to put the baby on the phone so she could listen to her gurgle and coo. Although Nivea and her mother were working on their fractured relationship, it was too soon to talk to Denise about the new man in her life. Knowing Denise, she'd find a way to put a damper on Nivea's happiness, find some major flaw in Malcolm, and Nivea wasn't ready to have her bubble burst quite yet.

She would be returning to her job soon and wondered if her lack of availability would have an effect on her relationship with Malcolm. *Relationship?* Realistically, she and Malcolm were only dating, and it probably was too soon to think of them in "couple" terms.

She wondered how Malcolm viewed their connection. No, she didn't want to go there. The only thing that mattered was that he made her happy. As far as Nivea was concerned, they could go on exactly as they were for the next twenty years and she wouldn't have any reason to complain.

They left Bleu Martini, and went back to Malcolm's place. In bed with her honey, making love, Nivea was engaging in her own version of skydiving as she skittered to the edge of ecstasy and then free fell over the abyss, screaming out Malcolm's name all the way down.

Thanks to Odette's flexible schedule, she was able to spend the night at Malcolm's, but by morning, she was anxious to get home to Mackenzie. *I miss my little Kenzie-Ken,* Nivea thought as she ran a red light. *I'd better slow down before I get pulled over.*

To ensure that she didn't exceed the speed limit, she forced herself to stop yearning for Mackenzie. Switching her thoughts to Malcolm relaxed her enough that she no longer felt compelled to shoot through red lights.

Home at last! She pulled into her designated slot and noticed a car pulling up beside her. Without bothering to look at the driver, she got out, armed her car and began to trot toward her townhouse.

"Nivea!" Someone got out of a dark-colored sedan, calling her name.

She slowed her stride and squinted at the man who'd emerged from the car.

It took a few moments for her to recognize Dr. Sandburg. She was accustomed to seeing him in his office—not outside her home. Furthermore, she'd only seen him wearing a lab jacket over his clothes, and today he was dressed in sports attire.

"We need to talk," he said. "I'm on my way to play golf and I won't take up much of your time."

Nivea looked him up and down sneeringly. He looked dumpy and unsightly in golfing shorts that revealed saggy kneecaps and veiny, pale legs. Dr. Sandburg had never been easy on the eyes, but today he looked worse than ever. Since her visit to his office, he'd started growing a beard that was gray and grizzled. Adding to his unsightly appearance, tufts of hair stuck out of the sides of his ball cap, and wiry, gray chest hair sprouted out at the top of his shirt. Ugh. She had to have been out of her mind when she fucked him.

Scrutinizing him further, Nivea noticed Dr. Sandburg's bad posture. He seemed a little stooped around the shoulders—like he had a bad back. His golf game probably sucked.

"What do you want to talk about?" she asked with a mixture of suspicion and impatience.

"I want to talk about my daughter."

Her eyebrows shot up. Hearing the old doctor referring to Mackenzie as his daughter was appalling, and Nivea visibly cringed. "Excuse me?"

"The DNA results came back..." He trailed off, waiting for his words to sink in.

"And?"

"It's been proven that I'm the father."

Nivea winced. The gray-haired oldster looked more like Mackenzie's great-grandfather than her father. "You're sterile, remember, so how could you possibly be my daughter's father?"

"Apparently, I'm not sterile. It appears I'm quite virile." His prideful smile made her want to punch him. "I brought the results." He hustled over to his car and retrieved an envelope from under the visor.

Nivea's hand shook slightly as she opened the envelope. The paternity test proved that Dr. Sandburg was Mackenzie's biological father. Nivea looked at him and cringed.

"So, what do you want?"

"I want to see my daughter. Make up for lost time and establish a relationship with her."

"That's not a good idea. Your wife made it clear she doesn't want word getting out about your adulterous behavior. She doesn't want Mackenzie in your lives, and that's fine with me." Nivea gave a shrug as if to say: *What can I tell you? It's out of our hands.*

He shook his head mournfully. "Rachel was upset about the results of the paternity test, and we've separated. She wants a divorce."

"Sorry to hear that." Nivea tensed up, sensing big trouble on the horizon. Her generous child support was funded with Rachel's money. It wasn't likely that Rachel would want to support a child after she divorced its father. Nivea gulped in fear, and then reminded herself that they had a binding contract. Whether she liked it or not, Rachel had to pay!

"I want visitation rights," the doctor blurted.

Her breath escaped in a long sigh. "Are you nuts? You can't suddenly pop into my child's life. She's not comfortable around strangers. No offense, but with that scraggly beard and all, you'll terrify her."

"It may take time, but she'll get used to me—I'm her dad," he said with a crooked smile, appearing to be pleasantly awed by the whole idea of fatherhood.

"Look, I've abided by your wife's wishes. I've signed a lot of paperwork, giving you guys the anonymity you requested. Now, you need to return the gesture, and leave my daughter and me alone."

"She's my daughter, too, and it's important that I participate in her life."

"Why the change of heart? When I brought her to your office, you didn't as much as glance at her."

"I was shocked, and I didn't believe she was mine. Now that I know the truth, I want to co-parent. I want to be the best dad that I can."

"I need time to absorb all this. I'll give you a call in a few days."

"Why can't I see her now? I won't stay long. Can't I have a quick peek?" Dr. Sandburg said in a rush of hopeful words.

"Absolutely not," she said in a harsher tone than she'd intended. Shaping her mouth into a smile that felt garish and fake, she tried to soften the blow. "You can't pop up on us like this." She waved her hand around, gesturing anxiously. "Your visit would have to be planned, you know, like, weeks in advance."

"Weeks?" Dr. Sandburg's cheeks puffed up, his eyes widened in incredulity. He pointed a finger at Nivea. "I have as much right as you do to spend time with our daughter. The next time you hear from me, it'll be through my attorney." He stalked over to his car, got in, and slammed the door with a resounding thud. As upset as he seemed, Nivea expected him to shoot out of the parking space in the heat of anger, but he slowly backed out, cautiously looking over his shoulder like a nervous elderly driver.

She wondered how old Dr. Sandburg was. He was definitely older than her parents—probably in his mid to late fifties. Maybe early sixties. Oh, God, she had to have been off her rocker, having unprotected sex with that doddering old man. It was unfair to Mackenzie that her biological father might be living in a retirement home, eating Jell-O and drooling before she reached her teens.

Inside her home, Nivea hurried to Mackenzie's bedroom.

Odette frowned and clicked her tongue. "I just put her to sleep. Why you wanna go and wake her up?" she asked in her thick accent.

Ignoring Odette, Nivea went to Mackenzie's room and lifted her from the crib. Hugging and kissing her, she held her daughter close. "Hey, Kenzie. Hey, girl!" Nivea gushed, trying to get her daughter to wake up and interact. Mackenzie's eyes fluttered open. She blinked at her mother, cracked a tiny smile, and then dozed off again.

Worrying about Dr. Sandburg's request to co-parent, Nivea clutched the sleeping child to her bosom, and paced the floor with her. He was trying to force himself into their lives, and Nivea wasn't happy about it. She hardly knew him. Sure, they'd had that sexual encounter in his office back when she was on the brink of mental collapse, but in all actuality, she hardly knew the man at all. She couldn't bring herself to think of him as Mackenzie's father, and she wanted him to stick to the deal they'd agreed upon and stay out of her daughter's life.

HARLOW

Drake had yet to explain where he'd taken the money. Whatever he did with it, couldn't possibly be legal. Only a person involved in unlawful activities would pack a briefcase with a large sum of cash and take off in the middle of the night.

He wasn't being forthright with her, and so Harlow didn't divulge her secret, either. She didn't enjoy being spiteful, but she had no desire to share such joyous news with someone whom she apparently didn't know very well. Did Drake actually want a baby, or had he been mouthing words he thought she wanted to hear? She pondered his possible reactions and could picture his face breaking into a forced smile, which was something she didn't want to see. Nor did she want to observe his brows knit together in displeasure. There was no way Drake would be genuinely happy about the pregnancy—not with their marriage in shambles.

Harlow had been sleeping in the guest bedroom for the past week. Trying to make a statement. Trying to make Drake realize if he wanted to save their marriage, he'd have to come clean. But he seemed so distant and preoccupied, it was as if he hadn't even noticed her absence.

Morning sunshine poured into the living room, filling it with an almost ethereal glow. Carrying a cup of tea, Harlow sat in her favorite chair, facing the park. She took a sip, set the cup down, and let out a sigh. The stunning view and the glorious sunshine were not cheering her up. Slumped over, she placed her head in her hands. This pregnancy was supposed to be the happiest time of her life, but she couldn't imagine being more forlorn than she was right now. Feeling this depressed and agitated couldn't be good for the baby.

Oh, Drake, what is going on?

She'd made excuses for Drake in the past, but now it was time to pull her head out of the sand and face the fact that her husband was a liar and some sort of criminal. A month ago, it would have been inconceivable that she could end up being a single parent, but today it seemed completely plausible.

She had to make a decision about her marriage—stay and pretend that everything was okay or face the facts that the marriage was over and that it was time to start packing her bags. But she felt stuck, marooned in the chair and unable to get up and get going.

Gazing at the beautiful view, she smiled wryly. She'd always thought if her marriage to Drake ended, life wouldn't be worth living. That she'd be suicidal. Or at the least, she'd have a nervous breakdown. But here she was, emotionally stable and possessing a strong desire to live. Not only for herself but also for her unborn child. Gathering strength from an unknown source, she pushed herself up from the chair and padded out of the living room.

Out of common courtesy, she left Drake a note:

Drake,

This isn't working. I don't know what you're into, but whatever it is, it couldn't be good. Or legal. I've decided it's best for us to separate. You should feel relieved that you no longer have to worry about me walking in on another mysterious money transfer. I'll be staying at a hotel for the time being and plan to contact a divorce attorney in a day or so.

Harlow

A great sense of calm washed over her the moment she left the apartment. Forty minutes later, she checked into a hotel, and stretched out on the bed. She thought about the responsibility of being a single parent, and though it wouldn't be easy, she'd put everything she had into being the perfect mother.

She spent most of the afternoon researching divorce attorneys online. It would have been helpful if she had an older and wiser friend who could advise her, but she didn't. She thought about calling Vangie and making up. Perhaps they could go over the list of attorneys together, but Harlow quickly changed her mind. Though Vangie had spoken the truth about Drake's dirty business dealings, it wasn't as if she'd verbalized her feelings with Harlow's best interest at heart. When she bad-mouthed Drake, she was being mean and spiteful.

And Nivea. Well, Niv would always be pretentious and self-serving. Harlow realized Nivea was only interested in getting closer to her in order to elevate her social status. Harlow's only other female friends were the wives of Drake's business associates, and she couldn't expect her husband's allies to assist her in a divorce battle.

The unexpected blare of the hotel phone caused her to jump in alarm. Collecting herself, she picked up, expecting to hear the courteous voice of the concierge on the other end of the phone.

But to her surprise, Drake was on the phone.

"I'm downstairs in the lobby. Would you come down? We need to talk and try to work things out."

"You've been ignoring me and refusing to answer my questions about that hidden money, so what else is there to talk about, Drake?"

He was quiet for a few beats and then said, "We need to talk about our baby."

Harlow's heart dropped and her voice came out shaky. "How did you find out?"

"There was a voicemail on the home phone. From a doctor's

office. Said you left the office without making a follow-up appointment for prenatal care."

Harlow felt so stupid. When she'd visited the first obstetrician when she was too ashamed to visit her own doctor, she'd given her contact information, never dreaming the day would come when she would feel the need to hide her pregnancy from her husband.

"When were you going to tell me?" Drake asked.

"I don't know. Eventually."

"Eventually? Like when my kid was three years old? You're not right, Harlow. First, I get hit with your goodbye letter; then I find out not only have I lost my wife, but she's trying to take my child away from me, too."

"Under the circumstances, I didn't have a choice."

"Can you come downstairs so we can talk, face to face? I promise, I'll explain everything."

Yeah, right. You'll explain with more lies. "I'll be down in a few."

Drake sent a sad smile Harlow's way when she stepped out of the elevator. He paced swiftly in her direction. "You look beautiful," he said.

"Thanks." It was odd that he was offering compliments now that she'd left him, but didn't even notice her while they were living under the same roof.

"I need a drink," he said, ushering Harlow to a lounge in the hotel.

When the waiter came to their table, Drake ordered cognac for himself and red wine for Harlow.

Harlow shook her head at the waiter. "No wine for me; I'll have water with a lemon wedge."

Drake smiled. "I forgot, you can't drink while you're pregnant. You're carrying my child; that's the best news I've had in a long time." He reached across the table and laid a hand on top of hers. "You've made me so happy, Harlow."

"I wish I could say the same, but I'd be lying. I mean, I'm thrilled that I'm going to be a mother, but our situation..." She paused and shook her head. "Our situation breaks my heart."

"I know, and it's my fault, baby. It's all my fault. There're things about me—about the business—that I've kept from you," Drake confessed.

Harlow held herself erect and fastened her eyes on his. "I'm listening."

"Something happened the day you saw me getting money out of the safe—"

"The safe that I didn't even know existed," she reminded. "Are there any other hidden objects in our apartment that I don't know about?"

"No, that's it."

She looked at him doubtfully.

He held up his hands. "Honestly, that's it."

"I can't believe you kept something like that from me."

"I thought it was best that you didn't know."

Harlow gaped at Drake, unsatisfied with his response.

"I was in a desperate situation the night you saw me emptying the safe. I received a package that day—it was delivered to the office."

"What kind of package?"

"A package that contained a severed finger...and a ring."

Harlow gasped. "Whose finger was it?"

"The finger was unrecognizable, but I knew the ring belonged to Lucio."

"Who's Lucio?"

"Someone who was like a father to me."

"Why am I just now hearing about him?"

"He's been in prison for a long time. He had so much time, he wasn't supposed to ever get out. But due to health issues and his advanced age, he was no longer considered a threat to society, and they released him."

"And…" Harlow stared at him.

"Lucio had a lot of enemies, and they got to him before I could get him safely out of the country. They beat him…tortured him until he gave up my name."

Harlow covered her mouth in horror. "Why would he give up your name? What kind of involvement do you have with this guy's enemies?"

"No direct involvement, but I was the only person who knew where his money was stashed."

"The money in the safe?" Harlow's eyes were large with fear.

Drake nodded. "I was holding Lucio's money for him."

"How much money and where'd it come from?"

"Several million. Lucio was into mob activities, and I was only a kid when he left that money with me."

"How many years have you been keeping it for him?"

"About fifteen years. No one ever suspected that a mob guy would leave millions of dollars with a kid from the hood."

"Is that how you got your business started—with dirty money?"

"All money's dirty, one way or another. I used a portion of it to get started, but my business is totally legit."

"Oh, Drake," Harlow uttered. "I don't like how any of this sounds. You're affiliated with a gangster who has people after him."

"Nobody's after him, now. I paid the ransom they were demanding, and Lucio's going to be all right."

"Are we seriously having this conversation? How dumb do you think I am? This crap you're telling me doesn't sound remotely believable. Sounds like something out of a bad movie."

"I don't have any reason to lie; it's true."

"Why didn't you tell me about this old man, Lucio? When I

told you about my mother…about my painful past, we made a promise not to keep any more secrets."

"I didn't keep secrets about myself. My life is an open book. It wasn't my place to share Lucio's past with you."

"But you never even mentioned him."

"I couldn't. After all that man did for me, I couldn't betray his confidence. Not to you…not to anyone."

"Have you been keeping in touch with him all these years?"

"Of course."

"How? Letters? Phone calls?"

"Yes, and I visited him several times a year. Kept money on his books."

"Visited him…where?"

"At the Federal Penitentiary in Florence, Arizona."

"How'd you accomplish that without my knowing?" Harlow smiled sardonically. "I get it. You visited him while pretending to be on one of your business trips." She shook her head. "I've been so stupid and naïve when it comes to you. What else do you do under the guise of business?" She glared at Drake. "So many lies; it's like you've been leading a double life."

"Not lies, Harlow. I simply didn't tell you everything about my past."

"You had an ongoing secret life—during our marriage—that you kept from me."

"I had no choice. I couldn't tell you about my relationship with Lucio. You wouldn't have understood."

"You're right, and I still don't understand."

"We'll get through this, Harlow. I love you, baby. Just come home with me where you belong. I can't allow my pregnant wife to live out of a hotel. That's crazy."

"No. You shut me out. If I hadn't left, there's no telling how long we would have been living in that big apartment like strangers. I'm concerned about the baby's health, and I can't be in an environment where I'm unhappy and uncertain. I can't deal with your lies and your secret lifestyle, Drake."

"No more secrets. You know all there is to know, now. I realize that it was unfair of me to shut you out, but I had so much on my mind. Those goons worked Lucio over pretty badly. Not only did they cut off his finger; they broke ribs. Broke the old man's jaw. He was messed up with internal bleeding…bruised kidney; I didn't think he was going to make it."

"Where is he now?"

"Still in the hospital. But as soon as he's able to travel; I'm putting him on a private jet to Naples to live with his sister."

"This story is so outlandish."

"It's the honest to God truth and I can prove it. I'll take you to the hospital to meet Lucio, tomorrow. And after that, will you please come back home?"

"I don't know."

Drake winced. "What do you mean, you don't know?"

"Are you a gangster, Drake?"

"No. Every dollar I have has been earned through hard work." Wearing a serious expression, he looked her in the eyes. "Come home, Harlow. Please."

"I can't; I don't trust you."

VANGIE

Depression consumed her for days after role playing with Alphonso. *Role playing?* The term sounded harmless and trendy, but who was she kidding? She hadn't been merely role playing. Beating Alphonso's ass with a riding crop and verbally abusing him was straight-up sadistic. She was a bitter woman—furious with the world because of her inability to snag a husband and her lack of financial success. And now that she'd lost custody of Yuri, she could add bad mother to her list of failures.

Sadistic behavior was an outlet for her rage, filling her with a temporary sense of power. But when it was over, and she was alone with her thoughts, she plunged into despair and an even greater sense of self-loathing. The money should have helped, but it didn't. With every dollar being turned over to lawyers, it wasn't as if she'd actually acquired any financial gain.

The apartment was so quiet and lonely without Yuri. She missed her son tremendously and couldn't wait for him to come home. But until then, she had to find a way to fill her time and take her mind off of her problems. A visit with Harlow would be the perfect medicine to cure her woes, but that wasn't possible.

Feeling as if she would start bouncing off the walls if she didn't do something with herself, Vangie thought about calling the masseuse in New York. Not for any lesbian activities, but simply for a relaxing massage. She couldn't remember the woman's name, but she could remember the strokes of her tongue. She searched through her junk drawer and found the woman's card. The name, "Frieda Reinhardt," was at the bottom.

Frieda. Yes, that was her name. Frieda with the magical tongue.

After wielding a riding crop, degrading and humiliating the man she formerly considered marriage material, she could use more than a massage. She was so wound up, she yearned to be touched, fondled, and slowly lured into sexual delirium by Frieda's skilled fingers and tongue.

And Vangie didn't mind paying. She smiled at the irony. Alphonso got off from being whipped and debased and was willing to pay for his fetish. And like Alphonso, Vangie didn't mind paying for her own sexual release. But she was only willing to pay a fraction of what she charged Alphonso.

Anticipating another taboo, erotic adventure, she picked up the phone to call Frieda. It would be nice if the masseuse was willing to travel to Philly, but if she didn't, Vangie would make the trip to New York.

Frieda's phone rang and rang, and then went to voicemail.

"Uh, I was wondering…" Uncomfortable leaving a message, Vangie hung up, midsentence.

Antsy, she didn't want to be alone. There were a few guys that she'd gone out with in the past that she could invite over for a drink, but she didn't want to deal with men right now. She was harboring so much anger and animosity toward the opposite sex, she was likely to turn into "Venus" if a dude said something that pissed her off.

She knew exactly where to search for someone similar to Frieda. Philadelphia's "Gayborhood," located from Chestnut Street to Pine Street, between Eleventh and Broad Streets, was known to have a large concentration of gay and lesbian-friendly businesses, restaurants, and bars. Hoping to snag a gay girl for a pleasurable, one-night encounter, Vangie put on a tight black dress with a plunging neckline and drove downtown.

She'd never been inside a gay bar in her life, yet she wasn't nervous at all. She selected a small bar on Chancellor Street called The Merry-Go-Round, and after driving in circles for ten minutes, she finally landed a parking spot.

All eyes were on Vangie when she strutted inside and boldly took a seat at the bar. While most of the patrons were dressed for comfort in casual attire, Vangie stood out in a slinky, short dress and five-inch stilettos.

With her legs crossed, her dress hitched up even higher than it already was, spectators were given a generous view of her thighs.

"Tonight's margarita night," a petite female bartender with a blue Mohawk said and pointed to a chalkboard that listed a long list of specialty margaritas.

Vangie scanned the varieties and asked, "What's in the Cadillac Margarita?"

"Tequila, orange liqueur, and lime juice. It's good," she assured as she took in an eyeful of Vangie's cleavage.

"I'll take your word for it," Vangie said, checking out the bartender as well as other women who were in her line of vision. The bartender looked all right, but she was a little too short and thin for Vangie's newly acquired taste in women. She preferred someone taller and bigger, someone more masculine-looking. Someone like Frieda.

As she sipped her drink, she could feel pairs of eyes assessing her—feasting on her. She was "new meat" in the bar and everyone seemed interested in her. She turned to her left and right, scanning the crowd, openly appraising possible sex partners. The women were of all shapes and sizes and ethnicities, but she didn't spot anyone who attracted her.

The bartender began placing one margarita glass after another in front of Vangie. She pointed to the parties who had sent them. "I'll pour whenever you're ready."

Vangie swiveled around and nodded at the generous ladies. She turned back to the bartender and said, "That's it—no more. If I accept any more drinks, I'll be stumbling out of here."

"Turning down free drinks is not proper bar etiquette," the bartender said teasingly. "You don't have to drink them all, but don't deprive the ladies of the joy of spending money on you."

Vangie laughed. "Okay. I guess I could learn a thing or two about proper bar behavior."

"I'm a good teacher." She winked, somehow aware that Vangie was a newbie on the gay scene.

Vangie bobbed her head and rocked in her seat in time with the pulsing techno music. So far, she was having a good time and was thoroughly enjoying all the attention she was getting. In a heterosexual environment, she wouldn't have stood out in the crowd, but here in this setting, she felt über beautiful and sexy.

The Cadillac Margarita tasted so good, she inhaled her first drink and immediately beckoned the bartender to fill one of the empty glasses. Drinking much slower, she smiled to herself. This was exactly what she needed. Good drinks and a lively atmosphere that was heavily charged with sexual tension.

After two drinks, she had to use the restroom. Her head swiveled as she checked out the clientele, looking for someone with a desirable masculine appearance.

As she threaded her way through the crowd, a group of rowdy beer-guzzling women ogled her, and one of them made guttural sounds, announcing her appreciation for Vangie's curves in a very uncouth way.

All of them were masculine in their appearance and demeanor,

Vangie noticed, as they closed ranks around her, blocking her path toward the restroom, but none had that special something she was looking for. Actually, they were a little too rough and rugged and sort of disgusting.

One of the rowdy bunch said, "How's it going, sweetheart? You're looking hella delicious—like hot buttered toffee."

The cheesy line made her friends laugh, their behavior reminding Vangie of obnoxious schoolboys.

Vangie regarded the woman who'd made the off-color remark, curious to find out if she was a potential bedmate. She wasn't. She was sloppy-looking with unsightly tattoos up and down her arms and a big, beer belly that swelled beneath an oversized T-shirt. A current of perspiration trickled down the sides of her face, pooling in the creases of her thick neck. Damp circles stained the under-arms of her shirt, giving her the slovenly look of a truck driver who had been on the road all day and all night.

Wrinkling her nose, Vangie imagined the sweaty chick smelled bad, too. Without bothering to respond to the crude comment, Vangie pushed through the unattractive group of women and continued to the restroom.

Inside the ladies room, Vangie came to the realization that she was wasting her time here. None of these girls were her type; per-haps she'd have better luck at a different place. She groped inside her bag and pulled out her phone. Online, she pulled up the list of lesbian bars in the area, and after perusing the reviews, she decided to check out a place called Fillies that was only a few blocks away.

She exited the restroom feeling pleased that Fillies was in walking distance. Finding parking spaces in this area of the city was next to impossible, and she was grateful she didn't have to move her car. Trekking two blocks in stilettos wouldn't be easy, and she considered the idea of carrying her shoes and going barefoot until she reached the club. But she quickly nixed that idea. Sticking grime-covered feet inside her expensive Gucci heels was absurd and out of the question.

The crowd had grown while she was in the ladies room, and it was taking a painfully long time to squeeze past the pockets of people who clogged the path to the door.

She hoped the bartender was too busy to notice her sneaking out. It was rude to vacate the premises without leaving a tip. Vangie wasn't deliberately being cheap, but the lewd truck-driver chick was perched on the stool next to hers, prepared to bombard her with crude comments and corny jokes. Vangie had no choice but to try and make a clean getaway.

She'd almost made it to the front door when it suddenly opened and an oddly gorgeous woman strolled in. Androgynous in appearance, she possessed the combined characteristics of a beautiful woman and a handsome man. Tall and athletically lean, she was the color of dark copper with a tinge of red. High cheekbones, dark, slanted eyes, a prominent nose, and plump, sensual lips gave the impression that mixtures of African, Asian, and Mediterranean cultures had contributed to the features of her face. Her natural hairstyle was shaved and dark on one side with a shock of chin-length, maroon-tinted, wayward coils on the other.

Vangie was mesmerized. She couldn't take her eyes off the woman who was wearing shimmery black tights that clung like a second layer of skin. Everything about the woman was a contradiction. She was both wild and regal. Feminine and masculine. And she moved with the grace of a goddess while seeming to possess the physical prowess of a gladiator.

Damn, she's hot. That's the kind of girl I want to get with. Desire clenched at Vangie's core in a way she'd never experienced before. Abruptly changing her mind about going to the other bar, she turned around and headed for the barstool and the drinks she'd been eager to abandon.

Luckily, the sweaty chick had moved on and was talking with an attractive older woman, staring into her eyes and caressing her hair.

"I was getting ready to clear this area; I thought you'd gone," the bartender said and nodded toward the line of margarita glasses.

"I was in the restroom."

"What'd you do…fall in?" She guffawed as if she'd said something hilariously original.

It was a tired-ass expression, causing Vangie to groan inside. But just in case the goddess was watching, she wanted to appear as if she was having a wonderful time. She threw her head back and released a burst of side-splitting laughter, as if the corny joke was as funny as a Kevin Hart routine.

Vangie glanced over her shoulder. Everyone in the bar seemed to know the hot-looking, androgynous chick. People were either waving at her from the other side of the room or rushing toward her to say hello. At least five-ten, maybe taller, she towered over the women she conversed with.

"That's Zenith," the bartender informed.

Zenith sounded like the name of a sex goddess or a superhero, and it suited her perfectly. Longingly, Vangie glanced in her direction.

"You don't wanna get involved with her."

"Why not?"

The bartender spoke in a confidential tone. "She's bad news. Every time she comes here, she leaves with a different girl. It's all a game to her, and she doesn't care who she hurts. You seem like a nice girl, and I thought I'd warn you."

"Hmm." Vangie couldn't think of anything to say.

The bartender leaned in close, her words emerging in an ominous whisper. "Her last girlfriend ended up slashing her wrists."

"She killed herself?" Vangie's voice was high and screechy.

"She tried to. Her name was Molly. A pretty girl with a promising career in advertising. Now she looks like shit and can't hold down a job. She got hooked on some kind of pills after the suicide attempt, and word has it she lives on the streets when she's not alternating between mental hospitals and rehab."

"That's a shame," Vangie muttered.

"Zenith ruined that girl's life."

It was a sad story, but not sad enough to dissuade Vangie from stealing glances at the sexy amazon.

"You need to watch out for her. I'm serious. She brings drama whenever she goes. I guarantee before the night is over, she'll have some poor girl crying in her beer while a few others will start tussling and trying to claw each other's eyes out over her."

"Wow."

"You're new blood, and I'm sure she'll be trying to get at you at some point tonight, so be careful," the bartender cautioned and then moved along, going about her tasks behind the bar.

The message had been delivered as a dire warning, but the possibility of getting to know Zenith better was more than appealing. It wasn't as if Vangie was looking to get engaged or married to the chick. A one-night stand with that hot-ass stallion of a woman was exactly what she needed to take her mind off her numerous personal problems.

Deciding to take the initiative and introduce herself to Zenith, Vangie took a big sip of her drink, giving herself a bit of liquid courage.

She scanned the crowd and spotted Zenith sauntering toward the deejay's booth. She had crazy swag, moving like a sleek, well-muscled panther that was creeping up on prey. Vangie couldn't help feeling letdown and envious of the female deejay whom Zenith had apparently singled out as her sex partner for the night. She couldn't get a clear view of the deejay, but the chick must have been really hot to snag Zenith.

While Zenith was cozied up with the deejay, Vangie had to practically fight off the several women who seemed desperate to get her in bed. Some made suggestive comments and others got their point across with lewd gestures.

Disappointed with the way the night had turned out, Vangie tried to drown her sorrows in Cadillac Margaritas. She guzzled down each and every drink that had been bought for her, and when she finished the last one, she still wanted more. She lifted her hand to beckon the bartender, but thinking better of the idea, she abruptly lowered it. She'd had more than enough to drink, and with all the trouble in her life, the last thing she needed was a DUI.

She had a meeting scheduled with her attorney first thing in the morning, and it would be wise to take her butt home and get a decent night's sleep.

She placed a twenty under her margarita glass, tipping more generously than usual since she hadn't spent a dollar of her money on drinks. With lots of thoughts running through her head, she was only vaguely aware that the playlist had changed from thumping party music to a slower and softer song.

No sooner had she recognized "How Many Drinks?" by Miguel when a low voice murmured in her ear, "I requested that song for you."

Vangie jerked her head to the left, her face scrunched in agitation. She was prepared to tell one of the horny broads to fuck off. She wanted one person and one person only, and the rest of the bitches could kiss her ass. She shot a disdainful glare upward, but her tense facial muscles instantly relaxed when she found herself staring into Zenith's beautiful, ebony eyes.

HARLOW

The wizened elderly man in the hospital bed looked to be around ninety years old. What kind of monsters could have beaten such a frail, old man within an inch of his life? The old man must have had a lot of grit to withstand the level of torture he'd endured. Harlow winced when her eyes fell upon the bandaged hand that was missing several fingers.

"I thought you said they cut off *one* finger?" she whispered to Drake.

"They only sent one."

"Oh, my God."

The old man's eyes blinked open. He moved his lips, trying to talk.

"You can't talk, Lucio, your jaw is wired shut," Drake said.

The old man's rheumy eyes shifted to Harlow and his lips twitched—his version of a smile.

"That's Harlow, my wife. And don't forget you still owe us a wedding present," Drake said with forced laughter in his voice.

"Hi, Lucio. Sorry to meet you under these circumstances. But I hear you're doing better, and you'll be out of here soon," Harlow said in a honeyed voice that she hoped was convincing. She felt like a liar. This man was so banged up, he didn't look like he'd live to see another week.

Lucio coughed and Drake immediately picked up a container of water with a straw and carefully inserted the straw between his lips. Lucio sipped and coughed, but never took his eyes off Harlow.

Uncomfortable under his gaze, she moved her chair a little closer to Drake's.

"Before you know it, you're going to be sipping vino all day in Naples. That's the life you worked hard for, right, man?" Drake patted Lucio's arm. "I have a little secret to share with you."

Lucio looked at him attentively.

"We're having a baby. If it's a boy, we're going to name him after you."

Naming their child after the old mobster was news to Harlow, but she managed a concurring smile.

"And don't worry, man. I'm not going to rest until I find those punks who did this to you. They're going to pay—an eye for an eye, Pops," Drake said with conviction.

Lucio worked himself into an upright position and banged his good fist down so hard on the bedside table; he toppled a pitcher of water and overturned a vase filled with flowers.

Somehow Drake and Lucio communicated. Lucio would grunt in different tones and Drake would respond.

Lucio let out a rumbling growl and Drake said, "Don't worry about how it's going to get done. All you have to do is relax on the vineyard I put in your sister's name years ago. I want you to spend your remaining years enjoying wine and women at home in Italy. When you start receiving body parts in the mail, you'll know I've taken care of those goons that hurt you."

Grunting and jabbing the air like a prize-fighter, Lucio's face was twisted in fury as he fought an invisible opponent.

"I know you want to take care of them yourself, but you're not in top shape. You're going to have to trust me to handle it for you, Pops. I got it, man. Okay?"

Suspicious, Harlow stared at Drake. "What are you talking about, Drake?" He gestured for her to be quiet, and she dropped the subject, for the moment.

A big guy dressed in scrubs and carrying a clipboard entered the room. "Lucio Pegliasco?"

"Yes," Drake answered for Lucio.

"He's scheduled to get some tests done. I have to transport him down to the radiology department. You can wait for him, but it's going to be a while."

"No, I have to get back to work. I'll see you bright and early tomorrow, Pops," Drake said, patting Lucio on the shoulder.

Harlow waited until they were in the parking garage to voice her concerns. "Your pal, Lucio, seems to be itching to retaliate. As badly as he's injured, I would expect him to want to live in peace at this point."

"Retaliation is all he knows. Lucio is the last of a dying breed. Most of his old cronies are either in old folks' homes or they're six feet under."

"Apparently, not all of them are elderly and incapacitated. Obviously, one of them is alive and vibrant—someone from his past is still holding on to a grudge."

"Nah, it wasn't anyone from his past. Whoever got to Lucio is new blood," Drake said knowingly.

"Who do you think did this to him?"

"I'm not sure, but it's probably someone he did time with. Lucio may have bragged to a cellmate that he had a big nest egg waiting for him when he got out. Who knows? But I'm certain this wasn't a mob hit."

"How can you be so sure?"

"Because Lucio took the fall for his mob family, and they gave him an extravagant payday for his trouble. If nothing else, those guys have honor."

Harlow stared at Drake for a moment. "One minute you're my loving husband and the next minute, you're a stranger who knows all about mob laws and prison conduct."

"I only know what Lucio has been telling me over the years."

"I still have a feeling that you're not being completely honest with me."

Drake groaned in irritation. "You met Lucio; you saw with your own eyes that I didn't make up the story. I don't know what else you want from me, Harlow. Seriously, what more do I have to do to prove that I'm being truthful?"

"I don't know. You claim to be a legitimate businessman and a law-abiding citizen, but that's not how you sounded in Lucio's room when you were telling him the gruesome ways you were going to avenge him."

"That was only talk, babe. For a man like Lucio, hearing that I'm going to seek revenge is music to his ears. I was only trying to make him happy. You know, giving the old man a reason to pull through this. Trust, the minute he's well enough to travel, he's out of here. He can spend his remaining years bickering in Italian with his sister, Gina."

There was a long silence as they walked to the car. Harlow had an uneasy feeling that she couldn't shake.

He opened the car door for her. "If you're worrying about our safety, you don't have to. We're going to be all right, Harlow. Please believe that I'd never risk your safety. You have to believe that."

"You paid those thugs, and who's to say they won't come back for more?"

"They won't." Drake got in the driver's seat and gave Harlow a serious look. "I'd insist that you stay in a hotel—I'd send you out of the country before I'd allow you to be in harm's way."

"But…"

"No buts." He placed his hand against her face. "I'd never let anything happen to you. Don't you know I'd die for you?" He gazed down at her stomach. "Do you think I'd jeopardize the life of my child?" He stared at her. "Answer me, Harlow. Do you honestly believe that I'd tell you we're safe, if we weren't?"

"No."

"Do you believe me?"

She nodded.

"Are you ready to come back home?"

"I am, but you have to promise me something."

"Anything."

"Stop hiding things from me, Drake. I'm not some weak little woman who can't deal with the truth. And please don't ever shut me out like that again. Thinking you'd stopped loving me was unbearable. I thought I was going to have to raise our baby on my own."

"I'm sorry I put you through that. I let my anxiety over Lucio get the best of me, and I was wrong. But I got a reality check when I read your note. When I saw the word, 'divorce,' my legs almost gave out. I honestly saw my whole life flash before my eyes. Do you think for a minute that I'd put myself though something like that again?" He gazed at Harlow. "No more secrets; I promise." He squeezed her hand. "I swear on my life."

VANGIE

Exactly as the barmaid had predicted, there was drama. As Vangie and Zenith were leaving, a white girl who turned out to be the deejay, ran up behind them and grabbed Zenith by the arm. "Where are you going?" she asked anxiously. She looked like a college student, dressed in hideously scuffed, brown ankle boots that were decorated with looping chains and metal studs, shapeless shorts and a David Guetta T-shirt. Her unflattering pixie haircut did not complement her round face. Wearing her hair a little longer might have given her a more angular look.

"It's all good; I'll get with you some other time," Zenith said as she extracted her arm from the deejay's clutch.

"I thought we were gonna get together after I got off."

"Yeah, but something else came up, sweetness. Some other time, all right?"

"It's not all right!" Desperation gleamed in the girl's eyes and Vangie wouldn't have been surprised if she suddenly grabbed onto one of Zenith's long legs and clung to her.

Embarrassed for her, Vangie gave the girl her dignity by looking away.

"You're such a bitch; it's not all right to treat people like crap!" Her tearful glare traveled from Zenith to Vangie. Her lips curled in anger as her gaze settled on Vangie's face. "You're the cause of this," she yelled at Vangie, seeming to be on the verge of attacking her.

Vangie cautiously backed up.

Zenith smiled in amusement at the girl. "Come 'mere, baby," she said, holding out her arms, and the deejay slumped into them, crying. Zenith consoled her, stroking her hair and speaking to her in soft tones that only made her cry harder.

"Shh. You're causing a scene. Don't do this, okay?"

"But you're the one who's being all heartless and cruel. Why do you always treat me like shit?"

"Pull yourself together; I'll give you a call tomorrow."

Vangie shook her head in amazement. The bartender had called it; she'd warned Vangie that someone would be crying tonight. That fights would break out. Vangie was relieved that she wasn't the one being left behind, weeping and wailing and she was also grateful that the deejay hadn't tried to attack her over Zenith. A bar brawl was the last thing she needed. Zenith was hot and everything, but Vangie had an open case, and she wasn't willing to go back to jail over some pussy or anything else for that matter.

Vangie, shifted from one foot to the other, feeling guilty and conspicuous. But she didn't feel guilty enough to bow out gracefully. She took a few more steps backward, drifting into the background, and waiting patiently while Zenith comforted the brokenhearted deejay.

She consoled her with gentle words and soft kisses. Zenith covered the other woman's face and lips with so many tender kisses, Vangie began to squirm uncomfortably. It would be so embarrassing if Zenith suddenly changed her mind and told Vangie she'd prefer to go home with the deejay.

Zenith finally disengaged from her weepy lover. "It's you and me tomorrow night," she told her, while reaching for Vangie's hand and squeezing it reassuringly.

"You sure?" the girl asked, sniffling and wiping away tears that were mixed with black eyeliner.

Other than Vangie's S&M sessions with Alphonso and the fight with Jojina at court, this particular scenario had to be the third most fucked-up situation she'd ever been involved in. She felt ridiculous and completely humiliated. *What the hell am I doing standing around and waiting while she's kissing on that cry-baby bitch? Zenith is no better than a grimy dude and I need to tell her to kiss my ass and go to hell.*

But Vangie didn't say a word. She stood there with her arms folded, waiting around like a groupie.

Zenith convinced the deejay that she was making a big deal out of nothing, and gave her a pat on the ass and sent her back to her post.

And then, hand in hand, she and Vangie left the bar.

Vangie felt victorious, as if she'd been hailed as the lucky winner of an amazing grand prize.

Striding down the street with Zenith, she told herself that the events of tonight and also the tryst with Frieda would be secrets she'd take to the grave. Never, ever would she breathe a word to anyone about her secret lesbian escapades.

In the morning, Vangie arrived at the lawyer's office fifteen minutes early, feeling positive and optimistic. Considering that she hadn't had a wink of sleep last night, it was a miracle that she felt so energetic.

Thoughts of last night with Zenith put a smile on her lips and gave her a quick case of butterflies. Though she'd planned to only hit it and quit it, the way things ended up, she was sure she and Zenith would be seeing each other again. She'd left her female paramour stretched out, sound asleep and naked in her bed. Zenith hadn't stirred when Vangie got out of bed and gently kissed her on the cheek. She looked so damn luscious, it had taken all Vangie's willpower not to fling off her clothes and dive face-first between those long, strong legs.

Being sort of a virgin and all, when it came to actually participating during lovemaking with a woman, it was astounding how quickly things had progressed between her and Zenith. Last night when Zenith told Vangie to follow her to her apartment in Northern Liberties, Vangie obliged without question. In her memory of their night together, she couldn't recall the details of the drive. All she recalled was standing in Zenith's living room and being taken by the hand and led into the bedroom, which was decorated with enlarged black-and-white photographs of female genitalia and asses. Framed pussies and asses everywhere. And it was beautiful.

In mere seconds, they were undressed and all over each other.

That first kiss would be seared into her mind for eternity. So soft and sensual. As Zenith had walked her backward to the bed, and gently had urged her onto the mattress, Vangie's body had throbbed in anticipation. Zenith had straddled her, and Vangie had reached for her, running a hand through the wild tangles of her hair.

At the spa with Frieda, Vangie had lain still and enjoyed herself while the masseuse had pleasured her, but being with Zenith had brought out a different side of her. The desire to touch her was so overwhelming, she couldn't stop herself from sliding her hand over her bare skin, starting with her collarbone, roaming up and down her arms, and trailing down to her toned abs. Yearning to touch her in more intimate places, her shaky palms had jerked behind her and anxiously had squeezed the swollen mounds of her ass.

"I love the way you feel," Vangie had confessed.

"Oh, yeah?"

"Yeah," she'd responded, fondling her lover all over, touching and exploring her body almost obsessively. A woman's skin felt so different from a man's. And it was weird the way this kind of taboo intimacy aroused Vangie so much more than having sex with Shawn or any other man.

"God, I want you," she'd moaned, licking the part of Zenith that was closest to her mouth, which happened to be her forearm.

"It's your first time, huh?" she'd said knowingly.

"Sort of."

"Have you ever sucked a pussy?"

Vangie felt her face flush and she'd almost choked. "No, I haven't. The only time I was with a woman…well, she went down on me," she'd answered sheepishly.

"There's a big difference in giving and receiving, and you need to know something about me."

"What?"

"I like my bitches to be on point with their tongue game."

Vangie had flinched. She didn't have any tongue game that she knew of. And she'd never been referred to as a bitch while in the midst of making love. But being so completely smitten by Zenith, her judgment was a little flawed, and for some sick reason, she didn't mind being considered as simply another bitch in the hot amazon's bed. It wasn't like they were a couple or anything. They were only indulging their sexual cravings.

She'd glanced down at the neatly trimmed triangle between Zenith's thighs. "My tongue game may be a little off, but practice makes perfect, right?" Vangie had hoped she sounded bold and daring when she was actually terrified.

"I can teach you, if you're ready to learn." Zenith's velvety voice had given Vangie a rush of warmth in her deepest part.

"I'm willing." *What the hell am I saying? I don't want to eat pussy;*

that's not even who I am. The only pussy she'd ever tasted was her own, and she couldn't say that it had a delicious flavor because it didn't. She'd tasted her pussy on Shawn's tongue after he'd gone down on her, and she'd tasted it on his dick after they'd fucked, and she honestly had never enjoyed the taste. It was acrid. Sort of tangy, giving her tongue a slight sting. It definitely was not sweet like honey or nectar, the way some men declared while they were eating it.

Vangie was scared to go down on Zenith. She'd gag if the texture of pussy ooze was gooey or gritty. And suppose it turned out to be slimy like snot? That would be even worse, and she'd surely throw up. It occurred to her that maybe they should take it slow. Kiss and grind and rub their clits together until they both climaxed. She wasn't ready for cunnilingus. Licking a woman's pussy might be too extreme for a newbie like her.

Zenith had leaned over, pressing her small tits against Vangie's C-cups. "I'm gonna kiss you and I want you to pay close attention."

"Uh-huh," Vangie had said tentatively.

"I want you to tongue my pussy the same way I tongue your mouth."

"Right." *Oh, God, I can't go through with this. What have I gotten myself into?*

The way Zenith had pulled Vangie into her arms was rather confusing. There was the softness of her womanly flesh, yet she'd held Vangie with the strong embrace of a man. Her tongue had glided slowly between Vangie's lips, snaking and twirling in a way that had caused twinges and sharp sensations between her legs.

The kiss was crazy. Sending all sorts of currents and jolts zinging through her body. Ready to take the plunge, she was no longer afraid. She'd wanted to completely explore Zenith's magnificent body and savor the bitter sweetness of her forbidden fruit.

Moaning softly, Vangie had pulled away from her and wiggled downward until she was beneath her and caged between her firm thighs.

With pussy hovering over her face, she had taken the opportunity to look at it. It was pretty, much better-looking than Vangie's vagina. Maybe it looked so well kept, tight, and youthful because it was a pussy that had never given birth. Nor had it been plunged into and bulldozed by numerous, uncaring men.

Vangie had sniffed at the opening, bracing herself and wondering what she'd do if there was any hint of an unpleasant odor. To her relief and surprise, Zenith's pussy held a wonderful, aromatic scent. Sort of reminded her of the fragrance, patchouli—in a raw and natural state.

Vangie had kissed it softly. Like she was kissing Zenith on the mouth, she'd parted the lips ever so slightly, using only the tip of her tongue. Stretching her tongue a little more, she shyly entered the unknown territory. The taste! There were no words to describe it except liquid lust with a hint of peaches, some kind of spice, and a dash of lime. She'd pushed her tongue in deeper, twirling it the way Zenith had demonstrated.

But doing those tongue tricks were too theatrical, and Vangie had contented herself with licking and slurping, and moaning the whole time. Following Vangie's rhythm, Zenith had begun to hump against her lips. Vangie had clutched her hips tightly, pulling her closer, stretching her tongue as far as possible as she'd strived to lick the silken lining right out of that tangy-sweet pussy.

The low rumble in Zenith's throat and the frantic pelvic juts had told Vangie that her girl was about to explode. And she was ready, with her mouth parted hungrily. Apparently, Zenith was a squirter, the blast of jism that saturated Vangie's tongue had the power of a man's ejaculation and the sticky sweetness of a woman's cum.

Vangie had held Zenith in place, still lapping at her juices as her body bucked and quaked. She didn't stop licking and she didn't release the grip around her hips until she'd sucked out the last drop of silky sweetness.

Zenith had rolled off her. Still panting, she'd lain on her back. "That was insane. You're a beast, girl. You sure you never ate pussy before?"

"Positive," Vangie had replied with pride.

"Well, you could have fooled me; I came like a motherfucker."

Allowing Frieda to chow down on her pussy had been out of character for Vangie, but eating pussy was totally crazy for someone like Vangie who'd never was bi-curious and had been somewhat repulsed by the idea of two women bumping pussies. If anyone would have told her she would be eager to lick cunt, she would have called them a damn liar. She had gone to the lesbian bar with the intention of picking up a dyke and giving her the exquisite opportunity to lap on her pussy. But Zenith was so fine...so other-worldly sexy, she had to get her tongue all up in it and suck out that big, splashing nut.

Vangie had felt like she was under some kind of lust spell. She had felt totally uninhibited, ready and willing to try all kinds of new and freakish things.

While Zenith had lain stretched out, trying to catch her breath, with her head resting on her palms, her titties were poked out and looking particularly alluring with the dark nipples pointed to-ward the ceiling.

Vangie's gaze had settled on Zenith's perfect breasts, and before she'd fully decided she wanted to kiss and suck them, her hands had already started inching forward. She couldn't get enough of Zenith. She was feeling all hot and bothered and really needed to do something with her hands.

Apparently not wanting to be touched, Zenith had brushed her hands aside and Vangie had felt the sting of rejection. "What's wrong?" she asked, her feelings hurt.

"Chill for a minute, baby," Zenith had said. "As soon as my heart rate calms down, I'm gonna fuck the shit out of you."

And she did.

She had put on a moderately sized, strap-on dick, and had walked across the room and then sat in a chair. Vangie's mouth was wide open. The way Zenith had glided across the room with her tall, sculptured body was poetry in motion. The shocking contrast of a dick jutting out of that gorgeous feminine body…well, it had taken Vangie's breath away.

Zenith had taken a seat in a chair and beckoned Vangie. "Come get on this." She had pointed to the realistic-looking dick. "Daddy's gonna make you scream when you cum."

Daddy? Hearing a pretty bitch like Zenith referring to herself as *Daddy* was unexpectedly sexy as shit. Vangie was weak in the knees and had walked slightly gap-legged as she'd made her way across the room toward Daddy's dick.

NIVEA

On her first day back at work, Nivea wore a clingy Givenchy wrap dress, showing her coworkers that motherhood not only agreed with her, it had improved her. Hours spent at the gym had her body nice and fit, and with her fabulous and extensive new wardrobe, she would never be seen rotating clothes, bags, jewelry, or shoes.

She deliberately parked in a slot in the front of the building to ensure that everyone saw her new Cadillac SRX. Of course, she'd be getting a company car to use during the course of the work day—a Mazda or a Toyota—something economical. She had every intention of letting it be known that she considered it a huge embarrassment to be seen driving around in a hooptie, considering the fact that she was accustomed to the best of everything.

The first half of the day, Nivea spent so much time showing off pictures of Mackenzie, she hardly got any work done. Right before lunch, she received a call from the receptionist, telling her there was a delivery for her at the front desk.

The flower arrangement that was waiting for her was so elaborate, with exotic flowers she couldn't identify. It looked so expensive—like it could have cost a thousand dollars, easily. A small group of people gathered as she opened the card. "It's from my boyfriend," Nivea told the onlookers. *"Hoping these flowers brighten your first day back on the old grind,"* she read aloud and then put a hand to her chest, demonstrating how very touched she was.

Eric had never gone out of his way to do anything nice for Nivea. Malcolm was a gem, too good to be true, actually, and she couldn't help fearing that her love story would not have a happy ending.

While on the phone with Malcolm, thanking him for the exotic bouquet, her boss poked his head in her office. "There's a staff meeting in the conference room in five minutes."

"Hold on, Malcolm," she said. "I didn't get a memo about the meeting," she said.

"The secretary probably forgot to add your name to the list. Don't be late. I have an important announcement," he said in his usual gruff manner and then strode off toward the conference room.

"I have to go, Malcolm. These people are starting to irk me already," she complained.

"You'll be all right. You have to expect that it'll take a little while before you get back into the swing of things."

"I know, but I hated my boss coming in here and demanding my presence while I'm on the phone with my honey."

"Do you think you can squeeze me in after work or do you have to rush home and relieve your nanny?"

"I can always make time for you. Luckily, Odette is flexible."

"No, that's okay; I'm being selfish. Go home; your little girl is probably looking out the window, waiting for you."

"She's only a baby, Malcolm. She can't look out the window, yet," Nivea said, laughing.

"Oh, well, I've never met her and I don't have a mental picture of her."

"I showed you pictures."

"She could have grown since those pictures were taken. Look, as you can tell, I don't know much about babies."

"I didn't either. I learned as I went along, but thank goodness for my nanny. She's excellent with babies. Mackenzie loves Odette as much as she loves me."

"Speaking of Odette, you talk about her all the time and I feel like I know her, yet I haven't met her or little Mackenzie."

"I know. I was trying to keep my home life separate. You know, for the time being. I hope you don't mind."

"No, I understand. Can't blame you for not wanting to expose your kid to every guy who comes down the pike."

"It's not that..." Nivea fell silent. "It's her father. He, uh..."

"Seriously, you don't have to explain. I understand."

She wanted more than anything to introduce Malcolm to Mackenzie and Odette, but with Dr. Sandburg hovering around and threatening to exercise his parental rights, it didn't seem like a good idea to at the moment.

"Listen, I better get to the staff meeting. I'll give you a call when it's over."

Nivea and Malcolm made kissing sounds in the phone and then hung up. How had she snagged such a winner? Malcolm was more than she'd ever dreamed herself worthy of. She was cursed with the dark-skinned-woman complex. A complex that was probably caused by her mother's obvious favoritism toward her lighter-complexioned daughter, Courtney.

A high-achiever like Nivea should have never settled for a bum like Eric. And now that she had Malcolm, she intended to work on herself. She wondered if her compulsive spending had anything to do with her own "Mommy" issues. This was the kind of conversation she should have with Harlow. Harlow had a bad childhood, although she never talked about it. But she did mention that she was seeing a therapist regularly. Maybe Nivea needed to, also. She cherished the relationship that she and Malcolm were building and didn't want to mess things up with the baggage she was carrying.

First chance she got, she was going to give Harlow a call and get her opinion on therapy.

❤ ❤ ❤

The work day had taken a toll. Not accustomed to putting in eight-hour days, Nivea left the office, bone-tired. Her boss expected her to go back out in the field by the end of the week, and that was going to really wear her out. As much as she wanted to spend time with Malcolm, she had to ask him for a rain check. All she wanted to do this evening was go home, get out of her heels, and relax in a warm tub.

Odette and Mackenzie greeted her at the door. Mackenzie was dressed in a tangerine and white romper and Odette had gathered up Mackenzie's thin strands of hair and snapped an orange barrette onto them.

Nivea took her from Odette's arms. "Look at you, Lil' Mama. You're finally getting some hair on your head. It's about time, Kenzie-Ken," Nivea cooed. Mackenzie smiled and tugged on Nivea's earrings.

"If you don't need me, I'll be leaving in a few," Odette said. "I fixed oxtails, rice, and collards. Your plate is in the microwave."

"Thank you, Odette. That's so sweet of you, but you really didn't have to."

"No trouble at all. I love cooking. When Miss Mackenzie is old enough, I'm going to teach her how to cook with a Caribbean flair." Odette turned toward the closet to get the drab canvas bag she always carried.

"Oh, by the way, a letter came for you that required a signature. I signed for it; it's in the kitchen with the rest of your mail."

Registered mail was never good news. Brows bunched together, Nivea carried Mackenzie to the kitchen. The letter was from the law office of Andrew Brackman. Nivea's first impulse was to throw the letter in the trash.

"I'll see you in the morning," Odette called but Nivea didn't respond. She was caught up in the words written by Rachel Sandburg's lawyer.

Dear Ms. Westcott:

I'm writing to inform you that due to the pending divorce of Rachel and Bertram Sandburg, my client, Mrs. Sandburg, will no longer be responsible for any amounts of child support that she willingly agreed while married to Bertram Sandburg, the biological father of Mackenzie Westcott.

Please have your attorney contact Bertram Sandburg directly if you have any questions regarding this matter.

Sincerely,

Andrew Brackman, Esquire

Nivea wanted to scream. She wanted to do serious bodily harm to Rachel, her lawyer, and Dr. Sandburg. They couldn't get away with this. She had signed documents that assured her and her daughter of a cushy life for at least eighteen years. Nivea didn't know who Rachel thought she was dealing with, but she hadn't just fallen off the turnip truck, as Denise Westcott would say. Nivea would get a top-notch attorney of her own. Married to the doctor or not, Rachel would be forced to honor their agreement.

Later that evening, after she put Mackenzie to bed, Nivea was still so agitated over the attorney's letter, she went on a wild, on-line shopping spree that came to a whopping $12,000. And she didn't shop for only herself and Mackenzie, she bought Odette a new handbag and she bought Malcolm a $3,000 watch.

VANGIE

Her new family lawyer, Felder Ross, was a distinguished-looking black man who appeared to be in his mid-forties. He knew his stuff and seemed genuinely appalled that Shawn and Jojina were trying to steal her son.

"Temporary custody is exactly that…temporary. From what you've told me, there's no evidence that you've been an unfit mother. So, the first thing I'm going to do is file a motion for you to regain your parental rights."

Vangie nodded briskly.

"If things go our way, your son will be back home in a week, maybe sooner."

"Really? Oh, my God, really? Yuri's gonna be home in a week?"

"I don't see any reason why the judge would prevent him from being with his mother."

"I can't tell you how good it is to hear you say that. When I found out my son's father had the audacity to enroll my son in a school in his neighborhood—a school I've never even heard of—I went ballistic."

Mr. Ross looked appropriately appalled. "Well, he's going to have to disenroll him."

Vangie nodded in agreement. Mr. Ross wasn't playing any games, and she liked his style.

"I realize you've been through a lot, but you should try to relax during the next few days. I can assure you I'm going to get a new court date as soon as possible."

"Okay, but suppose Shawn wins. Suppose the judge thinks I'm an unfit parent because I assaulted his fiancée."

"That incident has nothing to do with your parenting skills."

"You're right." Vangie exhaled in a long stream, her shoulders relaxing.

"I usually don't like to make predictions, but I feel comfortable saying that I believe your child will be returned to you—the custodial parent. It's very rare for a judge to take a child from its mother!"

Vangie wanted to believe that everything was going to be all right, but that damned Jojina had so many tricks up her ghetto sleeves, Vangie wouldn't fully relax until Yuri was safe and sound back home.

"You're not doing yourself any favors by constantly worrying. I've got this," he said, smiling as he slipped into street vernacular. Vangie smiled, too.

"I'll file a motion and all you have to do is relax, get out of the house, and live a little."

The attorney's voice had a soothing tone and his confidence definitely had a calming effect. "Okay, I'll try to stop worrying."

"Good." He stood up, indicating that their meeting was over. "I'll be in touch with you in a day or so."

"Okay." She'd only been in his office for about forty minutes, and it sort of felt like she was getting the bum's rush. For all the money she'd paid him, she had expected them to put their heads together and strategize for a couple of hours. But on the bright side, Mr. Ross had impressed her with his competence and he needed to get busy and start filing documents on her behalf. She rose from her seat and shook his hand. "I'm depending on you, Mr. Ross."

She'd taken a full day off from work, and now didn't know how to fill the extra hours. Go to another bar? No, it was too early in the day for that. Besides, she'd decided not to go to any more lesbian bars. At least not for a while. Zenith had fucked her brains out last night and she was fully satisfied. Her sex drive had never been high, and she probably wouldn't need any more sexual release for at least another month.

However, the way Zenith had put it on her had kicked her sex drive into high gear. Zenith was good in bed—an awesome lover— yet she seemed to be somewhat emotionally distant. The heartless way she rotated her lovers was scary. She had women standing in line, and Vangie didn't want to have to take a number in order to spend time with her. It was probably wise for Vangie to leave Zenith alone and seek her sexual pleasure elsewhere.

They'd exchanged numbers last night, but Vangie decided it was best to delete Zenith from her contact list. Besides, Vangie wasn't even a real lesbian. She was only exploring her sexuality. Merely experimenting.

Vangie walked to the parking garage and felt a pang of sorrow. The thought of going home to an empty apartment was depressing. She wanted to hug her child. Kiss him. She wanted to at least be able to hear his voice. But Yuri was in school and wouldn't be available for their daily phone chat until after three, and sometimes much later, depending upon whether Jojina had plans for the kids after school.

Shawn was allowing Jojina to call all the shots. That bitch, Jojina was the one who determined when Vangie could and couldn't speak to her son. Two nights ago, Vangie had checked Jojina's Instagram page and there was a picture of Yuri posing with Jojina's two boys. The picture was captioned: *My Three Sons.*

After seeing that photo, the back of Vangie's throat had started to burn—a precursor to a long crying jag. Never in her life had she felt so helpless. A weaker person would have to be on medication to get through this kind of insanity. Vangie was trying to stay strong and keep it together for Yuri. But there was only so much emotional abuse a human being could take. If Mr. Ross didn't hurry up and get Yuri away from that evil bitch, there was no telling what Vangie was apt to do. She'd been having some twisted thoughts lately. Picturing herself sneaking into Jojina's house late at night and snatching Yuri, and then shooting the rest of the members of the household while they were asleep in their beds.

It was a shame that Vangie's mother didn't have any helpful advice to offer. Every time she tried to talk to her about her dire situation, Barbara would get angry at Vangie and start criticizing and blaming the entire fiasco on her. Judging from the things her mother said, Vangie got the distinct impression that she was on Shawn and Jojina's side. And that hurt deeply.

Needing to confide in someone, she thought about calling Nivea to see if she was open to an impromptu visit. Or perhaps she'd be willing to hook up for lunch. She dug inside her handbag, searching for her phone. The moment she wrapped her hand around the device, like magic, it began to vibrate inside her palm.

Peering at the screen, her eyes widened in surprise. Zenith was calling! She'd forgotten to delete her number and honestly hadn't expected to hear from her anytime soon. She was both thrilled and perplexed by the fact that the womanizing chick was even bothering to call. She struck Vangie as the type who would get what she wanted and never look back.

The phone buzzed in her hand twice more, and she brought it to her ear and answered the call.

"Hey, sweetness. I was dead to the world when you ran out of here. Just checking to make sure you're okay."

"I'm fine."

"You sure are."

Vangie laughed.

"What's on your agenda today?"

"I took the day off work to handle some personal business. I finished a lot sooner than I'd expected. I have the rest of the day to do whatever I want." Vangie grimaced. She'd said too much. Zenith was probably yawning and mentally scrolling through her contacts, eager to call the next person on the list.

"Wanna hang out?" Zenith asked.

"Sure. Is there anything in particular you'd like to do?" she asked coolly, though she was completely taken off-guard and a little freaked out.

Would seeing Zenith for a second time make her officially gay? Vangie glanced in the rearview mirror, studying her reflection, wondering if she looked like a lesbian. No, her face looked the same, but she felt emotionally lighter. More hopeful. Happier than she'd been in a long time.

"Why don't you drop by my place and let me take some pictures of you?"

"What kind of pictures? I know you're not asking me to pose for porn."

"My work isn't porn. It's art."

"No thanks. I don't want my naked ass ending up on the Internet."

Zenith laughed. "I promise your ass will be as anonymous as all the other asses I've photographed. Now, come on over and pose for me. It'll be fun," she cajoled.

"Okay, I'll do it." Her attorney had told her she should take her mind off her troubles and live a little. And to be honest, simply hearing Zenith's voice again had her pussy purring. One last roll in the hay couldn't hurt, could it?

HARLOW

She wondered why they called it "morning sickness." Nausea hit Harlow at all times of the day and night. Although she didn't feel the need to rush to the bathroom to vomit, there was this overall feeling of dizziness combined with a queasy stomach. She kept saltine crackers on hand to calm her stomach, but the crackers didn't help at all. Oddly, the only thing that made her feel better was eating hot dogs with the works. And the works included sauerkraut, chili, cheese, ketchup, mustard, and onions. Sometimes she added salsa to the list of toppings.

Only in her first trimester, the baby couldn't have been much larger than a bean, but that tiny little fetus sure had Harlow doing crazy things. Like taking a cab to Nathan's Famous Frankfurters in Times Square and buying six hot dogs to go.

Back from a Nathan's run, Harlow was surprised to find Drake and Alphonso talking in Drake's study. Alphonso rarely came to their apartment, but she was glad to see him.

The moment she approached the room to say hello, she heard Drake mention Lucio's name.

"Hi, honey," she said, poking her head in the study. "Hi, Alphonso."

Even though Alphonso was no longer Drake's bodyguard, Harlow always felt Drake was a little safer whenever Alphonso was around. She was relieved that Drake had shared his Lucio problem with Alphonso.

"I heard the good news," Alphonso said with a cheerful smile directed at Harlow. "Congratulations. What are you hoping for Harlow, a boy or a girl?"

Though her heart was set on a girl, she gave the standard response. "Doesn't matter, as long as it's healthy."

Drake concurred with a head nod. "I see my baby is having cravings again," Drake said, eyeing the big container of hot dogs.

"If this doesn't let up soon, I'm going to weigh a ton," Harlow complained.

"It's all good. I want you to fatten up my son," Drake said. "I mean, my daughter or whatever we're having."

"Don't try to clean it up now, man. You want a little Drake, so admit it," Alphonso said teasingly.

"I knew he wanted a boy all along," Harlow added. "The way this baby has me eating, it has to be a big-headed, greedy boy." Laughing, Harlow left Drake and Alphonso to discuss business.

In the kitchen, she perched on a stool, closed her eyes and bit into a messy hot dog. Blissfully unconcerned about the conglomeration of chili and cheese that ran down her fingers.

The distant sound of Drake's and Alphonso's deep voices had a comforting effect. This was the way a pregnancy should be. Every child deserved to be welcomed into the world by happy and loving parents.

She wondered how Alphonso and Vangie were doing. Had Vangie broken it off with him or was she still dealing with the horrendous sex? She wished Vangie had never told her about her bedroom dilemma; it was hard looking at Alphonso without thinking about his chubby, sawed-off dick and his terrible performance problems.

In bed that night, Drake kissed Harlow's lips, moved down to her swelling breasts and then placed a kissed on her tummy. "Hello, son," he murmured.

Harlow giggled. "Now, I feel pressured to give you a son."

"I'm gonna love whatever we have, but in my heart, I know it's a boy."

"Is that right? Well, I hate to burst your bubble, but I can tell it's a girl."

"How do you know?"

"I don't. But since we're being truthful, I thought I'd admit that I kind of want a girl." Harlow ran her palm over the waves in Drake's hair. "How are Alphonso and Vangie doing? Does he ever talk about their relationship?"

"No, never. I got the impression they were only casually dating."

"It was a little more than casual. He takes her shopping all the time, but Vangie wants more. She was hoping he would pop the question soon."

Drake shook his head. "Alphonso's a confirmed bachelor. Tell Vangie she's going to have to look elsewhere for a man who's marriage material."

"I guess she's going to have to find out on her own. Vangie and I are sort of not speaking."

"What happened?"

"We had an argument while you were in England." Harlow gave Drake the side eye. "I guess you were in England…"

"Let's not go there. I was definitely in England."

"I know. I'm sorry; I don't know why I said that."

"You still don't fully trust me, babe?"

"I trust you, Drake. Forget that I said that and let's blame it on hormones. By the way, how's Lucio doing?" She wondered if Alphonso had assisted Drake in dropping off the money to the kidnappers. She certainly hoped so. Whatever gripes Vangie had with Alphonso didn't change the way Harlow felt about him. He had always been Drake's most loyal and trusted friend.

"There's been a little improvement. Not much. He wants to talk, though. I can tell that he's desperate to get his jaw unwired."

"When is that going to happen?"

"Hard to say."

Harlow nodded, grateful for her current circumstances. A loving and healthy husband and a bouncing baby boy on the way. *Baby boy? Now, where'd that come from?*

"In general, you should gain two to four pounds in your first one to three months of pregnancy and one pound a week for the rest of the pregnancy," Dr. Talbert said. "You've gained seven pounds since your last visit. What's going on?"

Harlow wore a guilty expression. "I can't deal with the nausea. It's the most horrible feeling in the world. Someone suggested saltine crackers, but they don't help, so I've been eating a lot of hot dogs to combat morning, afternoon, and evening sickness."

"Hot dogs?"

"Specifically, Nathan's hot dogs with the works."

"And how often do you indulge in hot dog binges?" the doctor asked with slight smile.

"Several days a week."

"How many is several?"

"Like four or five days a week."

"And how many of these hot dogs with the works are you consuming?"

Harlow sighed. "A lot. A half dozen or so."

"Hot dogs are not very nutritious. And that's a lot of sodium. I want you to substitute the hot dogs with carrots and celery sticks dipped in a low-fat, low-sodium salad dressing."

Harlow made a face. "That sounds so boring, and I don't think my baby is gonna like that. Can't you come up with a heartier substitute?"

"Cravings are psychological."

"But I'm not craving anything. The hot dogs help the queasiness."

"Humor me and try the carrots and celery. Let's see if they improve your nausea. In the meantime, I'd like to do an ultrasound to find out if there's anything else going on."

Harlow's eyes lit up. "Really, will we be able to find out whether it's a boy or a girl?"

"I can get a more accurate reading during the second trimester. So let's not concern ourselves about the baby's gender just yet."

"Are you worried that something's wrong with my baby?" Harlow's voice was filled with alarm.

"Not at all. Curious to see how big the baby has grown…that's all."

"That's a relief," Harlow said.

NIVEA

"This is the most unusual contract I've ever seen," said the attorney Nivea had hired.

"Can you cut to the chase? Doesn't that contract clearly state that I'm supposed to get five-thousand a month for life? As long as my daughter is a minor?"

The attorney shook his head. "You didn't have an attorney look this over before you signed, did you?"

"No. It looked like everything was in my favor."

"You didn't read the small print."

"What small print?"

"In this case, it's a figure of speech. At any rate, you didn't read between the lines."

Nivea didn't like the direction of the meeting with the attorney she had selected and was already considering cancelling the check she'd written for him. "I haven't mastered that skill."

"Well, the way I'm reading this contract, you were only entitled to the money as long as you kept good faith."

"What does that mean?"

"You agreed that Mr. Sandburg was not the child's parent when you signed the document. But according to the DNA test, he is the father and that's a deal-breaker for Mrs. Sandburg."

"But he's the father and he has to pay."

"That's true. But you're going to have to go after his money, not hers. Apparently, Sandburg signed a prenuptial agreement and he's not entitled to any of his wife's money. You're going to have to go after his. Exactly how much he has…I guess we'll have to find out."

"I don't think he has that much," Nivea said with a scowl.

"Well, we'll haul him into court and find out."

"I'm sure he's hiding his assets as we speak." *I'm so fucked.*

"You can't say that for sure; we'll have to find out."

"Oh, my God. How many times are you going to say that? It's so annoying." Nivea stood up and adjusted the strap of her Louis Vuitton bag. "Thanks for nothing." Punching numbers on her cell phone, she walked out of the lawyer's office. She called her bank and cancelled the check she'd written. He could sue her if he wanted to, but he was going to have to fight to get paid good money for the piss-poor job of lawyering he'd done.

In a short time span, Nivea had run through over a hundred grand. Ashamed that she didn't have anything of real value, she began looking at houses. She found a lovely little colonial-style home in Lower Merion, Pennsylvania and thought it would be the perfect starter house for Mackenzie and her. The 3,400-square-foot home had four bedrooms, two full baths, and two half-baths. Plenty of room for Odette to move in. And the chef's kitchen was magnificent. For a good cook like Odette, the kitchen would be her joyful domain. The half-acre of land surrounding the house would provide Mackenzie with lots of room to run and play when she got older.

Nivea was ready to make a more than reasonable down payment, when she was told she didn't qualify due to her poor credit score.

It was as if she'd never rid herself of the stench of having once been engaged to a fucking loser. Eric was the worst mistake of her life. The engagement ring that she'd allowed him to put on her credit card had never been paid off, and the cancelled wedding had also contributed to her credit rating. Had she been of sound mind at the time, she would have handled things differently. She would have made arrangements with all the wedding vendors she owed money, but instead, she ignored their bills.

She couldn't get her dream house unless she made a down payment of $90,000. And she no longer had that kind of money. She was suddenly sickened by the way she'd squandered Mackenzie's money on so many frivolous things.

Mackenzie's room was filled with an expensive doll collection that she wouldn't be interested in for years to come, and she was outgrowing her elegant clothes faster than she could wear them. Nivea wondered how much she could make if she sold the dolls and Mackenzie's clothes to consignment shops.

She sighed. Running around like a chicken with her head cut off, trying to sell her daughter's clothes and toys to the highest bidder was out of the question. She had too much dignity for that.

With a heavy heart, she resigned herself to buying a much cheaper condo in the same neighborhood as the house she'd coveted. Trying to feel better, she convinced herself that she didn't want to be bothered with keeping up the grounds of that stupid house, anyway.

Times like this, when she was filled with self-loathing, she could do one of two things. Get together with Malcolm and let him fuck her brains out until she felt better or she could shop some more.

Nivea chose to spend time with Malcolm.

But after driving to his place and bringing him Chinese food, Malcolm seemed more interested in *Monday Night Football* than in Nivea.

"Want another beer?" she asked, noticing his bottle was almost empty.

"Sure," he said absently, his eyes glued to the TV.

Nivea didn't like being ignored and was considering going home. Pouting and sighing, she went to the kitchen and gazed in the fridge. She didn't hear Malcolm creep up behind her.

He reached over her shoulder and grabbed a container of whipped cream, opened his mouth and pushed the nozzle, filling his mouth with the creamy dessert topping.

"Ew." Nivea frowned. "How can you eat it like that?"

"It's my favorite dessert, and I was just struck with a great idea." Grinning, he lifted his brows twice.

"What are you talking about?" she asked innocently, although she had a pretty good idea of his intentions.

"Take those clothes off and I'll show you."

After she tore her clothes off, Malcolm lifted her up and stretched her out on the kitchen island. Lying naked in the center of Malcolm's kitchen was so weirdly sexy, Nivea's skin began to tingle.

"Close your eyes," he said.

She did as he said and smiled when she felt the cool whipped cream being applied to each of her nipples. The way he licked and sucked the cream from her titties had her whimpering and murmuring his name.

He shook the can and she trembled with excitement when he decorated her pussy with a big puff of whipped cream that stood about six inches high. He lapped and sucked in the sugary treat until he'd worked his way down to her aching pussy. To gain better access, he held her knees apart and by the time his tongue flicked against her skin, Nivea was on fire and begging for dick.

"Not yet," he said. "You gotta do me, baby." He pulled down his pants, then sprayed his dick with the creamy, white coating. Nivea scooted off the island and knelt in front of him. By the time she finished sucking whipped cream off his dick, she had acquired a taste for her man's favorite dessert.

Sounds of a cheering crowd emanated from the living room. "Oh, shit, my team just scored. I'll finish you off during halftime."

Before Nivea could protest, and demand that he fuck her right now, he scooped her in his muscular arms and jogged from the kitchen to the living room without losing his breath or breaking into a sweat.

The strength and stamina of her big, ol' handsome, alpha-man made her hornier than ever. "How long before halftime?" she asked, rubbing herself as he lowered her on the couch.

"Fuck waiting for halftime. I want this pussy right now."

She showed him how much she agreed by spreading open her legs.

HARLOW

"As I suspected, you're carrying twins," Dr. Talbert told Harlow.

"Are you serious? Is that why I'm eating like a truck driver?"

"I wouldn't blame the babies for that. Twin pregnancies have an increased risk for preterm labor, premature rupture of membranes, high blood pressure, and diabetes. Therefore, I'm going to be monitoring you more closely to check fetal heart rate, levels of amniotic fluid and fetal growth."

"I'm excited and scared at the same time."

"There's nothing to be concerned about, but you should follow my dietary recommendations. I'm also going to prescribe extra vitamins and minerals."

"Okay."

"One more thing…"

Her life had been going so well; it was actually too good to be true, and so Harlow braced herself for bad news. "What is it, Dr. Talbert?"

"I was able to determine the gender of the twins. You're having identical boys."

Harlow wanted to jump up and hug the doctor. "Oh, my God. That's amazing news. My husband is going to be ecstatic."

"I'd like you to eat 2,700 healthy calories a day. By the way, did you give up those hot dogs?"

"Yes, and I'm ready to go organic. I want to feed my babies nothing except the most nutritious food."

"Don't go overboard and cut out meat. You can find organic lean meat."

"Okay, I will," Harlow said excitedly with a grin plastered on her face. Dr. Talbert handed Harlow a grainy ultrasound photo of the babies. "They're not much to look at yet, but we'll get a better image when they get a little bigger."

Harlow kissed the photograph, her heart swelling with love. She'd come a long way from the sexually abused daughter of a crackhead, and she silently apologized to her babies for feeding them so many unhealthy hot dogs. Harlow tucked the photo in her purse, vowing to be a health-conscious parent from now on.

Drake came home that evening wearing a somber expression.

"What's wrong, hon?" Harlow asked.

"Something's up with Lucio."

"What do you mean?"

"It's like he's trying to tell me something. And since he can't verbalize his feelings, I try to throw out suggestions that he can either nod to or shake his head. So, I asked if he was sick of being on a liquid diet. He shook his head. I asked if he was in pain. Again, the answer was no. I went through a long list, including if he was worried about being broke. He nodded to that, and so I assured him that I would personally replace his money—"

"How much was it, you never mentioned an exact amount."

"Five million dollars."

"Wow."

"That won't break our bank, baby. I want to do whatever I can to give the old man a little peace of mind. But even after I offered to replace the money, he was still agitated. I don't know if he's legitimately worried about something or if he's getting senile."

"I wish I had the answer for you, Drake." She wanted to press him for details about where he'd delivered the ransom money and if he was absolutely sure the kidnappers wouldn't come back for more. But she kept her questions to herself.

"I'm going to take a shower and call it a night," he said, loosening his tie.

Drake stood at his bureau with a worried expression as he took off his watch and placed it inside his jewelry box.

Harlow had wanted to share the good news, but decided that tonight wasn't a good time.

At Whole Foods, she cheerfully loaded her cart with organic produce and then went to the meat counter and selected organic chicken and lean beef. She went up and down the aisles, and carefully read the labels of every item that went into her cart. Only foods with natural ingredients were good enough for her babies.

The classical music piping through the speakers added to her good mood. She'd never enjoyed classical; she'd discounted it as music undesirable for someone who had grown up listening to hip-hop and R&B. She wondered what it would be like to attend an evening at the symphony. She'd made a mental note to find out which symphonic orchestras were in town. Chuckling to herself, she imagined Drake's scowl when she insisted that he escort her to a concert. She'd wait until after she told him they were going to be the parents of twins and then inform him that she'd read that classical music was soothing for the fetus while in utero.

And that wasn't a lie. She had read in a pamphlet at Dr. Talbert's office that studies suggested that fetuses can hear and react to sound by moving. Classical music was thought to stimulate the baby's developing brain. Drake would definitely want to ensure that his kids came out healthy and smart.

There was no reason to wait until they went to a concert when she could go to iTunes and start downloading a classical music collection for her babies. Drake would make sure they were sports enthusiasts, but she would make sure their cultural pursuits were well balanced.

She pushed her cart outside and waited for the Town Car that had brought her to the market to pull up close to the entrance. She looked from left to right, but the car was nowhere in sight. Ordinarily, she would have had the groceries delivered, but today she wanted to be more hands-on.

The black Town Car finally glided into the parking lot. The driver must have taken a little spin while waiting for her. She stepped forward and waved and he stopped directly in front of her.

"Mrs. Morgan?" said a driver who was much younger than the one who had brought her to Whole Foods. "My name's Otto. Sorry, if you've been waiting for very long."

"No, not at all. What happened to the other driver?"

"His wife went into labor and the boss asked me to replace him."

"Oh, he mentioned that his wife was expecting, but he didn't tell me she was due any day. You know, I'm expecting, too," Harlow said brightly. It wasn't like her to tell her personal business, but she was over the moon with happiness. Then her face clouded with worry. She hoped Drake wouldn't be on the other side of the world when she went into labor. They'd have to have a serious discussion about him limiting his traveling.

"You don't look like you're expecting, ma'am," the driver said, looking uncomfortable discussing pregnancy.

"I'm still in my first trimester." She wanted to blurt out that she was having twin boys, but it didn't seem right to tell a stranger when Drake didn't know yet.

The driver loaded her bags in the trunk. "You don't have to worry about carrying these bags, ma'am. I'll get them in the elevator for you and I can ride up with you and carry them inside your apartment if you'd like."

"Thank you. I appreciate the offer." The packages weren't very heavy, but Harlow didn't want to overburden herself if she didn't have to.

During the ride to her apartment, she pulled out her phone and perused classical music on iTunes, and quickly learned she didn't know what was good and what wasn't. Listening to samples, she discovered a preference for string instruments, particularly violins.

When she finally lifted her head, she realized they were going in the wrong direction. "Uh, did you make a mistake? I live on the Upper East Side."

Otto didn't turn around, but she could see through the rearview mirror that his pleasant expression had turned to stone. "We're not going to the Upper East Side, bitch. So shut your mouth and enjoy the scenery."

NIVEA

Malcolm taught at a skydiving school in Montgomery County, Pennsylvania, but when he wasn't teaching, he liked to change up the scenery and jump from various places. Today, they were at a skydiving school in New Jersey. Nivea and Malcolm sat in the waiting area with the other daredevils who were suited up and ready to risk their lives by jumping out of an airplane.

Malcolm was dressed in his skydiving gear: a helmet, a backpack containing his parachute, and he was wearing a jumpsuit. He looked super-hot in the loose-fitting, one-piece garment.

"Nervous?" she asked him with a teasing smirk.

"Not at all. I'm cool, calm, and collected."

"You can still back out, you know."

"Are you kidding? I live for this."

When Malcolm's turn came to walk out on the field and get into the small plane that looked old and rickety, Nivea wanted to grab his hand and forbid him to go through with the ridiculous stunt.

"Seriously, you don't have to prove anything to me or anyone else. I know you're a virile man," she said, sort of kidding, but mostly serious.

"You're nervous for me, aren't you?"

Nivea pantomimed biting her nails. Malcolm laughed and then

pulled her into an embrace, kissing her on the cheek before trotting across the field toward the waiting plane.

Sitting on a bench in the spectator area with the other skydivers' family and friends, Nivea watched as the small aircraft, a Cessna 182, climbed higher and higher. Much, much too high for her comfort level. Her palms began to sweat when she saw Malcolm's silhouette appear at the opening of the distant plane. He jumped, and for a moment, he appeared to be suspended in midair. Then he began to fall slowly, and it seemed to take forever for his parachute to open. Nivea began to panic, wondering if everything was okay. A few seconds later, when the parachute still hadn't opened, she clamped a hand over her mouth while her heart pounded in her chest.

Finally, the rainbow-colored parachute blossomed in the sky, and it was the most beautiful sight Nivea had beheld, second only to when she'd first set eyes on her gorgeous baby girl.

Ten thousand feet in the air, Malcolm soared through the sky, his arms stretched out, reminding her of Superman. Floating downward, his descent was beautiful—poetry in motion. And she raced across the field to greet him when his feet gracefully touched the ground.

He lay on his back, murmuring, "That was incredible. Wow! The view was surreal. I don't think I'll ever get used to seeing the bay, the bridge and land from that angle." He flashed Nivea a grin. "It's better than sex, babe. You should try it."

Nivea crouched down beside him. "Don't ever invite me here again."

He sat up and looked at her with confusion. "Why not?"

"It was too scary. I almost had a heart attack watching you being so reckless and foolhardy. I just can't do it; I love you too much." She gasped and her eyes widened when she realized what she'd said. "Oh, my God, I didn't mean to say I love you. I meant to say, you know, that I really like you a lot," Nivea blubbered. She felt like an idiot and she could feel the warmth of embarrassment rising in her cheeks. She could have kicked herself for blurting something so mushy and stupid.

Malcolm didn't respond or react. He maintained a prone position.

"Are you okay?" she asked, trying to decode his body language.

"Not really."

"What's wrong?" she asked worriedly. Had she frightened him by using the "L" word so soon?

"My adrenaline is pumping and I'm ready to go again. You wanna skydive with me, baby?"

Nivea swatted at Malcolm playfully as he pulled himself upright. "Are you crazy, boy? I value my life too much to even get inside that rickety-looking, little plane."

Malcolm made no mention of her love confession, and for that, she was relieved. But her words hung in the air like the proverbial elephant in the room. Nivea hoped she hadn't scared him off by blurting out those three words. She'd cringed thinking how desperate and love-starved she must have seemed.

Looking back and recalling how much she despised him when they'd first met, it was amazing that she'd grown to care so much for him. Though her feelings were strong, what she felt was far from love. She'd misspoken and would explain that to him later on, when they had some quiet time together.

Malcolm climbed to his feet. "Jumping from planes burns a lot of calories. I'm starving; how about you?"

"I could go for something to eat."

With their arms wrapped around each other, they walked back toward the building where Malcolm could change clothes. As they approached the spectators sitting on the benches, there was a

chorus of applause as the crowd acknowledged Malcolm's successful free fall.

❤ ❤ ❤

Avoiding traffic, Malcolm took back streets for a few miles and
then turned off on a deserted dirt road. Malcolm had one hand on
the steering wheel and the other gently clasping Nivea's hand. It
was a sweet moment, but instead of basking in it, Nivea found
herself stressing over her dwindling finances.

Malcolm made a sudden turn, snapping Nivea out of her worri-
some contemplation. She gave him a curious glance. "We're going
to a restaurant in the woods?"

"Not exactly a restaurant, but we're having lunch at my favorite
spot."

"What do you mean?"

"I brought lunch for us. It's in a basket—on the floor in the back."

Nivea twisted around and spotted the basket. "A picnic basket?"

"It's a Christmas gift from my Aunt Estelle, two years ago. She's
always asking if I've used it yet, and she'll be glad to hear that I
finally have."

"I feel so special."

"You are special." He looked her up and down. "You look real
nice today, but then, you always look nice." He parked under a
tree, leaned in and kissed her, his hand running beneath her skirt.
"Smell good, too."

"Keep it up and we may have to skip lunch," Nivea said. "But
I'm really hungry, so let's eat first."

Malcolm laid out a gourmet spread that he'd purchased from a
specialty shop. Next, he uncorked a bottle of vintage wine and
poured them both a glass. "I want to propose a toast."

"All right."

"Uh, to our future…I hope."

"You hope? What are you saying?"

"I have to tell you something."

"Oh, no. I can't take any bad news, Malcolm."

"The business is folding and my partners and I may have to file bankruptcy."

"You can't be serious. The gym seems to be doing a killer business."

"We overextended ourselves and we're barely able to keep the doors open with all the salaries we have to pay. Recently, we were approached by a buyer. A corporation. And if we sell quickly, I can get back my investment and also have enough to pursue my dream to market my health drink."

"That's good news; isn't it, Malcolm?"

"In a way. The only glitch is that I have to move to the West Coast."

"Why?" Nivea shrieked in alarm.

"That's where the bottling company is located and my potential investors are out there. It's where I need to be."

"Are you breaking up with me?"

Malcolm had a sad look in his eyes. "Sort of."

"Sort of?"

"My first thought was to ask if you could possibly deal with a long distance relationship, but we both know they don't usually work out. And I can't ask you to relocate when I don't know what the future holds for me. If I lose everything I have, I can always tough it out, but you have a baby and a career in this area. It would be selfish of me to even expect you to run off into the unknown with me."

"But this is so sudden," she said sadly.

"I know and I'm sorry. I care for you, deeply; I honestly never intended to hurt you."

"I'm heartbroken, but I'll bounce back. I've gotten used to being disappointed by men."

"I had good intentions, Nivea."

She sighed heavily. "I'm sure you did."

"Do you want to finish the picnic?"

Nivea shook her head.

He pulled off the gleaming watch she'd given him. "I feel I should return this gift."

"Keep it. Please, just take me home."

During the drive home, Malcolm filled the silence with steady chatter while Nivea only grunted and murmured one-word responses. Her world had suddenly shattered, and she was fighting back tears, trying hard not to reveal how totally devastated she was.

HARLOW

With a gun stuck in her side, Otto forced Harlow inside the basement apartment of a dilapidated building somewhere in Queens. The place was a mess with girlie magazines strewn about, and old pizza boxes were stacked atop tables and counters. The trash was overflowing in the small, unkempt kitchen and dirty dishes were piled sky-high. He guided her to the living room, which was also cluttered with everything under the sun. It appeared that no one had cleaned the place in years.

In the apartments overhead, she heard people speaking in foreign languages, children squealing in delight, rock music pumping, and babies crying. There was so much life above her, yet she'd never felt more alone and terrified.

Otto pushed her into a raggedy chair that was covered with cigarette burns and then went through her purse, removing her wallet and sticking it in his back pocket. Then he popped the battery out of her cell phone and tossed it onto a cluttered table.

"Why'd you bring me here?" she asked Otto, though she had already deducted that he was involved with the men who had kidnapped and tortured Lucio.

"If you wanna keep that pretty smile, you need to shut your trap. Ask another question and I'm gonna knock some teeth out when I stuff your mouth with my fist." He held up a beefy fist. Harlow recoiled, noticing that his fist bore the ominous tattoo of a spider caught in a web.

This couldn't be happening. Drake had promised they were safe and now not only was her life in danger, but also the lives of her unborn babies.

Otto's cell phone rang and he flinched at the sound. Jumpy and nervous, he obviously wasn't a seasoned criminal. Maybe she could talk him into letting her go.

"Yeah, can you hurry up. I gotta get rid of the car. The driver's in the trunk." Otto listened for a moment and then barked, "I don't know if he's breathing or not. The last thing I heard him say was, 'Please don't shoot me; I have a pregnant wife.' Right now he's covered with a bunch of grocery bags and I don't know if he's dead or alive. I couldn't hang around the Whole Foods parking lot, so excuse me if I didn't have time to check his fuckin' pulse. Just get here as soon as possible. I'm not feeling good about this."

The original driver with the pregnant wife was in the trunk of the Town Car, possibly dead. This situation was not looking good at all.

As Otto spoke softly into the phone, his eyes constantly darted at her, making sure she didn't try to escape.

"Nah, she's not wearing a diamond. I don't know what kind of stone it is. Something pink."

Harlow's frightened eyes shot down to her ring finger. Were they going to cut off her finger and send it to Drake or did they simply want her ring? She twisted off her engagement ring and wedding band and held them out. "This is pink sapphire. It's worth a lot. Here, you can have it," she said in an urgent voice. "And... and my wedding band is platinum. Please take them both and let me go."

"She said it's pink sapphire, whatever the fuck that is. I don't know if it's worth anything or not."

"It is," Harlow shouted. "You can pawn it and get a lot of money."

Otto ignored Harlow and continued his phone conversation. "He instructed us to snip off her finger and pack it together with her wedding ring."

Oh, my God, no! Harlow pictured herself trying to change diapers with a missing finger and she didn't like the imagery.

"We should keep the sapphire ring and tell the boss she was only wearing the wedding band. He won't care as long as the husband gets the message loud and clear. Look, man, I did my part; now hurry up and get here so you can do the cutting. I get dizzy when I see blood."

Oh, Jesus! I've got to get out of here.

"All right; I'll go check the dude in the trunk, but that's it. I need to get paid for all the work I put in so far."

Otto walked toward the front door and then looked over his shoulder. "The front door is made of solid steel. There're bars on every window, so don't even think about trying to get out. I'll be right outside and if you even think about yelling, I'll come back in here and staple your mouth shut if I have to." Otto said something in the phone and then said, "Tape her mouth shut with what? This was a spur-of-the-moment assignment. The bitch got in the Town Car and I followed like I was told to do. I didn't have time to stop at Home Depot and pick up duct tape. All I have at the crib is a staple gun."

Harlow shuddered and was crying softly by the time Otto slammed the heavy door and locked it. Trapped inside the ratty basement apartment, she tried to figure a way out of her predicament, but no sooner had Otto left than she heard his key turning the lock.

Otto looked more agitated than before. "So what if he saw my face! That driver doesn't know me from a can of paint," he said into the phone. "If you want to finish him off, then come and do it. And hurry up; I'm tired of babysitting this broad." Otto looked at Harlow with disgust.

An hour later, three soft bumps followed by two hard bangs sounded on the door. Otto went to the door that didn't have a peep hole and pressed his ear against it. "Who is it?" he said in a hushed voice. Again, there were three knocks and two thumps.

Harlow realized it was some kind of code when Otto opened the door, admitting a big guy with a Russian accent. He had a deeply etched, crescent-shaped scar on his right cheek. The big guy was carrying a canvas bag. Harlow didn't even want to think about what the bag could possibly contain. She wasn't in suspense very long.

The big guy unzipped the bag and took out a roll of duct tape. Harlow let out a frightened whine. The big guy's eyes glimmered as he tore off a piece of the tape and swiftly covered her mouth. He took out plastic zip tie cuffs and Harlow went into a panic, struggling to prevent him from securing her hands.

"Cooperate, bitch!" he barked and gave her a hard slap across the face.

Harlow's body went rigid and tears spilled from her eyes. After he cuffed her hands, he put another zip tie tightly around her ankles.

"You're lucky the boss has a soft spot for you," he said to Harlow. "He says we don't have to remove that pretty little finger for now. But your husband has exactly one hour to drop off the money." He turned his attention toward Otto. "Give me the rings."

"Both of them?"

"Yeah, both of them."

"I thought we were gonna keep the sapphire."

"If I leave it with your junkie ass, you'll run off and pawn it and I won't ever see my cut."

"You can trust me; I wouldn't do you like that, man."

"I'm not foolish enough to put trust in your word. No honor

among thieves; haven't you ever heard that expression? Now, let's go dump that body and get rid of the car."

The body? Was the poor driver dead? Harlow wondered.

He eyed Harlow and pulled a large, menacing knife out of the canvas bag. "Sit tight, pretty lady. If you so much as move a muscle, I'm going to give you a scar exactly like mine."

"His and Her scars; that would be a riot," Otto said, laughing. "But I couldn't watch you do it."

"Yeah, I know, a little bit of blood makes you woozy. You're such a pussy," the big guy spat.

Suddenly, there was the familiar pattern of knocks at the door. Three soft raps and two more forceful knocks.

"Oh, shit; it's the boss. He's probably pissed about the car," Otto said with fear in his eyes.

The pattern of knocks occurred again and Otto fixed a wide-eyed stare on the big guy.

"Let him in, man. You have to answer for botching up the job. I didn't have anything to do with the car or the driver," the big guy said.

Looking apprehensive, Otto unlocked the door and pulled it open, and to Harlow's utter surprise, Drake walked in.

VANGIE

Vanilla ice cream trickled down Vangie's right butt cheek. Positioned on her hands and knees, she held the bizarre pose while Zenith, standing directly behind her, aimed her camera and clicked.

"Beautiful," Zenith exclaimed and then used Handi Wipes to remove the ice cream trail. "Let's try a smudge of strawberry ice cream for the next shot. That'll look hot."

Vangie had been nervous about the idea of posing nude even though Zenith promised not to expose her face. In the beginning of the photo shoot, she was trembling so badly, Zenith couldn't get a good shot. She offered Vangie a joint to calm her down, and after a couple puffs, Vangie was relaxed enough to hold still while she poked her ass out.

A few minutes later, the dread and mortification that caused her body to quake began to morph into a wondrous feeling similar to empowerment. Vangie's ass was photographed with drippings of ice cream, syrup, and in some shots, her ass was decorated with pieces of candy that were held in place with body glue.

"That's it; we're finished. Thanks for posing for me," Zenith said as she wiped sugary residue from Vangie's buttocks.

"It was fun in a weird way," Vangie replied, lying on her tummy on Zenith's bed.

"Would you mind if I include your photos in my show?" Zenith sat next to Vangie on the bed.

"What show?"

"My agent has connections and she strong-armed somebody into giving me a show next month. It'll be my first exhibit." Zenith beamed and Vangie realized she'd never seen her smile so brightly.

"Congrats. That's fantastic."

"I know, but I'm so nervous." Her long fingers fluttered to her chest. Zenith was usually overly confident and such a badass, it was refreshing for Vangie to see her vulnerable side.

"What are you nervous about; your work is fabulous." Vangie gestured to the numerous photographs that adorned the walls.

"I have a lot more. My apartment was overflowing with my work, and I had to put most of my pieces in storage." She lit another joint, puffed on it and passed it to Vangie.

She blew out a cloud of smoke. "Do you only take pictures of pussies and asses?"

Zenith laughed. "No, I'm going through a phase right now. If you want to see my other stuff, you'll have to come to my opening."

"I'd love to. And in response to your question, I'd be honored if you added my ass to your collection…as long as it remains anonymous."

"All my asses are anonymous," Zenith said, and then she and Vangie both broke out laughing. Laughing hard and unable to stop. The weed had Vangie acting stupid. She hadn't smoked the stuff in years. She took another puff and the feeling of relaxation, happiness, and overall peace with the world that engulfed her was so pleasurable, she wondered why she'd given up smoking pot. With all the recent turmoil that had occurred in her life, she felt she deserved to unwind. A little bit of ganja never hurt anyone.

"Tell me about yourself, Vangie. When did you become interested in women?" Hovering over Vangie, Zenith rubbed the back of her neck.

Vangie blew out a thin stream of smoke. "It wasn't something I'd ever given any thought to, you know? It wasn't like I had a secret attraction toward women that I'd been trying to hide. I've always been into men. This is a brand-new experience for me."

"So, how'd you find your way to The Merry-Go-Round?"

Vangie shrugged. "Looked it up online. But, for all I know, this could be a phase I'm going through. Anyway, it all started when I had an argument with my best friend…well, my former best friend."

"What happened?"

"I was being a cranky bitch and said something mean that I couldn't take back. I said something about her husband. A thoughtless remark that hit below the belt. There's a little more to it than that, but that's the gist of it. Now she won't talk to me. Won't accept my apology or take my calls."

"An argument with your friend led you to a gay bar?"

"No. There's more to it than that."

Zenith gave Vangie a look that encouraged her to go on.

"Well, she was angry and at the last minute, she canceled a spa date we'd planned. I went alone, and this freaky masseuse gave me a "happy ending," if you know what I mean. It was like the most intense orgasm ever, and a few weeks later, I found myself wanting to have another sexual experience with her. I couldn't get her on the phone, and so I looked online for a gay bar. I was only looking for recreational sex. Wasn't trying to get emotionally involved with another woman or anything like that."

"That's a pity."

Vangie rose up on an elbow and looked at Zenith. "Why do you say that?"

"Because I like you. I want to see more of you, and I was hoping you felt the same."

"You're nothing but a player. I've seen the way women throw

themselves at you. We both know you can have your pick of sex partners, so why are you trying to act like you're looking for something more than a quick fling?"

"I'm not a player; I'm far from being that. The way I act at the club—it's all a front. Hard exterior but soft and mushy right here." She touched her heart with one hand and reached for Vangie's with the other.

Vangie started to bring up the subject of the girl who had tried to commit suicide over Zenith, but she didn't think it was the appropriate time to dig into her past. Needing to feel connected to someone, she gave Zenith her hand. With their fingers intertwined, they were both quiet for a few moments as if silently agreeing to a pact.

Vangie squeezed Zenith's hand, tightly, as if holding on to a lifeline. She could feel her eyes becoming glassy as they began to well with tears. "There's so much going on in my life right now, and I've been trying to escape the pain."

"You wanna talk about it?" Zenith's voice was low and compassionate, barely above a whisper.

"My son's father took him from me, and I've been trying to stay strong while I fight to get him back…but it's so hard. I'm almost at my breaking point. You know? Fighting this battle all by myself is wearing me down. And the idea that I might go back to jail…" Vangie's throat tightened, and she couldn't speak.

"Jail? What are you talking about?"

Vangie told Zenith about her fight with Jojina and the short but traumatic time she'd spent behind bars. "You wouldn't believe how much money I've spent on lawyers, and I don't have any idea how this is going to turn out." There was a lump pushing at the back of her throat that seemed to grow larger by the second. Unable to swallow it down, she succumbed to tears.

Displaying an unexpected rush of compassion, Zenith gathered her in her arms and murmured in her ear. "You don't have to be alone anymore. I like you, and I want to be a part of your life—let me."

"I want to. But I don't want to lead you on. I don't think I'm gay, you know what I'm saying? I'm still attracted to men. I want to get married one day. Have a big wedding and the clichéd house with a white-picket fence. I can't see myself involved in a serious relationship with a woman. I'm sorry, but I'm not that way."

"I understand."

"You do?"

"Yes. You're tripping on the labels. Straight, lesbian, gay. Those terms don't define us. You feel me? We're two human beings who like spending time together. Two people who enjoy experiencing the beauty of making love with each other."

Zenith's words struck a chord and Vangie nodded her head in understanding.

"I don't want to rush you into something you're not ready for, so I'm gonna fall back and let you set the tempo. Okay, sweetness? I'm not trying to pressure you. Take your time and let this play out at a pace you're comfortable with."

"Okay," Vangie said, sniffling and crying softly.

With her thumb, Zenith wiped away the tears that rolled down Vangie's cheek. That tender gesture touched Vangie's heart and made her cry harder. She dropped her head on Zenith's shoulder and openly wept.

"Don't cry, baby. It's gonna be all right. I won't let you down; I promise," she whispered, stroking Vangie's hair. "Put your fears aside and give us a chance. Don't be afraid. Be with me. Let me show you that I'm more than a man."

Vangie lifted her head and through teary eyes, she gazed at Zenith, leaning toward the idea of getting into a relationship with her.

"Like you, I've been hurt before. Hurt down to my soul. And the cavalier attitude that you saw at the bar—I've already told you—that's a fake persona. Pretending to be cold and hard is my way of putting a protective fence around my heart."

The words she spoke resonated within Vangie. She could relate to every word Zenith had spoken. She stared at her for a long time, struggling with the idea of taking a chance with a relationship that would alter her entire identity.

As if reading her mind, Zenith said, "You'll always be safe with me. I'll take care of you and treat you like the queen that you are." She lightly brushed a hand over Vangie's breasts. "I love these pretty titties," she murmured.

Vangie blushed and shook her head. "You know my breasts look a mess. They're all saggy and unattractive. I wish I could get a breast lift."

"You better not change a thing about those beautiful titties." She lowered her head and kissed each nipple. Vangie shivered and released a soft moan.

"Tell me what you want, baby. What do you need me to do?"

"I only need you to be on my side. I'm so tired of feeling like it's me against the world."

"That goes without saying. It's me and you." She aimed two V-shaped fingers at her eyes and then flicked them in Vangie's direction. "From now on, we're on the same side."

Comforted by her words, Vangie smiled.

"What else do you want?"

"I only want you," Vangie admitted shyly in a voice that cracked.

"Do you want Daddy to go get his dick and fuck you?"

Vangie's eyelids fluttered closed as she nodded her head. Too embarrassed to look Zenith in the eyes and expose her shameful, burning desire.

Zenith rose from the bed, and Vangie cracked her eyes open, delighting in the sight of her paramour's long legs striding across the room. Zenith stripped out of her clothes and stood magnificently naked, toned and strong like an otherworldly sex goddess. She opened a drawer and retrieved the plastic penis, and Vangie gawked at her with raw lust brimming in her eyes as she watched Zenith strap on her dick.

HARLOW

"What the fuck!" Otto yelled.

Drake held a gun with a silencer attached. He aimed it at Otto's chest, pulled the trigger, and Otto went down. Harlow watched in horror as a widening red circle appeared on the front of Otto's white shirt. Before the big guy could move, Drake was holding the gun to his head. "Call your fucking boss if you want me to spare your worthless life."

Harlow began shaking and whimpering.

"It's okay, baby. I can't risk taking the tape off your mouth. I need you to be quiet until I take care of this. Okay, baby?"

She nodded her head. She and her babies were going to live through this disaster and for that, she was more grateful than she'd ever been in her life.

The big guy held his phone in his hand. "What do want me to say to him?" he asked Drake.

"Tell him the woman shot your boy and she got away. Tell him she's hiding in one of the apartments upstairs and you need his help."

He nodded and pressed a button. Like an award-winning actor, the big guy began shouting, "Boss. That bitch got away. I don't know. She shot Otto while I was outside dealing with the car. But she didn't get very far. She's in one of the apartments above us, but I don't know which one. You're going to have to help me find her, boss. No, he didn't get the ring off her finger, but I swear none of this is my fault." He cut a nervous eye at Drake as he continued, "Okay, boss. I'll sit tight until you get here."

The big guy ended the call and asked Drake, "How'd I do?"

"You gave a great performance," Drake said and pulled the trigger. Blood and brains splattered the walls, and Harlow's muffled screams went unheard.

Drake cut the zip ties from her hands and feet. "I'm so sorry you had to go through this, Harlow. It's almost over, baby, and you're going to be safe and sound." He slowly removed the tape from her mouth.

"Drake, oh my God. Who are these people? How did you know how to find me?"

"I put a GPS on your phone."

"What?"

"To make sure I knew where you were if something like this happened. I watched the big Russian guy when he knocked with the secret code. That's how I was able to get in."

"But you said—"

"I know what I said, but we're going to have to talk about that later. Right now, I need you to go in the bedroom and wait until this is over."

"Why can't we leave, Drake? Let the police handle this."

"If we leave, it'll never be over. Lucio's enemies will hound us relentlessly. They're not going to stop until I make them stop."

"You told me we were safe. You promised on your life that it was over."

"I thought it was. I truly did. Trust, it ends tonight."

"You can't do this all alone. Why didn't you bring Alphonso with you? You need him, Drake."

"I sent him out of town, babe. With you being pregnant and Lucio all messed up, I'm trying to cut back on some of my business trips. Besides, this isn't Alphonso's problem; it's mine."

"I'm so scared, Drake."

"Whoever shows up at that door is going to lead me to each and every one of Lucio's enemies." Drake closed his eyes for a moment and shook his head bitterly. "Listen, you've seen enough bloodshed. I want you to go in the bedroom and wait there for me." He bent down and pulled a small gun from an ankle strap. "Take this gun and use it if you have to."

Holding the gun in a trembling hand, Harlow stepped over pools of blood and two dead bodies. She wandered out of the cluttered living room and made her way down the narrow hall.

Harlow wasn't religious. She hadn't been raised in the church, but she believed in God. And she asked Him to forgive Drake's sins. And to please have mercy on the souls of her unborn children.

She stiffened when she heard those eerily familiar knocks on the door and wondered if she and Drake were going to make it out of there alive.

Moments later, she heard a man's anguished yell. She considered hiding in the closet, but she had to get to Drake. Following her impulse, she raced toward the sound of the yell.

"Just tell me why?" Drake yelled with his gun pointed at an injured man.

Down on one knee, with a bullet wound in his shoulder, was Alphonso. Shocked, Harlow covered her mouth, muffling a cry.

"We're supposed to be partners, but what do I really have?" Alphonso said with his hand covering his bleeding wound.

"You've got a couple million." Drake sneered at him. "Plus the five you pocketed when you set up Lucio with the information you got from me. I trusted you and never once suspected you were involved in this. How could you torture an old man like that? An old man who'd been a father to me!"

"Man, fuck that old mobster. What was he gonna do with all that bread?"

"Why did you go after Harlow? How much was the price for my wife's life?"

"I wasn't going to hurt her. I just wanted a few more millions so I could be sitting as financially comfortable as you are."

"You're disgusting. So, what did you do with Lucio's money?"

"If I tell you, will you take me to a hospital? This shit is burning the fuck out of my shoulder."

"Where's Lucio's money, Alphonso?"

"It's in a box behind a false wall in my bedroom."

"All right. You get credit for cooperating. But suppose one of those stupid goons would have fucked up and hurt my wife. Hurt my child she's carrying. How could you put her at risk like that, man?"

"You can always make more babies. If not with her, then with some other ho. She got you soft, man. You're nothing like you used to be."

"I'm not so soft that I'm willing to spare your life," Drake said with a deadly look in his eyes. He raised his gun.

"We go too far back for all this, Drake. I told you where the money is. Now, let it go."

"Let it go?" Drake said incredulously.

"How many times have I put myself in the line of fire for your ass? Doesn't that mean anything? Are you seriously gonna let an old man, a bitch, and a baby come between the partnership we've built?"

Harlow had heard enough. Drake was hesitating, as if Alphonso had him mesmerized. She didn't recall her brain sending a signal to her legs, but suddenly found herself walking. Gun in hand, she moved across the room. And right before she got to Alphonso, Drake put a bullet through his head...right between his eyes.

Harlow frowned at the three bodies. "What are we going to do, now?"

"We're going home, baby. I'll have someone come and clean this up. It'll be like these three animals never existed."

"What about the driver?"

"They'll clean that up, too."

"His wife was pregnant, and now he's dead because of me."

"I'll make sure she's generously compensated."

"You act like money can fix everything."

"Maybe not, but it helps ease the pain."

VANGIE

Felder Ross had exaggerated when he said he could get a hearing in a few days. It took almost a month for Vangie to have her day in Family Court, and unfortunately things didn't go the way she had expected. Her high-priced attorney, with his tailor-made suit, strutted around like a peacock, showing off his extensive vocabulary by spouting big words. Each time he spoke on Vangie's behalf, he waved his hands around with dramatic flourish. But his posturing didn't accomplish a thing, except to annoy the judge.

Shawn's attorney looked unkempt in a cheap suit and dull, worn shoes. He even had an unsightly piece of lint stuck in the back of his hair, yet despite his appearance, he was able to impress the judge. The judge was so impressed she came to the conclusion that Yuri was better off remaining in his father's custody until the end of the school term.

When the judge offered Vangie weekend visitation, she gasped and desperately urged her attorney to do something. As soon as Felder Ross opened his mouth, the judge shut him down. But she allowed Shawn's attorney to emphasize that Vangie was on probation and was likely to return to prison after her assault and battery trial.

Vangie felt dizzy and swayed to one side. Her mother had accompanied her to court for emotional support. Barbara patted Vangie's hand and asked if she needed water.

"No, I'll be all right," Vangie said in a flat voice while looking dazed.

"Are you sure?"

"I said I'm all right!" Vangie's voice rose in agitation.

"Well, you don't have to bite my head off; I'm only trying to be helpful. My goodness." Barbara rolled her eyes and sprang up from her seat, exiting the courtroom as soon as the hearing was adjourned.

Felder Ross looked sheepish as he approached Vangie. From the corner of her eye, she could see Shawn and Jojina giving each other high-fives. Her life was an unending nightmare.

"I did the best I could."

"Really?" She rolled her eyes toward the ceiling.

"We were lucky to get weekend visitation."

"You didn't tell me that visitation was the most I could hope for when you accepted that fat-ass check I gave you. You led me to believe that it was only a matter of time until my son would be back home where he belongs."

"I'm sorry it didn't work out that way. But don't worry; I'm going to continue to pursue this. Of course, we'll have to wait for the outcome of your criminal trial."

She sucked her teeth. "I'm sick of spending money on you crooked attorneys. None of y'all fulfill your promises," Vangie said belligerently and then stormed out of the courtroom. When she reached the corridor, her heavy footsteps came to an abrupt halt. She gaped in disbelief, as she witnessed her mother grinning and talking with Shawn and Jojina as if they were her family.

"Mom!" Vangie bellowed.

Barbara made a comment to Shawn and Jojina that Vangie couldn't hear, but judging by her mother's expression, Vangie determined she had made some sort of apology for Vangie's rude behavior.

Shawn and Jojina headed for the bank of elevators, and Vangie made long, angry strides toward her mother. "What the hell is your problem, Mom?"

"What are you talking about?"

"You know damn well what I'm talking about."

Barbara gave Vangie a sidelong glance. "You done lost your damn mind. You better watch your mouth, little girl. How dare you fix your lips to disrespect me? I'm not one of your friends, you know. I'll slap that sass right out of your mouth," she threatened, getting close to Vangie and threatening her with a hand that trembled with fury.

Vangie backed down. "I'm just saying, Mom. Why would you be over there consorting with the enemy?"

"I don't have a quarrel with Shawn. I'm trying to keep the peace so I can maintain a good relationship with my grandson, whom I haven't seen in far too long. If I leave it up to you, Yuri will be a grown man before I see him again. Now you can act all crazy if you want to...getting into fights and whatnot, but I'm going to conduct myself in a civilized manner and try to get along with folks, whether you like it or not!"

Vangie had spent so much money on Family Law attorneys; she couldn't afford to pay her defense attorney's fee. He was replaced with a public defender in her assault case. The public defender was a nice man, young, and ambitious. Still, she doubted if he would actually be able to get her out of the mess she was in. Everyone knew that public defenders hardly ever won their cases. She feared that she'd be going back to prison and began to mentally prepare herself.

❤ ❤ ❤

Zenith's place had become a refuge. Vangie threw clothes in an overnight bag, grateful that she had someone to run to in her time of need. Without Yuri, her apartment was as quiet as a tomb, and she was a nervous wreck waiting for the days to pass until their first weekend visit together.

In the midst of packing, Zenith called.

"Hey, baby. I'm almost finished packing. I'll be there soon."

"I was thinking we could use a change of scenery, so how about you invite me over. Let me spend the night at your place for a change."

"That's not a problem, Zenith. As long as we're together, it doesn't matter if we're at my place or yours."

"That's what I wanted to hear; I'm on my way."

"Hurry up, baby; I miss you," Vangie said with a smile.

❤ ❤ ❤

The glow of candlelight illuminated the bouquet of white roses with pink tips that Zenith had given to Vangie. Cuddled together, naked in Vangie's bed, they shared a pint of ice cream while watching a rerun of *Zane's The Jump Off*.

"Those brothers are hot enough to make me rethink my sexual orientation," Zenith commented with a laugh.

Deep in thought, Vangie didn't respond.

"What's wrong, sweetness?"

"Nothing. I was staring at the flowers and thinking how lucky I am to have you in my life. You're not only beautiful; you're so thoughtful and sweet."

"Beautiful? You mean handsome, don't you?" Zenith said with a crooked smile.

"You know what I mean. With you, I get the best of both worlds."

"I don't know what you mean. Explain it to me."

"I feel like we have this shared bond of sisterhood. But when you're making love to me, when you're deep inside me, you possess the sex appeal, the strength, and the power of a man. You're everything I want. The missing piece in the puzzle that's been my life." Vangie lowered her eyes. "I didn't plan to, but I can feel myself falling hard. I don't know what I'd do if I didn't have you." She shook her head and an unhappy expression formed on her face.

Zenith tucked a finger under Vangie's chin and tilted it up. "What's up with the sad face?"

"I'm sprung. And that scares me."

"That makes two of us, so cheer up. If what we're feeling is love, let's embrace it. There's no reason to be afraid of it. Now, stop hogging the ice cream." Zenith took the container of ice cream from Vangie's hand.

The sound of keys jangling outside the front door startled Vangie and Zenith.

"Who the fuck is coming in here?" Zenith asked, staring at Vangie in astonishment.

"My mom, I guess. She's the only person who has keys. But I have no idea what she's doing here." Vangie jumped out of bed and ran to the closet, and as she reached for her robe, she heard the lock turn.

"Is anybody in here? Vangie? Are you home?" Barbara yelled from the hallway.

"Yeah, Mom. Don't come back here; I'll be right out." Vangie was panicked, and it was on the tip of her tongue to ask Zenith to hide. But before she could formulate the words, her mother was standing in the doorway of her bedroom, looking from Vangie to Zenith with her mouth hanging open.

"What are you doing here, Mom?" Vangie threw on the robe and Zenith pulled the sheet up, covering herself.

"Who is she and what the hell are you doing, Evangeline?"

"I…we…" Vangie looked at Zenith helplessly.

"I'm Vangie's girlfriend, Zenith. It's nice to meet you."

Frowning, Barbara reared back. "You're Vangie's girlfriend?" She shot a hostile look at Vangie. "And when did you plan on telling me you turned gay?"

"I don't consider myself gay."

Barbara snorted. "Well, what do you call it when you're laying up in bed with a naked woman?"

"I call it being in love."

"Oh, really? Well, I call it being nasty and disgraceful and acting like Satan's daughter. You should be ashamed of yourself, Evangeline."

Vangie sighed. "Why did you come over and use your key without telling me?"

"When I talked to you earlier today, you said it was hard to sleep here without Yuri and you were staying the night with a friend. I thought you were referring to a decent friend, like Harlow, but I was obviously wrong." A look of distaste crossed Barbara's face as she gazed at Zenith.

"My plans changed, Mom. I decided to stay home, but what are you doing here? Do you come around, snooping through my personal things whenever I'm not home?"

Barbara's face showed fierce indignation. "I don't have time to be snooping through your shit. I came over out of the goodness of my heart because Shawn called and asked me if I could pick up Yuri's football cleats. He's going to sign Yuri up for a Pee Wee League in his nice, new neighborhood."

"Why are you still communicating with Shawn? He shouldn't even be calling you. And anyway, I paid for those cleats—not Shawn. You should have told his cheap ass to go out and buy Yuri a new pair."

Barbara's eyelids fluttered; her lips tightened. "I don't know who you think you're talking to, but you had better watch your language when you're speaking to me."

"I apologize, Mom. But for real, though—"

Barbara threw up her hand. "I don't want to hear it. Now if you two deviants don't mind, I'm going—"

"Why we gotta be deviants? That's not even right, Mom." Vangie sent Zenith an apologetic look for her mother's ignorance.

"There's no way to sugarcoat it; the behavior I just walked in on is deviant and perverted."

"I think I better leave," Zenith said quietly.

"You got that right. Take your depraved ways on out of here… corrupting my child's morals," Barbara said with her arms folded.

"Mom, stop it! Don't talk to her like that. This is my apartment; you can't come over here, telling me what to do."

"Oh, so you're gonna take the side of a goddamn bulldagger over your own mother?"

"Mom, you're embarrassing me, and you should be ashamed of your ignorance."

"Oh, I'm embarrassing you, am I?" Barbara asked incredulously. "Well, I hope the hell you don't think I'm proud of what your nasty ass is over here doing. How long have you been involved in this funny business, Evangeline?"

"What I do in my personal life is none of your concern."

"You're right about that. I don't want anything to do with this mess. Do me a favor—please don't ring my phone anymore. Because as far as I'm concerned, I no longer have a daughter."

And on that note, Barbara whirled on her heels and hurried out of Vangie's room. She could be heard bumping around in Yuri's room, and then there was the loud bang when she slammed the front door.

"Wow. Please tell me what just happened?" Zenith asked, making a funny face in an attempt to lighten the mood.

Vangie tried to laugh with Zenith, but her mouth began to twitch before she burst into tears.

NIVEA

As if things couldn't get any worse, her new condo had a terrible mold issue that conveniently went undetected until after she made settlement and after she'd given up her townhouse. Her cash flow was running perilously low and making matters worse, with the income Dr. Sandburg had declared, he was ordered by the court to pay her only $1,500 a month. It was an embarrassment to have a child by an old, supposedly wealthy doctor and end up with only a pittance.

And she missed Malcolm so badly, it seemed that her very soul was crying out in agony.

She and Mackenzie were staying at a hotel, which was expensive and terribly inconvenient. Most of their wardrobe and personal possessions were in storage, and Nivea hated living like a gypsy.

Needing to lash out at someone, she called Dr. Sandburg and called him every name in the book. "Do you realize your daughter is residing in a goddamn hotel? God only knows how many diseases she could pick from living like a transient. You know damn well you can afford to pay much more than you're giving me. This is a disgrace. You should be ashamed to call yourself a father."

Dr. Sandburg couldn't get a word in edgewise until Nivea finally took a breath.

"You're right. My behavior has been deplorable," he said. "I was upset and blamed you for the demise of my marriage, but it wasn't your fault. I apologize."

Nivea's heart didn't soften. "Your apology will not pay my bills. How can you look in the mirror knowing that you're not doing anywhere near what you should be doing for your only child in the world?"

"I have a great deal of guilt," he moaned.

"Well, what are you going to do about it?"

"I'm going to set up a trust fund for Mackenzie. Make sure she has a nest egg when she becomes an adult?"

"How is she supposed to survive in the meantime?" Nivea yelled.

"I don't know. I'm not in my right mind. My marriage is over," he repeated and actually began to cry. "I've been married for most of my adult life. I don't know how to be by myself. I can't make wise decisions. I'm lost without Rachel's guidance," he wailed.

"You and Rachel are divorced now. So you need to get over it and man up. You need to take care of your responsibility and stop whining like a child."

He sniffled into the phone. "That's the way Rachel always spoke to me. She was my backbone. She was the person who toughened me up."

"Well, I'm the one who's going to toughen you up, now."

"You are?"

"Yes. I want to go back to court and I want you to declare your true income."

"I can't do that."

"Yes, you can. For your daughter."

"My money is well hidden and I don't want any problems with the IRS."

"Stop being so selfish, Bertram. When you're a parent, your children have to come first. Don't you understand?"

"In a way."

Nivea took a deep breath, trying to keep her temper under control. "Bertram, how much money do you have stashed?"

"Millions."

Nivea's heartbeat picked up. "How many millions?"

"I don't know, exactly."

"Over ten million?"

"Absolutely."

"And you don't want Mackenzie to benefit from your money until she's grown?"

"I think that's best. She can't appreciate it now."

"But I can," Nivea said in soft tone. "You said you're accustomed to being married to a strong woman who can guide you. Well, what better woman than the mother of your child?"

"You're not as strong as Rachel."

"Yes, I am. Without me, you wouldn't have ever known about your virile, baby-producing sperm. If you marry me, I'll control you with an iron fist; I promise you, Bertram."

Nivea thought about the way her mother had always worn the pants in their family. Her dad never seemed to mind. In fact, he seemed to delight in her mother's domination. Nivea had grown up watching the dynamic between her parents, and she knew exactly how to give Bertram what he needed. Most of all, she knew how to get his money and make it her own after she became his lawful wedded wife.

It didn't matter that she didn't love him and he didn't love her. Each had something that the other needed to feel secure. Her thoughts turned to Malcolm and she shook her head. Sooner or later, men like Malcolm always broke a woman's heart. At least with Bertram, her heart would never be broken again.

Bertram's money would give Nivea a bigger thrill than any orgasm she'd ever had.

Imagining the way her mother spoke to her father, Nivea said, "Bertram, we need to pick our rings as soon as possible. But I won't stand for anything cheesy."

"Well, I have a jeweler friend who could—"

"No, no, no, your taste in jewelry is horrid. I'll handle everything."

"Yes, dear," Bertram said.

VANGIE

So many things had changed about Yuri. In the weeks he'd been living with his father, he seemed to have sprouted several inches taller and had put on extra weight. *What's Jojina feeding my child?* Vangie noticed other changes. A subtle difference in his vocal quality and his pattern of speech. There were nuances in his facial expressions that reminded her of Shawn, and his conversation was peppered with slang words that she assumed he'd picked up from Jojina's little thugs.

Her son was no longer the cuddly, high-spirited, cheerful kid he once was. He was quiet. More serious—practically sullen. He'd stiffened in her arms when she greeted him with a tight hug, and it was like pulling teeth trying to get him to open up and communicate with her the way he used to.

On the way to her car, she reached for Yuri's hand and he balled his fist and kept his arm pressed against his side. That rebuff hurt Vangie's feelings, but she let it go.

"What do you want to do, Yuri? This is our special time together, and we can go to the movies, the arcade…whatever you'd like to do."

"I don't care," he said with an indifferent shrug.

"*Monsters University* is playing. Or we could go see *Despicable Me 2*," Vangie said exuberantly.

He frowned and then looked at her like she was crazy. "I'm not a baby." The snorting sound that followed his statement made it clear that he considered his mother's film recommendations as absurdly childish and beneath him.

"What about *Man of Steel* or *World War Z?*"

His frown deepened. "I already saw both those flicks."

Flicks? She winced as if Yuri had used profanity. She'd never heard him refer to a movie as a flick. It was new terminology and another painful reminder that someone other than she was raising and influencing her child.

"We don't have to go to the movies if you don't want to. You love Dave & Buster's; wanna go there?"

"I guess," Yuri muttered disinterestedly.

Before he climbed into the back seat, Vangie ruffled his hair. He reacted with an almost imperceptible wince, as if he didn't want his mother to touch him.

"What's wrong, Yuri?"

"Nothing."

"Okay, but if something's bothering you, we can talk about it."

"I'm good."

"You're good? When did you start saying that?"

"I don't know."

Vangie sighed in resignation. "Buckle your seatbelt, honey."

"My dad doesn't make me."

"I'm not your dad; buckle up," she said firmly.

Discontented, Yuri muttered under his breath, and Vangie didn't call him on it. She had to pick her battles carefully if she wanted to win back the affection of her son.

She spent much more than she should have at D&B, but she wanted to make sure Yuri had a good time. It was nice to see a smile finally blossom on his face, even if it took three containers stuffed to the brim with redeemable tickets to make it happen.

"Why do you keep staring at me, Mom?" Yuri asked while he and Vangie were side by side, playing Skee-Ball.

"Because I've missed you so much and I can't get over how mature you've gotten."

The compliment brought another smile on his face and Vangie felt relieved that she and Yuri were finally breaking the ice between them.

"Do you want to eat here or get pizza at Little Caesars?"

"I like Domino's better."

"Since when? You love Little Caesars."

"Not anymore."

So much had changed, and Vangie had to accept it. If she could do it all over again, she would have never attacked Jojina at court. But she couldn't undo what she'd done. All she could do now was move forward, work on rebuilding her relationship with her son, and pray that the public defender could work a miracle and get her off with only probation.

They finished their pizza and were headed for the car. "Do you wanna get water ice at Rita's?" she asked with a big smile.

"No, I'm ready to go home."

"Really? I'm surprised you're ready to call it a day, already. It's only seven o'clock."

Yuri lifted a shoulder in response.

"I'll tell you what, when we get home, I'll let you download a game for your computer. But I'm not spending more than ten dollars. Okay?"

"I don't want a game; I want to go home," Yuri whined.

"What's wrong, honey? Don't you feel okay?" Vangie pressed the back of her hand against his forehead, checking to see if he was warm.

"I'm not sick; I'm just ready to go home."

"We're going home," Vangie said in annoyance. She'd bent over backward, trying to make sure she and Yuri had a nice day, and now that the fun was over, he was getting cranky for no reason.

They rode in silence for a few minutes, and when she exited the expressway, Yuri leaned forward with his face in a panic. "This isn't the way home."

"Of course, it is. What are you talking about?"

"I don't want to go back to your apartment. I want to go home to *my* house."

Vangie was too stunned to speak.

"The whole family's going electric kart racing at Speed Raceway tomorrow. I wanna go, too. Can you take me home? Please, Mom. I'm ready to go."

"But you just got here," she said in a pleading tone. "I can't believe you want to leave, already."

Her hands were shaking so badly, she had to pull over to the curb and try and collect herself. "Listen to me; the judge says you have to stay with me every weekend."

"I don't wanna be with you every weekend," Yuri yelled.

"I'm your mother, and I've been missing you like crazy. Haven't you missed me at all, Yuri?"

"Sometimes," he mumbled.

"I'm sorry for the way your life was disrupted, and I take full responsibility. But we have to move forward. Do you understand?"

"I don't want to stay the whole weekend."

"Why do you keep saying that? Do you realize how much you're hurting me?"

"I'm sorry, but I'm ready to go home." Tears of frustration spilled from Yuri's eyes.

Vangie felt helpless and heartbroken. After being separated for such a long time, she'd expected Yuri to be ecstatic about spending time with her. But he was forlorn and shedding tears as if being with her was a harsh punishment.

"You're angry with me, Yuri. I get it. You think I abandoned you.

But I didn't; I got locked up for fighting Jojina and I lost custody of you. I've been fighting to get you back ever since. I'm not proud of the behavior that led to that and I hope you can forgive me for not being there for you." Vangie had been avoiding the topic of prison all day, hoping that Shawn had shielded Yuri from knowing the sordid truth, but she could no longer avoid the subject. She had to come clean and explain why he was no longer living with her.

To punctuate his displeasure, Yuri kicked the back of the passenger seat and cried harder.

"Please, sweetheart, don't kick the seat. Mommy's sorry."

"Everybody's always teasing me."

"Who teases you?"

"Devontay and Javarious. They said you had to eat cats while you were in jail."

Vangie frowned in confusion. "What? Don't listen to those ignorant little future convicts. They don't know what they're talking about. The food was terrible, but we weren't fed cats or any other house pets." Vangie shook her head in disbelief.

"Devontay said he heard Jojina telling one of her friends that you probably started licking a lot of cats while you were in jail with all those women."

Vangie gasped, suddenly grasping the true meaning of the crude comment. Ironically, she was attracted to women now, but her sexual preference had nothing to do with the three days she'd spent in jail.

Shawn and his girlfriend were poisoning her son against her. They were also teaching him to be homophobic. There was no telling how they'd react once they found out about her relationship with Zenith.

She could no longer lie down and accept the judge's ruling. She had to fight harder to get her child back.

Additionally, she had to stop acting like a guilty, unfit mother; it was time to start using tough love when dealing with Yuri. Today would be the last time she would ever try to buy her son's affection with expensive outings and junk food. From now on, they were going to talk about their feelings, and for the duration of this visit and all future visits, she expected him to treat her with respect.

"Listen to me, Yuri."

"I don't wanna listen."

"Listen to me, dammit!" she yelled. Yuri's eyes bulged and he sat up straight.

Vangie twisted around in her seat and pointed a finger at him. "Your bad attitude has got to stop. Now, it hurt my feelings when you first arrived and refused to give me a hug. But I'm over that now. You don't have to hug me if you don't want to, but all the mumbling under your breath and the smart little comments you've been making have got to stop." Getting worked up, Vangie wagged her finger in Yuri's face. "And if you ever kick the back of my car seat or anything else, I will whip your little ass. Do you hear me?"

Sniffling, Yuri nodded his head.

Clearly, their relationship had been fractured, and it occurred to Vangie that she and Yuri might need family counseling. There was no point in asking Shawn to join them. He was much too narrow-minded to agree to therapy.

HARLOW

Sitting in a wheelchair, Lucio wore a solemn expression as Drake pushed him across the tarmac and toward the waiting plane. Harlow and the nurse that was hired to tend to Lucio during the flight walked behind them, side by side.

Lucio wistfully reminisced about the good old days when he was a force to be reckoned with, when he was feared. A time before he'd become a weak old man. No man would have dared to confront him, much less kidnap, torture, and leave him for dead. And anyone who had the balls to try would have paid dearly. Lucio would have methodically taken the perpetrator's family out, one by one. Saving the best for last, he would have had the brazen cocksucker begging and pleading for a merciful death.

As a hint of a smile began to form, Lucio's reverie was interrupted by Drake's voice. "After our child is born and is old enough to travel, Harlow and I are coming to Italy to get drunk with you in your sister's vineyard."

"My vineyard," Lucio corrected. Though his jaw had been recently unwired, it was difficult for him to enunciate more than a few words at a time.

"All right, but you're going to have to dispute that issue with Gina," Drake joked.

Drake stepped aside, so the nurse could adjust the lap blanket that was placed across Lucio's frail thighs.

Moments before boarding the plane, Lucio frantically grabbed Drake's hand. "It was your friend," he told Drake. "He left me for dead."

"I realize that's what you were trying to tell me while your jaw was wired shut. But don't worry, I took care of him."

Lucio jabbed his fists at the air, his way of saying, "Yes!"

He's sleeping with the fishes," Drake said with a wink.

"Did he suffer like I did?" Lucio's voice was garbled and scratchy.

Drake took a velvet pouch out of his pocket and gave it to him. Lucio peeked inside and upon seeing a severed finger wrapped in plastic, his lips curled in satisfaction.

Drake left out the fact that the finger had been removed postmortem. But what the old man didn't know wouldn't hurt him.

Harlow and Drake watched in silence as Lucio's plane disappeared from sight. Glancing up at her husband, Harlow noticed a single tear streaming down his face. No words were necessary. Harlow squeezed his hand reassuringly. Still staring off into the distance, Drake brought her hand to his lips and kissed it.

It had been a long emotional day and Harlow was glad to be home. She undressed and put on a powder-blue nightie and crawled into bed next to Drake. He turned over and kissed her cleavage.

"I'm really loving these big ol' pregnant boobies," he said and kissed each swollen breast. His hand skimmed down to her stomach and he gave her a curious look. "Wow, seems like your tummy grew overnight. You been feeding my boy power shakes?" he joked.

"Who said it's a boy?"

"I say it's a boy. How much do you wanna bet?"

"A night at the symphony?"

"A night where?"

"I've developed an appreciation for classical music. I want us to get dressed up and go to a New York Philharmonic concert."

"Uh, sure. But if it's a boy, you have to spend a week in Italy with Lucio and his sister."

"You don't have to bribe me; I want to visit Lucio. I've grown quite fond of the old man."

"Thanks, Harlow. That means a lot. So, when are we going to find out the sex of the baby?"

"Actually, I already have." Harlow pulled open the drawer of her bedside table. She took out the most recent ultrasound picture and handed it to Drake.

He squinted at the image. "I don't know what I'm looking at. Seems like I'm seeing double."

"You are. Those are our sons. Identical twin boys. Do you know how rare that is?"

"We're having twin boys? Really? Oh, man, I'm ready to start handing out cigars, right now."

"Do people still do that?" Harlow asked.

"I don't know. But I'm definitely going to be handing out the most expensive Cuban cigars I can find."

Nestled in Drake's strong arms, Harlow felt a peace she'd never known wash over her. Filled with gratitude, she began, "You know, I never would have imagined this life I've shared with you. Never thought I deserved this kind of happiness, but here I am. Sweetheart, despite the mistakes we've made in the past and despite what we believe we do or don't deserve, these babies are a sign from God that we've been forgiven, and we're doubly blessed."

"Triple-blessed because I have you. I love you so much, Harlow."

As Drake's lips brushed across Harlow's open mouth, she murmured, "I know Drake and believe me, I love you, too."

VANGIE

Sunday evening at six, Vangie dropped Yuri off at the designated hand-off spot.

"Hey, man," Shawn greeted Yuri without giving Vangie as much as a glance.

Vangie slid down the window. "Can we talk, Shawn?"

"Get in the car," he told Yuri. And then gave Vangie a scornful frown. "What do want?"

"Can't we be civil toward each other? For Yuri's sake, we should make an effort to smooth this friction between us…we need to try and get along."

He blew her off with a rude hand gesture. "Man, I'm not trying to hear shit you have to say." He turned away and sauntered toward his car.

"Fuck you, Shawn. You Section Eight-living, bum!" she yelled, losing her temper.

Shawn laughed tauntingly, and kept walking as if Vangie was too insignificant to trade insults with.

Fucking asshole. I hate him so much. Nerves rattled, Vangie turned on the radio, hoping music would calm her down. Times like this, she was grateful to have Zenith in her corner, and was eager to get to her girl's place to relax and unwind.

When her phone rang, she expected the call to be from Zenith, and was surprised to see her mother's name on the screen. Vangie took a deep breath before answering.

"Hi, Mom," she said pleasantly, but was braced for a big argument with her mother.

"I can't believe you didn't bring Yuri over to see me. Is he still with you?" Barbara asked in a pissed-off tone.

"No, Shawn just picked him up."

"It was very inconsiderate of you not to bring my grandson over to see me."

"The last time we talked, you were upset with me. I didn't want any drama during the short amount of time that Yuri was with me."

"Oh, it's my fault that you're disgracing yourself and offending the Lord?"

"You're being offensive and I don't want Yuri to be subjected to your hateful words."

"I guess you never heard of grandparents' rights, huh?"

Vangie sighed. "I'm not trying to keep you from seeing Yuri; but I won't allow you to poison his mind. His father and his girlfriend are already doing that."

Barbara sighed heavily. "I have a question for you."

Here we go. "What's that, Mom?"

"Has the devil left your body yet?'

"What are you talking about?" Vangie turned the radio down in order to hear her mother more clearly.

"You know exactly what I'm talking about. I'm talking about you and that big bulldagger."

"Her name is Zenith, and I'd appreciate it if you didn't make homophobic slurs."

"Mmm-hmm. Whatever. All I'm gonna say is, God will never bless a mess."

"Who are you calling a mess? If that's the case, you shouldn't look for any blessings, either. You're shacking up with Mr. Harold, and he's a married man."

"Harold has been legally separated for five years."

"He's still married and in the eyes of God, you're fornicating."

"The Lord doesn't tolerate disrespect to parents. All that kissing, fondling, and having relations with another woman is going to send you straight to hell. You will be struck down and burned in hot flames, and Satan's wicked face will be smiling down at you."

"You sound deranged, Mom. For real."

"You need to repent, Evangeline. I want to see my daughter in heaven. I'm not only looking out for your physical body; I also care about your soul. After that nasty mess I witnessed at your apartment, I planned to never speak to you again, but as your mother, it's my duty to try to get you back on track. Vangie, get a hold of yourself; don't let the devil win."

"You're really going overboard, Mom."

"I'm speaking the truth."

"Oh, yeah? I'm going to hell, but all your sins are forgiven, huh? I finally found someone who's kind and caring. We have something very special, so why can't you be happy for me?"

"What is wrong with you? Did that new fella, Alphonso, dump you, too? Are times that hard that you don't think you can get another man? No one could have ever made me believe that my daughter would turn into a rainbow person. What's next—marching in parades so you and that big bulldagger can have some gay rights and get married?" Barbara grunted in disgust. "I swear, homosexuality is taking over the world."

"Mom, I'm not looking for your approval—"

"Hush, Vangie. That's not you talking; the devil has a hold of you, girl. Oh, good Lord, please help this child of mine," Barbara pleaded, launching into fervent prayer. "Have mercy on her wicked soul. She's lost, Lord, and she needs Your guidance. Help her, heavenly Father."

Vangie took a deep, tired breath. "Mom, please. I can't deal with this right now."

"Why not? Are you too busy for the Lord? I feel sorry for you; your soul is lost, child. If you don't believe me, listen to these passages. I have the Bible right here in my hand and it says: *You shall not lie with a male as with a woman. It is an abomination. Nor shall you mate with any animal, to defile yourself with. Nor shall any woman stand before an animal to mate with it. It is perversion. Do not defile yourselves with any of these things; for by all these the nations are defiled, which I am casting out before you.* That's from the Book of Leviticus, honey. I gave you the Lord's holy word!"

"Yeah, well, while you're reading your Bible, you need to find the passage about fornicating, and playing the numbers," Vangie said and then hung up on her mother.

She immediately called Zenith. "Hey, baby. I'm on my way over. Do you want me to pick up anything from the store?"

"Nope. Just bring your sexy self. I can tell you need some TLC."

"How do you know?"

"I can hear the stress in your voice. When you get here, I'll have champagne and a hot bath waiting for you, and while I'm bathing you, I'm going to hand-feed you sushi."

❤ ❤ ❤

After a relaxing bath with a glass of champagne and sushi platter, Vangie and Zenith never made it out of the bathroom.

Their bodies were still soapy and wet when Zenith began kissing a trail down Vangie's moist arm, all the way down to her open palm. Soon she was lapping at Vangie's fingers and sucking each one. Wasting no time, her hands explored Vangie's body, lavishing her with the soft, feathery touches that made her body arch and tremble.

She gently squeezed breasts as if checking the ripeness of fruit. Vangie whimpered and opened her legs for Zenith.

"Fuck my pussy, Zenith," she pleaded.

"No, you're not ready yet."

"Yes, I am." Vangie spread her legs wider, displaying an open pussy with swollen lips that were glistening and dewy with lust.

Pressing her mouth against Vangie's vaginal lips, Zenith's tongue darted and probed. Her tongue circled and flicked against Vangie's sensitive nub, causing friction on her clit that increased the tension in Vangie's writhing body. Each tongue thrust ignited fireworks— little rockets of passion bursting inside her until Vangie's groans increased in volume.

Vangie moaned as she dug her hand into the thick mass of coils on one side of Zenith's head, grabbed a fistful and yanked as she cried out. "Fuck me, baby. I'm ready to feel you inside me."

Zenith's tongue remained busy as she stealthily reached behind her and opened the bottom drawer of a wicker chest and retrieved her dick. As she pulled her mouth away, Vangie begged her not to stop.

"I got something else for you, baby." Zenith said, strapping on the male apparatus. She mounted Vangie and spiraled into her. Making love with slow, sensual movements that filled and touched her in all her most sensitive places. She gave Vangie deep and unrelenting dick strokes while kissing her passionately at the same time.

"I'm coming," Vangie murmured as slow waves of warmth crept up her body. Recognizing the beginning of an orgasm, she wrapped her arms around Zenith, as if anchoring herself against a storm that could potentially sweep her away.

"Let it go, baby. I want you to explode."

Vangie lifted up a little and gave a hoarse yelp as her inner walls contracted and clenched multiple times around the plastic device that felt better than any human dick that had ever entered her body.

"Get it, baby," Zenith encouraged and Vangie held on tighter. She didn't release her iron grip around Zenith until her body stopped shaking.

Vangie looked into Zenith's eyes and exclaimed, "If this isn't love, I don't know what it is. I really love you. I mean it. Do you love me?" she asked, her voice cracking, fearful that Zenith would deliver bad news.

Zenith gazed at Vangie and didn't speak for a long moment. Brows furrowed as she carefully chose her words, she finally said, "I don't want to get caught up in the 'L' word. Like I told you, my heart's been broken to pieces more times than I care to count. Words are easy to say. Let me show you how I feel by the way I treat you. Respect, kindness, and going that extra mile equal love. Now, do I have to tell you I love you?"

"I guess I'm a little insecure, but doesn't compromising play a big part in a healthy relationship?"

"Yeah, I suppose so."

"Then why don't you tell me what I want to hear," Vangie persisted.

"I love you, Vangie," Zenith said with a soft smile.

VANGIE

Zenith and Vangie were in bed watching *Ancient Aliens*. Vangie didn't particularly like the show, but Zenith was crazy about everything on The History Channel. The back of her head was pressed against Zenith's bare chest, and Zenith's arms were wrapped loosely around Vangie's waist. The feeling of their naked skin on skin was so soothing, it enabled Vangie to endure the weird, alien program.

During a commercial break Zenith said excitedly, "My exhibit is next Friday night. I can't believe it's finally happening. My agent is expecting a huge turnout. She's already sold some of my pieces. They'll be hung with the others, but a card that says, 'SOLD,' will be placed beneath those photographs. I'm thrilled but I'm also really nervous."

"There's nothing to be nervous about. Your work is amazing and you know it. You're going to be a celebrated photographer," Vangie said, giving Zenith an encouraging smile.

"Yeah, I'm self-assured about most things, but when it comes to my work, I feel vulnerable. Like I'm walking around naked while other people examine my body, looking for and pointing out the flaws."

"Well, if that's the case, you should be feeling completely confident because your body doesn't have any flaws. You're built like a female gladiator."

"Shut up," Zenith said, laughing. "Are you deliberately trying to make me blush?"

"I'm being serious. Did I ever tell you how I felt the first time I saw you?"

"No, but I'm curious."

"You didn't look real."

"Huh?"

"You looked so amazing and extraordinary; it seemed like you should have been wearing a cape. Like Wonder Woman or Super-girl."

Zenith laughed louder. "Stop fuckin' with me."

"I'm dead serious. And I had to have you. Then the bartender tried to burst my bubble by telling me that you're nothing more than a heartless bitch. She said some chick tried to kill herself over you."

Zenith lowered her gaze. "There's some truth in that."

"Really?" Vangie's eyes widened.

"Her name was Molly, but what she did to herself wasn't because I broke her heart."

"Well, what happened?"

"She had a boyfriend back in her hometown. She told me she broke it off with him, but he came to visit her, and I found out she'd never told him she was playing on the other team. So, I told him, which was really immature of me. I've grown a lot since then. Her boyfriend threatened to tell her family and hometown friends, and Molly couldn't deal with it."

"How do you feel about her living on the streets now?"

"I try not to think about it."

"That's your solution?"

"Don't judge me, Vangie. You don't know what I've been through with that girl and her addiction. I put her in rehab again and again.

I've let her stay here with me. But she repaid my kindness by stealing from me. Money. Credit cards. Jewelry and my camera. My fuckin' camera! After she stole my camera, I was finally through. How much abuse is a person supposed to withstand?"

"Okay, I get it. But, I had to ask you about it."

Zenith nodded. She had a sad, faraway look in her eyes.

Vangie stroked her softly on the arm. "I'm sorry I brought up the past. Okay, baby. You look so sad; what can I do to cheer you up?"

A little smile appeared on Zenith's face. "You can be my date at my show."

"Oh, the show on Friday night?"

"Yes, and I want you to wear something super sexy. I'm wearing a custom-made tuxedo jacket over tights that have hand-sewn crystals going up the outer legs. The designer is a local woman. And she's not charging me a thing," Zenith exclaimed with joy sparkling in her eyes and ringing in her voice.

"I'm so sorry, but I can't go to your show."

"You're kidding. It's the biggest moment of my life and I want to share it with you and you don't want to go? Why not?"

"I get visits with my son every weekend; you know that."

"Yeah, but the show only lasts a few hours. Can't your mom babysit Friday night?"

"It's not that simple. Yuri is sort of detaching from me. His father and his fiancée are poisoning his mind against me. And you heard what my mother had to say about us; I can't trust her not to fill his head with her opinions. Besides, I've been away from my child for so long, I can't afford to lose one minute of the time we have together."

"Okay. No problem, there're plenty of bitches who'd love to take your place."

"Come on, Zenith, don't be like that. Give me some time to

rebuild the bond between my son and me. I'm all yours every day of the week, but I have to devote my weekends to Yuri."

"I said I understand. What I don't understand is why you can't give me three fucking hours on such an important night? Three fucking hours! I think you're being ridiculous, Vangie. My feelings are hurt. But I'm not a mother so I don't fully understand what you're going through." Zenith caressed Vangie's face. "I'm sorry for blowing up. Forgive me?"

Vangie nodded.

"Hey, I have an idea. Why don't you and I take Yuri somewhere fun on Saturday? Don't you think it's time that I meet your little man? We need to start having family outings so he can start getting to know me."

"I can't do that. I can't subject Yuri to my sexual preferences. He's young and impressionable and it'll embarrass him."

"Am I hearing you right? Did you use the word, 'subject'? You said that as if introducing your son to me is akin to subjecting him to a disease."

"I didn't mean it that way."

"Then how'd you mean it?"

"I only meant… Well, he's going through a hard time. His step-brothers are teasing him about the time I was incarcerated. They've been throwing slurs and alluding to the fact that I've been having sex with women."

"Well, you have, so what's the problem?"

Vangie shrugged. "I'm not ready to share that with the world."

"Oh, it's okay to eat my pussy and suck my dick behind closed doors. It's okay to bust multiple nuts on my strap-on. As long as your family doesn't know."

"I'm confused. It's too soon to tell people about us. I'm sort of still attracted to men, you know."

"This is bullshit. You told me you loved me, forced me to say that shit back, and now you're telling me you're still yearning for a man?" Zenith's hands began to shake.

"I do love you. Honest, I do. But I'm not sure if this is the kind of lifestyle for me to drag my son into." Vangie rubbed Zenith's arm, trying to soothe her.

Zenith pulled away from her. "Don't touch me. In fact, put your goddamn clothes on and take your ass out of here before I beat the shit out of you."

"Zenith!"

"I'm serious!" Zenith spoke through clenched teeth. She grabbed a hank of Vangie's hair and yanked it hard.

"Ow, you're hurting me."

"That's why you need to hurry up and go while you can still walk, you fuckin' shady bitch!" She gave Vangie a hard shove that sent her crashing to the floor. Zenith glared down at her. "The old me would be stomping your ass for the way you played me. You're lucky I have a lot more self-control."

Vangie dressed quickly and by the time she made it to the front door, she could hear Zenith sobbing. It was a heartbreakingly mournful sound.

Vangie sat in her car crying as hard as Zenith had. But she had to put her child first. Yuri was going through the most difficult time of his young life, and now was not the time for her to indulge her own selfish desires.

It would be different if she'd raised him to accept and understand same-gender sex and love. But to her discredit, she hadn't. All his life he'd heard homophobic slurs from all the adults in his life.

It was time to begin the dialogue and teach him that people had a right to love whomever they chose. But it would be irresponsible of her to force him into suddenly accepting his mother's relationship with another woman, when she wasn't even sure if she'd lost her desire for men.

Additionally, if Shawn and Jojina caught wind of her relationship with Zenith, they'd use it against her in court and who knows how the judge would feel about it. Right now, she still had a fighting chance to get Yuri back, but after Shawn got finished dragging her sexuality through the mud, Vangie could easily lose Yuri for good.

She wiped the tears from her eyes and before starting the engine, she gave Zenith's apartment building one last look. *I'm sorry, Zenith. A part of me really loved you. But I love my son more.*

VANGIE

She was late for work when her phone vibrated in her purse. She retrieved it but didn't recognize the number.

"Hello?"

"Vangie! It's Mike Bening from the Public Defender's Office. I wanted to share some information with you."

"Sure, what's up?" Vangie's heart thumped. The public defender guy sounded excited, like he had good news.

"I have a friend at the District Attorney's Office in Delaware County, and I found out that Jojina McElroy has a bench warrant for selling prescription drugs from her home. Apparently, she receives SSI benefits and claims to be disabled with chronic pain, depression, and a host of different phobias. She gets lots of prescription meds for her various conditions, and she's been selling her pills illegally for quite a while. She got busted last week, made bail, but didn't show up for her court date, and it's not likely she'll make an appearance when your case comes up at the end of the month. And even if she does, which I doubt, it's not likely that the judge will show favor toward a drug dealer. Her residence is obviously not a fit home for a minor child. So, it looks like you'll be getting your boy back real soon."

"Am I dreaming? Are you serious?" Vangie knew that Jojina was doing something illegal. All those weaves and bags and all that cosmetic surgery had to cost more than a welfare check and Social Security benefits could pay for.

"You can probably get temporary custody, right away. After that, you shouldn't have any problem regaining full custody. I can fax the paperwork on Ms. McElroy to your Family Law attorney tonight if you'd like."

"Yes, please. Oh, my God. This is a miracle. Thank you so much."

"My pleasure. You're a nice person and I'm glad I could help."

Vangie sat still for a moment and absorbed the public defender's words. With tears falling from her eyes, she shouted out loud, "Thank you, Jesus. Thank you, Lord."

After talking to Felder Ross and making arrangements to file for temporary custody of Yuri, Vangie called her mother.

"I don't talk to the devil's daughter," Barbara barked into the phone.

"I wanted you to know that I'm getting Yuri back."

"You are! When?"

"I'm on my way to pick him up, right now." Vangie told her mother what she'd found out about Jojina's drug dealing and the warrant for her arrest. "I wanted to know if you'd like to go to dinner with Yuri and me tomorrow night. I'm sure he misses you and I think if we put up a united front, he'll feel safe and loved."

"Yuri knows I love him with all my heart, but that doesn't mean that I intend to share a meal with someone who's breaking one of the Lord's most sacred vows."

"I broke it off with Zenith, Mom."

"Hallelujah. Thank you, Jesus, for putting my wayward child back on the path of righteousness!"

Her mother was such a hypocrite, but she had to make peace with her on Yuri's behalf.

"I have coupons for Olive Garden. And Yuri loves their Cheese Ravioli," Barbara said.

"He sure does," Vangie recalled fondly.

Vangie was grateful to have her mother back in her life and maybe in time, she and Shawn could put aside their differences and co-parent their son. All Vangie could do was pray.

Losing Zenith was a high price, but it wasn't their time. Fighting tears that threatened to start flowing again, Vangie turned her car around and steered it toward Thornbury.

NIVEA

In hushed whispers, people talked about Nivea and her gray-haired groom-to-be. Though they were undeniably ill-matched, no one could say anything unflattering about the beautifully decorated wedding venue. Or the bride's lovely gown that was revealed when her father escorted her down the aisle.

Inside the main ballroom of the Rittenhouse Hotel, cameras flashed, capturing Nivea's beauty from various angles. It was the day she'd been dreaming of for most of her life, yet so many aspects of it were wrong. Standing at the altar, her bridesmaids, Harlow and Vangie, gave each other the cold shoulder, but sent warm smiles in Nivea's direction. The man she would soon marry was older than her father and would require medication to consummate the marriage—not that Nivea was in a great rush to do that.

Clutching her father's arm, she stepped slowly. Carefully. Her mind was focused on her daughter's bright future. Eleven-month-old Mackenzie was on the waiting list of an elite, French-speaking preschool. The idea of her baby being refined and cultured brought a slight curve to Nivea's downturned mouth.

Nivea had handed in her resignation at work several months ago. Women of her stature didn't toil at jobs. From now on, she'd devote her free time to charity and being the best mother she could be.

The new home Bertram had bought for their family was a luxurious piece of real estate, replete with private quarters for Odette.

She was being kind by allowing Bertram to keep his house-keeper, but the woman had to meet Nivea's standards if she wanted to keep her position.

Closer to the altar, she could see Bertram's eager face. Over the past few months, he'd claimed to have grown to love her, but she believed it was her harsh words and demanding nature that had turned him on.

I'm truly my mother's daughter; I don't need love in order to be happy. Money and power are all I need.

With all the wedding preparations of recent months, her mind had been constantly occupied, keeping the heartache at bay. But now, as she stepped closer to the altar, she could feel the fissure as it seemed to jaggedly rip through the center of her heart.

Finally, she reached the altar and her knees felt week. Tears slid down her cheeks while Bertram's voice droned on, seemingly from a distant place, as he recited his vows.

When it was Nivea's turn to speak, her mind went blank and she couldn't remember a single word she had planned to say, and so she quickly came up with a new speech.

"This is the special day I've waited for my whole life. Unfortunately, I can't go through with this. I'm sorry, Bertram. I can't."

The audience gasped.

"You can't back out now," her father whispered, cutting an eye at his wife who was sitting in the front row and looking extremely perturbed.

"Yes, I can back out. I don't have to do anything I don't want to do. I thought I was like Mother, but I'm not. I don't want a man who can't think for himself. I don't want to be married without love and passion."

"Nivea?" Bertram said, waiting to be told what he should do.

"Go home, Bertram. The wedding is cancelled." She flung her bridal bouquet to the floor and dashed down the aisle and out of the ballroom. Sobbing, she repeatedly jabbed the button of the elevator, in a hurry to get to her hotel suite, where Mackenzie and Odette were waiting.

"Why aren't you at your wedding?" Odette asked, her eyes wide with surprise. "I called it off," she said, taking Mackenzie from Odette's arms.

"So, you're a runaway bride, are you?" Odette said with laughter and Nivea laughed, too. "I didn't think you were the kind of woman who would marry a man for his money. Not my Miss Nivea. She's too nice of a girl."

Nivea sighed. "I'm not nice."

"Yes, you are and you will be blessed. Your cell phone has been ringing and ringing. Probably some out-of-town guests needing directions. I don't know, but I finally shut the thing off so the baby could enjoy her nap."

There was a sharp knock on the door.

"I don't want to talk to my parents or Bertram," Nivea told Odette.

Odette looked through the eyehole. "It's your bridesmaids—the pregnant girl and the other one."

Realizing she needed privacy with her friends, Nivea turned to Odette before opening the door for Harlow and Vangie. "Can you do me a favor, Odette?"

"Of course."

"I need some time alone with my friends. Would you take Kenzie to your room, please?"

"Not a problem. Come on, Kenzie, my girl. Let's go to my room and play with your toys." Odette reached out her arms and Mackenzie happily leapt into them. The nanny and Mackenzie exited through the door that adjoined the two suites.

Nivea opened the door, admitting Harlow and Vangie whose faces were creased with concern.

"Are you okay, Niv?" Harlow asked.

"I'm fine. I know I made the right decision. Did Bertram leave?"

"He left the building like you told him to," Vangie responded.

"My head is killing me. I'm so stressed about money. I don't have a job. Hardly any money in the bank, but at least I have my condo."

Harlow patted Nivea on the shoulder. "I'm proud of you for doing the right thing. You would have been miserable being married to that fat, old man. You don't need to sell your soul for money. You're highly qualified; you can always find another job."

"Actually, I could have dealt with being married to Bertram. He's easy to get along with. And he does everything he's told."

"So, we notice," Vangie piped in. "So, what made you change your mind?"

"For the first time in my life, I found someone to love. Someone who also loved me. I want another chance at that kind of happiness. Marrying for money would have hardened my heart and robbed me of any chance of happiness. That love I lost came and went in a flash. It was so fleeting, we never even called it love. But now that I know how love feels, I won't be satisfied until I find it again."

"I don't know, Niv. If you're looking for lost love, maybe you should have taken the money and kept it moving," Vangie said.

Harlow shook her head. "Don't listen to her. I married for love and I couldn't be happier. With twin boys due any day now, I couldn't ask for more."

"As rich as you are, it's no surprise that your days are filled with joy," Vangie said, rolling her eyes.

"Money doesn't bring happiness, Vangie."

"I can't believe you two are still going at it. Don't you think it's about time you made up?" Nivea asked. "And by the way, Vangie, whatever happened to that guy, Alphonso, whom you wanted to marry so desperately?"

"Ask Harlow; he's her husband's partner. He vanished from my life. I haven't seen or heard from him in months, and frankly, I don't care."

"I don't get into Drake's business affairs. All I know is they ended their partnership. I heard Alphonso left the country. That's all I know."

"Well, good riddance to Alphonso with his chunky, little stubby dick," Vangie said with a sneer.

Harlow shared a look with Vangie and they both giggled.

"His stubby dick?" Nivea asked, perplexed.

Vangie and Harlow laughed harder. "It's a long story," Vangie said, elbowing Harlow, exactly like old times.

Catching up, the three friends laughed and talked for over an hour, until Drake came upstairs to collect his wife. "You all right, Nivea?"

She nodded.

"Well, I hate to break this up, but my very pregnant wife is supposed to be on bed rest and I have to get her home."

Harlow and Vangie embraced each other and Harlow whispered, "I forgive you, Vangie."

"Thank you, Harlow. Please know I'm truly sorry." Vangie squeezed Harlow's arm.

"I know and we're going to rebuild our friendship, okay, girl?"

Vangie nodded. After Harlow and Drake left, she said to Nivea, "I can stay with you if you don't want to be alone."

"No, I'm okay."

"You sure?"

"Positive." Nivea said. "I'm glad you and Harlow finally made up."

"Me, too. I've been angry with her and missing her at the same time. Now I can let those feelings go."

"Were you in love with Alphonso, Vangie?"

"No. I was looking for security. He wasn't a very nice person, and he's not missed at all."

"Are you seeing anyone?"

"No. I was. But we broke up."

"Who?"

"A girl named Zenith."

"A girl?"

"A woman. An amazing woman."

"You're gay?"

"Yes. I am."

"What happened between you and Zenith? Wait, don't tell me. I bet you were worrying about what folks thought about you."

"You're so right."

"Vangie, if you know like I know, you'd better hold on to love in whatever form it comes in."

"I hurt her and I'm ashamed to go crawling back."

"If she loved you, she'll understand."

"Where's all this wisdom coming from, Nivea?"

Nivea shrugged as she walked Vangie to the door. "Like I said, I've loved and lost."

Vangie left, and Nivea had the rest of the evening to clear her head and try to figure out what she was going to do with the rest of her life. She took off her wedding gown, then sat at the dressing table. Staring at her reflection in the mirror, she began wiping her makeup off. As she went through the mundane task, it occurred to her that she'd have to return the wedding gifts. Maybe her mother would assist her with that. Denise Westcott was in charge of the gifts and though Nivea dreaded talking to her, she had to face the music and deal with her mother's disappointment.

She turned on her cell phone and noticed there were seven calls from an area code she didn't recognize. And there was a message. She entered the numbers to retrieve her voicemail and listened:

Hey, Nivea, it's Malcolm. I'm in town for a few weeks, drumming up some business for my company. Things are working out much better than I could have imagined. I was hoping we could get together…if you're not too busy. Listen, I really miss you, Niv, and um, if you give us another chance, I promise, I won't give up so easily this time. Looking back, I realize I should have put more effort into keeping us together. For that, I'm sorry. Anyway, when you get this message, I hope you'll give me a call. And by the way, I'm still hoping you'll be brave enough to do a tandem jump with me.

A smile spread across her face. *Damn, right, I'm brave enough to do it. I'm brave enough for a lot of things. Like a move to the West Coast if you still want me to. I'm willing to face financial uncertainty as long as I'm with you. And yes, my love, I'm more than ready to free fall from the sky with you.*

Imagining a promising future with Malcolm, Nivea swiped a finger across the screen and returned his call.

ABOUT THE AUTHOR

Allison Hobbs is a national bestselling author of twenty-two novels and has been featured in such publications as *Romantic Times* and *The Philadelphia Tribune*. She lives in Philadelphia, Pennsylvania. Visit the author at www.allisonhobbs.com and Facebook.com/Allison Hobbs.

WANT TO REMEMBER HOW VANGIE,
HARLOW AND NIVEA GOT TO THIS DAY?
BE SURE TO PICK UP

PUT A
RING
ON IT

BY ALLISON HOBBS
AVAILABLE FROM STREBOR BOOKS

CHAPTER 1

C all it a woman's intuition. Call it a sixth sense, but instead of driving home after work, Nivea felt an urge to swing by her fiancé's old apartment.

When she rolled up in front of the building where Eric used to live, she gave the place a smug look. Eric's former apartment building was a dump. She had no idea why he'd been so resistant to the idea of moving into her upscale townhouse.

But that was water over the bridge. She had introduced Eric to a better lifestyle and she was proud of that fact.

Nivea did a double take when she noticed the Highlander parked at the curb. Her heart rate began to accelerate when she recognized Eric's license plate. *What's he doing here? He's supposed to be working overtime.*

With the motor running, she jumped out of her Mazda and removed a couple of lawn chairs that were holding someone's nicely shoveled parking spot. Brows joined together in bafflement, she parallel parked, cut the engine, and then got out.

Nivea peered up at the second floor apartment that Eric had left six months ago when he'd moved in with her. She could see the twinkling colored lights that adorned a Christmas tree. She frowned at the Christmas tree. It was the first day of December, too soon to put up a tree in Nivea's opinion.

Eric had sublet the place to one of his unmarried friends. *Which one?* She couldn't remember. Feeling a rush of uncomfortable heat, she unbuttoned her wool coat, allowing the frigid evening air to cool her.

There had to be a good explanation for Eric being here. Something really innocent. *He didn't have to work overtime after all, and decided to stop by and visit his buddy,* she told herself.

Even though moving into Nivea's townhouse was a step up for Eric, it had been hard convincing him to give up his crappy bachelor's pad. She was so elated when she'd gotten him to agree to move in, that she hadn't bothered to question him about the details of his rental transaction.

But she was concerned now.

Carefully, Nivea climbed the icy concrete steps that led to the front door. Inside the vestibule area, another door, this one locked, prevented her from forcing her way to Eric's old apartment. She read the name that was centered above the doorbell of apartment number two: D. Alston.

Who the hell is D. Alston? She jabbed the doorbell twice, and then pressed the button without letting up.

She heard a door open on the second floor. "Stay right here. Let me handle this," Eric said gruffly.

Who the hell is Eric talking to?

Eric thumped down the stairs, causing a vibration. At the bottom of the stairs, he looked at Nivea through the large windowpane that separated them. She expected a smile of surprise, but Eric gawked at her, displeasure wrinkling his forehead.

He turned the lock, cracked the door open, and poked his head out. "Whatchu doing here, Niv?"

"I should be asking that question. You're supposed to be at work!"

"Yeah, um…" He scratched his head.

"Who's renting the place now?"

"Uh…"

Refusing to give him time to gather his thoughts, she pushed the door open, and zipped past Eric.

"You can't go up there, Niv."

"Hell if I can't!" Nivea took the stairs two at a time, the heels of her boots stomping against the wooden stairs. Eric was up to something, and she had to know what the hell was going on.

Eric raced behind her. He roughly grabbed her arm. "You outta pocket."

She yanked her arm away and spun around. "Let me go, Eric!" Eric was a big, stocky man, but she gave him such a violent shove, he fell backward, stumbling down a couple of steps.

Motivated by a suspicious mind, Nivea bolted for Eric's apartment, which was at the top of the stairs. The door was slightly ajar. She pushed it open.

A woman, who appeared to be in her early twenties, stood in the kitchen, clutching a baby. One glance told Nivea that the woman was street tough. Hardcore. She was not cute at all. Light-skinned, reed-thin with a narrow, ferret-like face. The Kool Aid red-colored weave she was rocking looked a hot Halloween mess. Anger flickered across the woman's mean, sharp-featured face.

"Who are you?" Nivea asked, hoping to hear, *I'm Eric's cousin.* Hell, she was willing to accept childhood friend, or even long lost sister. She'd happily go along with any relationship, except jumpoff. She stole a glance at the baby that was buried beneath blankets.

The skinny chick looked at Nivea like she had sprouted a second head. "How you gon' bust in here axin' me who da hell I am?" Her bad grammar and attitude confirmed Nivea's suspicion that the chick was a hood rat.

Nivea scanned the kitchen quickly. The appliances were as outdated as Nivea remembered, and the cabinetry was still old and chipped, but the room was spotlessly clean and somewhat better furnished than when Eric had lived there. Nivea took in the rather new, but cheap-looking kitchen set that had replaced Eric's old one.

The female tenant had tried to brighten up the dismal kitchen. Matching potholders and dishtowels were on display. The former dusty mini blinds that had once hung at the kitchen window had been replaced with ruffled curtains.

What is Eric doing here with this ghettofied heifer and her child?

As if she'd read Nivea's mind, the thuggish chick turned toward Nivea. Holding the baby upright, she gave Nivea a full view of the infant's face. Nivea felt her heart stop. The little boy, who looked to be around four or five months old, was a miniature replica of Eric.

"Oh, my God!" Nivea squeaked out. She grimaced at the child who was Eric's spitting image.

Okay, I'm imagining things. That child can't possibly be Eric's baby!

CHAPTER 2

Eric barreled into the apartment. Nivea suspected he had been hanging out in the hallway, trying to get his lies together.

"You need to check yourself, Nivea. You know you dead wrong for running up in the crib like this."

Nivea was stunned that Eric, her gentle teddy bear, was growling at her like a vicious grizzly bear.

Nivea stared at the baby and then at Eric. She swiped at the tears that watered her eyes. "What's going on, Eric?"

The skinny chick bit down on her lip, like she was struggling to control her temper. "I'm not with this shit, Eric. You'd better handle it."

Eric tugged Nivea's coat sleeve. "This ain't the time or the place, Niv."

"Have you lost your mind, Eric? You told me you were at work. I need to know what the hell is going on. Get your coat!" She motioned with her hand. "Talk to me on the way home. We're out of here!" Nivea waited for Eric to go get his coat, but he didn't budge.

The ghetto chick snickered, and then looked down at the baby. "Don't worry, Boo-Boo; Daddy ain't going nowhere."

Daddy! No way! That is not Eric's child, Nivea told herself. With a hand on her hip, she glared at Eric. "Who is this bitch? And why are you here with her?"

"My name is Dyeesha. I ain't gon' be another bitch, *bitch*. I don't know who you is, but you trespassing." The woman with the bad grammar spoke in an annoying scratchy tone, her nostrils flaring as she furiously patted her baby.

"Eric! Tell this girl who I am!" Nivea spoke through clenched teeth.

Looking like a cornered rat, Eric was at loss for words and could only come up with utterances and sputtering sounds.

"How you expect him to remember the name of e'ry hooka he done slept with while I was pregnant with his son," Dyeesha said with a sneer.

The abrasive sound of the girl's voice, her assumption that Nivea was a stripper and a prostitute, and her terrible grammar…it all grated Nivea's nerves. "For the love of God, will you please tell this ignorant-ass, ghettofied, hood chick who I am!" Nivea yelled.

As if his lips were sealed with Super Glue, Eric was mute.

"Ghettofied! You da one acting ghetto." Dyeesha contorted her lips. "For your information, I'm Eric's baby mama. In a few weeks, I'ma be his wife." Dyeesha shot a hot glance at Eric. "I can't believe you let one of your tricks run up on me like this."

"Stop calling me a trick! You're not marrying Eric. I am! Our wedding is in June," Nivea shouted.

Dyeesha grabbed the doorknob. "Keep dreaming. Now bounce, bitch. Take your trick ass back to that strip club you crawled out of."

Nivea stared at Eric. "Are you gonna just stand there while your jumpoff insults me?"

Dyeesha snorted. "You da damn jumpoff! Now take your home-wrecking activities somewhere else!" Dyeesha tried to pass the baby to Eric. "Hold your son cuz I'm 'bout to go on her trick ass!"

Nivea gasped. She wasn't expecting to get into a fistfight with a street tough thug chick.

Eric calmed Dyeesha by rubbing the length of her willowy arm. "I told you, I got this."

The gentleness in Eric's voice, the tender strokes he delivered to Dyeesha's sweater-covered arm…and the baby! It was all too much to bear. Hotly jealous, Nivea felt her anger rising like steam. She pounced on Eric, trying to claw at his face. "You lying, cheating, broke ass, no-good scumbag. I should have never gotten involved with a damn warehouse worker!"

Dodging Nivea's fingernails, Eric tossed her off of him, knocking her into the fridge. Too wound up and too furious to feel any pain, Nivea kept fighting, jutting her kneecap upward as she aimed for Eric's groin, which in her opinion, was the real culprit in this triangle of lies and deceit.

She missed the intended mark, but Eric grunted in pain as Nivea's kneecap rammed his inner thigh.

"Get that bitch, Eric. Fuck her up," Dyeesha goaded.

Holding the baby, Dyeesha followed Nivea and Eric as they scuffled along a short hallway, ending up in the small living room.

"Stop acting crazy!" Eric demanded as he grabbed Nivea by the shoulders and gave her a brisk shake. To Eric's credit, he hadn't actually hit Nivea; he'd merely tried to restrain her.

Nivea maneuvered out of his grasp and landed a hard slap across his face.

"Ow! Shit!" Eric rubbed his cheek.

Dyeesha sucked her teeth. "Hold the baby, Eric, so I can whoop that ass."

"I got this!" Eric insisted as he lunged for Nivea.

Swinging both hands, kicking, and scratching, Nivea was prepared to fight to the death. She wasn't leaving the premises without her groom in tow. In the midst of the squabble, Nivea noticed a series of photos in silver frames. There was one with Eric holding the baby. Another with Dyeesha and the baby, and the third silver-framed photo held a family portrait.

Feeling lightheaded, Nivea stumbled, bumping into the small Christmas tree that sat atop a table, the one she'd seen twinkling through the window.

Three red and white stockings were thumb-tacked to the wall: Eric, Dyeesha, and Eric, Jr. was printed in glittery letters.

Nivea punched Eric in the face. His large form toppled the Christmas tree. Glass balls shattered. Mini lights crashed against the floor.

The baby screamed. Dyeesha pressed the baby against her bosom. "Bitch, I know you don't think I'ma let you fuck up my family's first Christmas together."

Eric pulled himself to his feet. "Get the baby out of here. I got this, Dyeesha," he mumbled, picking up the dwarfed tree, trying to get it to stand up straight.

"You better get this trick outta my house before I call the cops."

"Stop calling me a trick. I'm his fiancée." Nivea held up her ringed finger as proof.

Dyeesha looked at the diamond ring and snorted. "Pole dancers make lots of money. You bought that bling and put it on your own finger."

Nivea drew in a breath. The truth hurt. She had put the expensive ring on her credit card, telling herself it was okay as long as Eric made the payments, which he hadn't done at that point. And with this horrible turn of events, it wasn't likely he'd be making any payments in the future.

Eric stepped in front of Nivea. "What's wrong with you, girl? Why you tryna make me hurt you?" He drew his lips together in a threatening manner. Nivea couldn't believe her eyes or her ears. *What the hell?* Eric had been such a pushover. The way he always let her have her way had endeared him to her. Now he was threatening to hurt her.

"When were you going to tell me about your secret family? On our wedding day?"

"He ain't marrying you!" Dyeesha hissed.

"Oh, yes he is," Nivea insisted. She knew that she should have turned around and walked away the moment she saw that baby's face, but she had put so much time and effort into Eric…into her wedding, she couldn't walk away.

In an act of desperation, Nivea reached for Eric's hand. "We can discuss this at home."

Refusing the gesture, Eric placed his hands behind his back.

"I guess you didn't get the memo, trick. The only wedding that's going down is mine and Eric's." Dyeesha rolled her eyes at Nivea. "Tell her, Eric," Dyeesha coaxed.

Eric lowered his head. He stuffed his hands inside the pockets of his jeans, and began jiggling change. He spoke in a low tone. "I should have told you about Dyeesha. I can't go through with it. The wedding is cancelled, Niv."

Dyeesha puffed up with pride. "You hear that, trick! Your imaginary wedding is cancelled."

The wedding is cancelled! Nivea opened her mouth and began shrieking as if someone had thrown a pot of boiling oil in her face.

The baby screamed along with her.

"Yo, get a grip. You scaring the shit outta my son," Eric said.

"But you don't have any children," Nivea replied dumbly.

"That's my son," Eric confirmed. "I wanted to tell you but I ain't know how."

Any normal bride-to-be who was getting hit with one bombshell after another would have been lying prone on the floor, while awaiting an emergency ambulance team to rush in and recharge her heart, but Nivea didn't have time for heart failure. She appealed to Eric's sense of reasoning. "My gown, Eric. What about my wedding gown? I'm scheduled for my next fitting in a few weeks."

Eric blinked at her, held his hands up in the air.

Dyeesha's mouth was twisted, like she'd eaten something rotten. "Don't nobody care about your raggedy-ass gown. You better get your damn deposit back. Eric's not leaving me for you or any other trick-bitch."

Dyeesha's slanderous words had lost their sting. Nivea was deep in thought. Like a broken record, *the wedding is cancelled*, repeated inside her mind.

It was unbelievable that Eric had been leading a double life. Nivea tried to imagine sitting her parents down, and telling them this horror story, but it was too humiliating to ponder. She had to figure out a way to fix this awful mess.

"You gotta go, Niv," Eric told her. "You're upsetting my family."

"Fuck your family!" Finally giving into the rage that was bubbling inside, Nivea grabbed both silver-framed photographs and sent then zinging toward Eric's head.

Eric hit the floor. His eyelids fluttered as blood oozed from an open wound on the side of his head.

"Help!" Dyeesha screamed. Dyeesha raced out of the apartment and out into the hallway. Neighbors began to open their doors.

"Help. There's a crazy bitch in my crib. She's tryna kill my whole family," Dyeesha shrieked.

With the single thought of escaping punishment, Nivea left Eric moaning and bleeding on the floor, and ran out of the apartment.

"There she is. Somebody catch that trick." Dyeesha's voice climbed higher. "Don't let her get away!"

Whizzing past several puzzled neighbors, Nivea bounded down the stairs and out the set of doors.

Nivea rushed along the slushy pavement. Slip-sliding across the icy street, she jumped in her car. *A few stitches should take care of Eric's head*, she told herself. She gnawed at her bottom lip as she pulled the Mazda forward. The tires thudded against a mound of hardened snow. *Fuck!* She had to get out of the tight parking spot before the police arrived.

Suppose he's dead! Nivea grimaced. The idea of doing jail time for murder was far more distressing than being dumped six months before her wedding.

Ramming the car behind her, she forcefully gave herself room. As she zoomed away from the scene of the crime, hot tears splashed against her face. Eric deserved to be dead, but for the sake of Nivea's freedom, she needed him to live.